P9-DKF-580

Losing You

A Novella Collection

Also by Candace Meredith

Contemplation: Imagery, Sound & Form in
Lyricism

www.ctupublishinggroup.com

www.amazon.com

Losing You

A Novella Collection

Candace Meredith

www.ctupublishinggroup.com

HANDLEY REGIONAL LIBRARY
P.O.¡¡BOX 58
WINCHESTER, VA 22604

Losing You Copyright © 2018: Candace Meredith. All rights reserved. No part of this book may be used or reproduced in any manner whatsoever without written permission except in the case of reprints in the context of reviews. This Collection is protected under U.S. and International Copyright laws.

CTU Publishing Group

a division of Creative Talents Unleashed

Po Box 605 Helendale, Ca 92342

www.ctupublishinggroup.com

www.creativetalentsunleashed.com

info@ctupublishinggroup.com

1st Edition
Printed in the United States of America.
ISBN: 978-1-945791-54-3
Library of Congress: 2018940353

Book Introduction: Candace Meredith
Cover Design: Raja Williams
Editor: Shelley Mascia

HANDLEY REGIONAL LIBRARY
P.O. BOX 58
WINCHESTER, VA 22604

Introduction

Losing You is a compilation of three Novellas titled *Dear Caroline*, *Not My Daughter* and *The Marathon Runner* that deal with loss in some way.

Dear Caroline is a story about a man who loses his wife; even at the age of seventy-four Jimmy feels he has lost his wife too soon especially when her death was so unexpected. The story gravitates to the surreal in a fantastical kind of way while the protagonist writes to his beloved wife almost on a daily basis – from behind prison bars. Jimmy feels he still has a connection with his wife in a metaphysical sense but that doesn't go over well with his daughter who vehemently disagrees with his actions and is devastated about his incarceration.

Not My Daughter is also about losing a wife but the story gravitates more toward the loss of a mother as the protagonist Kristi mourns her loss; the story develops further as Kristi is found to have a relationship with William who had been with Marissa Shaw on the night of her death. Kristi dates a man who her father disregards all-the-while trying not to mourn the man who was responsible for the loss of her mother. The finale is a collision course of loss, death and potential forgiveness.

The Marathon Runner delves into the loss of a friend that at some point can be re-kindled if the protagonist plays his cards right: a man who is easily confused as a bum who has no job and is virtually homeless despite his relationship with a store owner. Maverick wants nothing more than to move forward from the past and think of the future but finds himself at the hands of his ex to his dismay. This is the story of a man who wants to re-kindle the past while being constantly reminded of his present.

Losing You is comprised of three stories that are written to move the reader through intense fantasy and a surreal reality.

Contents

Not My Daughter

Prologue

Evening had settled upon the small town in Western Appalachia where her body was discovered among the sooty streets of Grand and Pennsylvania Avenue. Condry left his quarters at 5 am, where he worked nights at the Western Corrections Institution. On that morning, he nearly took her arm off with his left front tire. She looked to be in her twenties, pale and pasty, and her tangled, wet ponytail was fastened to her head with a red band; her waitressing apron was beneath her as she laid face-down with her arms out-stretched.

The young woman didn't show signs of assault or trauma: no head wound, no bloodshed, no bruises, no strangulation that he could see; he stood transfixed upon her lifeless gaze and ruby red lips.

"Everyone called her Peaches," a voice said as he turned around to see the figure, a mere shadow, illuminated by a rising sun.

"Who are you?" he questioned.

"Names William," the voice explained.

"You know this girl?" he asked calmly.

"She jumped right out of my car," William responded.

He knelt beside the young woman, inhaling the fragrant smell of eucalyptus. *Why would she do that?* He thought.

"You call the police? An ambulance?" he asked.

"Should be here any minute," William explained, "my cell was dead, had to use the charger in the car."

Condry gave one more look the young woman – the girl whose friends called Peaches, when the police showed up. The police took down his basic information, but he knew there was little he could offer them and he knew the story remained with the driver, William, and the story he would give the police: *she just jumped out of my car.*

But as Condry lay in bed, waiting for sleep to come, those words didn't resonate with him. The scent of eucalyptus in her hair and those ruby red lips were conducive to someone who cared about themselves. By word-of-mouth, he would later learn that the young woman – named Marissa Shaw – had died of a spinal injury.

Chapter One

Many years later, the death of the girl still weighed on his mind. Condry, who stood at 6'4" and 280 pounds, employed in corrections enforcement, had a sixth sense for convicts in the twenty years he worked for WCI.

Condry was a man for truth, justice, and conviction. He spoke of the law eloquently when his own wife died in her car. She was hit head-on when a drunk driver ran a stop light and the impact upon her Jeep Liberty caused her to die instantly. That was four years prior to the death of the young woman, who, at 24, was the same age as his daughter. Condry felt that his wife called to him to take that detour through town that night when he had usually stayed on the interstate.

"It's July again," he says, stepping into the break room of the WCI facility.

"And the wettest damn season in twenty-five years," Ed, his second in command, replies.

"Rained out my daughter's vacation plans last month, now it's going to rain on the festival it seems."

"My wife intends to go to that dang Heritage Festival – when is it?" Ed inquires.

"It's today," Condry nods, "daughter sent me a text a few minutes ago – it's raining like hell out there."

"Well, there's always next year."

Ed's head falls, "Oh man, I'm sorry brother – I didn't mean to…"

"It's alright man," he interjects. "It'll be five years ago next week."

"How is Kristi holding up?" Ed asks.

"She's still selling those angels made from her mother's old jeans, but the dang rain is too much for anyone to want to go outside," he shrugs, grabbing a cup of coffee.

"Well, she still got that little store down in Bedford?"

"Oh yeah man, doing pretty good," Condry sips and grimaces. "She's still with that loans officer from the PNC bank," he grabs a few packets of sugar from the communal counter.

"Any plans for a wedding?"

"There would be," he shrugs, "but she's not making any plans without her mother."

"Still hard to believe it's been five years already," Ed says, shifting his feet.

"Yeah, well, you know what they say," he says, "feels like yesterday. It changed Kristi, she was only nineteen then.

Rick actually told her the other day she should go back to college, for her and no one else."

"What she say to that?"

"She thought he was being an asshole," Condry snickers.

Ed laughs as he glances at the clock, "Well it's time to get out of here," he zips his parka and grabs his bottled water from the fridge.

Condry returned home to an empty fridge and a six pack of beer; the home he shared with his wife has gone stale over the years. Old news and dated magazines litter the kitchen table and torn grocery bags lay forgotten on the floor. Bed sheets cover the furniture.

Kristi bends slightly over her mother's grave. It's the third consecutive day of rain, but she doesn't care. She places fresh yellow roses before a headstone that reads:

Miranda R. Sullivan
Beloved Mother and Wife
01-29-1960 to 07-24-2010

Kristi kisses the last rose before she drops it to the ground. The geese at "At Rest

Memorial Garden" fly overhead; the pond's waterfall hums in the background. In the five years since her mother's death, Kristi recalls how her mother's killer served eighteen months in prison and was released in January 2012, the same month her mother would have turned fifty-two years old.

Condry removes a 5 x 7 photo frame from the wall, places it onto unkempt newspapers on the end table and takes a seat on the flannel bedsheet covered sofa. He leans back, propping his feet on an ottoman and cracks open his cold beer. The photo features Kristi and her mother ten years before her mother's death. Kristi was 13 in the photo and she looked like her mother even then.

His wife was a petite 5'1", 120 pounds with her coffee-toasted hazel eyes, round pouty lips, long eyelashes, thin brows and exceptional hips: all the minute details that made her beautiful – down to her long cinnamon brown hair. Kristi was close to a carbon copy of her mother: how their ponytail swayed and leaned with each bend, how they could be wedged beneath Condry's arm and everything from her skin tone to eye and hair color.

Condry shifts his weight in the soft cushion of the couch, bending one side while wedging the sheet in the other direction– taking only a sip of beer with each lingering thought while noting that beer isn't good when warm. His mind wanders to Marissa: dead and gone in her early twenties – how she will never age, being the age Miranda had been when Kristi was born, and how Marissa and Kristi could've been friends – inviting one another over for dinner. But that would never happen.

Kristi swipes wet bangs from her forehead and fixes the yellow roses in the white marble vase. Each petal feels like velvet in the steady rain that sops beneath her open-toed sandals. She turns and stomps through the puddles to get inside her warm and dry car. While she dabs the strands of her hair with her palms and smooths the wrinkles of her shirt, she notices a large black Silverado idling close by; the driver is familiar, but she can't place it and shrugs it off as she drives away.

Two hours later, she dressed in slacks and a blouse with her heeled shoes in anticipation for her interview scheduled at 5

9

p.m.; her clock shows 4:53 p.m. – although she was accustomed to showing up in the nick of time, she was rarely late. She turns into the parking lot at The Hub and shuts off the engine. Kristi quickly walks through the glass door and peers at the busy crowd, wondering why an interview would be scheduled during peak restaurant hours. Servers wearing black steady their trays across one shoulder and pour their guests' refills. Guests seated at the bar are packed together; many stand and hover. The television shows the local minor league team winning 7 to 3 and the town supporters are wearing red. They clap during the final run, with a single hit taking three to home plate.

The Hub is sterile in comparison to Kristi's desired style which is wholesome, earthy, and inviting. The Hub is comprised of booths and tables that surround the center bar, the walls are adorned with flat screens that display sports or sports news. The lighting is dim, and the place settings were made of paper. A skinny, frail blond with a well-kept bun and glossy eye-shadow, as blue as her eyes, wearing a manager's pin, greets Kristi.

"You are my second interview today, but I'll be wrapping up the other interview in just a minute," she says, and guides Kristi to an empty table that seats two.

"Thank you," Kristi replies, and walks past one of the two bartenders, who peers at her from over the bar. Having forgotten to clean her contact lenses, she cannot make out the details of his face with the cloudy lenses. She parks herself at the green suede booth and places her purse by her feet.

"Okay, so here we are," the manager says and flops on the bench before her.
"Yes, hello," she says, offering her hand to shake. "I'm Kristi."

"I'm first shift manager here and my name's Sandy."

"It's nice to meet you, Sandy," Kristi says and extends one arm across the table to shake hands.

"Kristi Sullivan," Sandy briefly shakes it. "I have your application right here."

"Great," says Kristi with a half-smile.

"So, you have serving experience?"

"Yes I do," says Kristi.

"I see here you have fine dining experience…"

"Yes, I've been there for several years."

"What makes you want to leave your current job?"

Kristi sighs, "Business slowed after a change in ownership and my hours have been cut."

"I see," murmured Sandy, looking over her resume, "you looking for full-time?"

"Yes, I am," replies Kristi.

"Are you a student?"

"No, but I run a small store three days a week and have been working mostly in the evening."

"Not a problem," Sandy waves her hand, "we work around a lot of hours here."

"That's really helpful," Kristi smiles.

"So, what are your hours at the store?"

"I open Monday, Tuesday and Thursday mornings," Kristi explains.

"Perfect," says the manager, "we don't open until 11a.m. and stay open until 1 a.m. except for Friday and Saturday we stay open until 2 a.m.– and we're open every day. How soon can you start?"

"I can start after a week," responds Kristi.

"Well, then, let's get started by showing you around."

Chapter Two

Kristi gave up her writing degree when her mother died; she was six credits away from completion. Rick had tried to convince her to return to college, but Kristi has recently been doubting college, as well as her relationship. She wants to set out on her own again – to live freely and independently which is why she is waiting tables five nights a week and working at the store for three. Her relationship with her father and younger brother had always been bleak – and she misses her mother terribly. Today is the day her mother died five years ago, it is miserable enough being a Wednesday, and she is due to begin work at The Hub in two days. Kristi opens her business at *A Touch of Rain* on mornings when she doesn't have to put in busy hours waiting tables – the same as she had done when working at the other restaurant.

A Touch of Rain was inspired by her mother, whose middle name was Rain. She dominated Kristi's thoughts when she decided to open the small store in the old town district of Bedford – about a twenty-minute drive from the Western Appalachia region of Maryland. *A Touch of Rain* was organized by Kristi primarily with the help of her friend Lisa, who works at the Bedford Coffee Shop. They were students at state university together.

Lisa helped Kristi decorate the store with soft white curtains. They found inventory from the locals of the old town district comprised of scarves, hats, gloves, jewelry, clothing, jackets, pottery, and photography. Kristi learned how to sew her mother's jeans and other articles of clothing into decorative angels that could be placed around the house, hung from decorative shelves or on a Christmas tree. She fastened her mother's buttons as smiles, eyes and hearts. The store opened during the week and business was steady with tourists who'd visit during the day – so Kristi hadn't needed to open on the weekend, which were the hours she'd make the most in tips at the restaurant.

Kristi's relationship with her brother, who's three years younger, has been nearly nonexistent since their mother's death. Only sixteen when their mother died, Jake had gotten into booze and drugs. He often didn't visit, preferring to stay with friends and girlfriends – their father always liked working night shifts and hadn't been home. Kristi picked up more hours waiting tables to avoid the silent house. Her relationship with her father was strained and nearly robotic in tone. They mostly communicated through text messages now that her father took up using a mobile device.

On this day, Kristi decided to open the store. Kristi stopped visiting her mother's grave on the day of her death – it felt too contrived – so she would visit throughout the year, bringing fresh flowers from her garden. Kristi's mother had taught her how to garden when she was younger, and yellow lilies and roses were her mother's favorite: she even gave Kristi the middle name Lily, and if Jake had been a girl, he would have been named Rose.

Kristi's store clerk, Kim, works part-time and on off days has another job working in sales. While Kristi works on the inventory in the store alone, she wonders about Jake, thinking about what new girlfriend he has and if he is using heroin. She last saw Jake at the Pit-N-Go where she bought a lime soda. Jake had been smoking cigarettes and wreaked of alcohol.

The extra inventory is from an artist named June. Earlier she accompanied Kristi at the coffee shop in the morning where Lisa worked. June had finished her collection of stained glass pendants for the Heritage Days festival, but didn't make many sales due to the rain. She asked Kristi if her collection

15

could be added to the store's inventory. The stained-glass pendants sparkle nicely aside the angels that are on display.

"Now you all come back to see me," Lisa had said when Kristi and June were leaving the coffee shop that morning.

"I know I will," said June, "and I'm sure Kristi will, too."

"Oh, yes, absolutely," Kristi replied. Then, Kristi and June hugged goodbye.

Kristi stands at the counter of her store, watching out the storefront window, at the pedestrians gathered on Pitt Street, who stroll by on bike while others push strollers. Kristi's thoughts turn to Rick: the man she thought she'd marry, had her mother not died, the man she felt she loved but she longed for something new. She longed for something she could immerse and find herself – a self she felt she lost. Perhaps, she thinks, that she is like her father. That she too could not replace her mother, that there was a huge gaping hole, she had to fill.

Condry lay in bed, not asleep, his thoughts on Marissa – the girl he found dead in the road a year ago today – and his own wife five years ago – today. He concentrates on the fact that his wife would be fifty-five and the young girl, like his daughter, would be twenty-five. He thinks about her red lipstick, fragrant hair, and work uniform – he wonders where she had been going at five a.m. still holding her waitressing apron: *she just jumped out in front of my car* William had said – but the restaurant, The Hub, closed at two. Hence, Condry thinks less about where she was going and more about where she had been.

Kristi steps into The Hub two days after her mother's anniversary of the day she died. She had signed out of social media after she found the profile of her mother's killer; she had been contemplating sending him a message – curious to know if he felt an ounce of guilt.

Her mother's killer, Carl, was only twenty years old when he ran the stoplight – too young for alcohol, but he left the fraternity drunk thinking he'd make it home, but hadn't. Kristi felt enraged they were about the same age, but they went to separate high schools – he went to Allegany and her at Fort Hill. They knew nothing of one another, but he killed her mother – that she did know.

Serving tables is second-nature to Kristi – she works flawlessly while serving a ten-top table in a crowded Friday night restaurant. She's already earned $200 in tips and the night is still young – three hours to go. Even though the bar is crowded, one of the bartenders has been peering at Kristi all evening. His slight grin, pearly white teeth and side-parted jet-black hair are all familiar, but she can't place it. His build is average at about 5'10" and 180 pounds. His biceps are defined beneath a tight black tee that is tucked into matching black trousers. The Hub is loud with background music playing the local classic rock station and the muted television stations feature the ballgame: The Washington Nationals versus the Baltimore Orioles. The female bartender wears orange and black.

The evening shift manager stands amid the guests at the bar and gazes as servers busily tend to the tables. The day is still wet from last night's rain. Kristi entered her shift at opening at 11 a.m., and leaves at the start of the evening shift at five. Her typical work hours begin at five, but a co-worker needed to trade shifts to attend her son's appointment.

"Will, I need a mango mimosa a-s-a-p please," says one waitress across the bar.

"Got it," replies Will, the bartender.

Will, thinks Kristi, and peers over her right shoulder.

Kristi shuffles her feet through the door at a little after five when the manager approaches.

"Kristi," says Sandy, putting an arm out to stop her, "I need someone to cover second shift tonight – girl called out – think you can fill it?" Without much time to respond, Sandy adds, "I really need you," she says, "you'll bring in the cash tonight to make up for it – I got a party of eleven to fifteen coming in – it's all yours."

"I don't have any plans tonight," Kristi says, "I can stay."

Sandy tosses her arm across Kristi's shoulder, "That makes it easier," she says and removes her jacket. The light is breaking from the clouds as Kristi peers out the open window, noting that the rain has stopped.

Kristi greets a party of twelve at 6 p.m., which consists of all senior citizen aged women, wearing an array of red and purple decorative hats with feathers and pins. The women each order a drink from the bar, a martini, mixed margarita or frozen daiquiri, with flavors like strawberry and peaches.

"I need a peach daiquiri," Kristi says across the bar as the bartender makes direct eye contact. Kristi gazes briefly at his strikingly beautiful green eyes. "Thanks," she says, as she lifts her serving tray filled with ice-waters and a lemon.

Another three hours and The Hub is at full service without a single empty seat. Kristi's feet and legs ache from the double shift hours – hoping she can leave at the start of the third shift. As Kristi rounds the manager's office in the back breakroom, Sandy calls her name.

"Kristi," says Sandy, as she clangs the phone onto the receiver, and Kristi pokes her head through the door.
"Yes?" She responds.

"You'll be cut by eleven," she says, "if you can hang in there – we've got a full crowd tonight."

Kristi nods, "No problem," she says, making a mental note to call Rick. They have been distant lately – or perhaps it is Kristi who has been distancing herself from Rick after their conversation about moving in together a few weeks ago. Kristi is not ready to leave her cozy apartment, feeling that Rick's more urban condo near DC is too public, and Kristi prefers remote and quaint.

The evening over, Kristi leans over a table to remove empty dishes. Business has slowed with a few guests seated at the bar. A few servers have already left for the evening,

and Kristi prepares to roll her silverware before she can clock out. A quick glance over the counter, Kristi meets a gaze from the bartender and wonders how long he has been watching – and why.

"You've got several more hours to go?" She questions discreetly but directly.

"I've got to clock out of here in a few minutes," the bartender responds.

"Oh yeah," says Kristi, "not closing house tonight?"

"Not tonight," he responds as he places glasses into the bleach water at the bar.

Kristi folds her napkins and rolls the silverware for the next shift, then arranges sugar packets and salt and pepper shakers on her table section and removes an empty ketchup bottle.

"My replacement has just arrived," the bartender nods as a woman enters the bar.

"I'm about ready to go myself," Kristi says as she heads through the door to the kitchen. Kristi grabs her coat and slides her card through the time slot, re-entering the restaurant – the bar tender waiting patiently at the counter, arms folded.

"Not bad for the first night," he says.

"Oh, yeah," says Kristi, "well, I've been waiting tables for nine years."

The bartender smiles. "But not here," he says.

"No, not here," she says.

"I've never seen a *newbie* serve tables like that on the first day."

"Well, like I said," says Kristi, "I'm not new. I'm old."

The bartender laughs, "You're not that old."

Kristi tosses her arm through her jacket sleeve and zips it slightly.

"A jacket," asks the bartender, "but it's July?"

"And a lot of rain these past few weeks," she pulls the hood up over her head. "Well, I'm ready to go," she says.

The bartender waves with his hand, pointing toward the door, "Here," he says, "let me walk you out."

"Sounds good," Kristi says as the bartender holds the door for her as she walks out into a breezy July night. The stars shine and a crescent moon gleams over-head.

"That's my truck right there," he points toward a large black Silverado with an extended cab.

"That's your truck?" Kristi asks.

"Sure is," he responds, "that's my baby."

Kristi stutters slightly, taken aback, "I think I saw you a few days ago."

"Oh, yeah," he says, "Where is that?"

"At the cemetery."

The bartender lowers his brows, "It's funny that you saw me there…," he says, "but not funny as in haha…but funny like a coincidence."

"Yeah, what are the odds?" Kristi mutters under her breath. "If you don't mind me asking," Kristi says, "what were you doing there?"

The bartender walks toward his truck, opens the door and tosses his wallet into the glove compartment. "I was visiting a friend," he explains. "And how about you?"

"My mother."

"Oh, man," he says, "I'm very sorry to hear that."

"Me, too," says Kristi.

"Maybe we can talk about it sometime," he says.

"Yeah, maybe so."

"You're name's Kristi, right?"

"Yes it is," she says, "and you are…"

"Name's William," he says, "but people call me Will."

Chapter Three

Condry researched William McLean on Maryland Judiciary Cases – he inquired into public records on the federal level and came up with nothing. William was clean as a whistle. The court system, Condry thought, must've had no evidence of foul play. Condry wasn't buying his story; he felt deeply that there must be more than a willing jump from a moving vehicle.

Condry opens the break room door at the WCI facility and finds Ed knee deep in papers and his lunch. "Got a mighty sub there," Condry says.

Ed chuckles, "Meatballs, onions and all the sweet and hot peppers they got."

"Heavy on the peppers," Condry says.

"Yeah, I know," says Ed, "should try it sometime."

"I'll pass," Condry says with a wave of his finger, "too bad with indigestion – my gut can't handle it."

"This guts made of iron," says Ed, slapping his palm to his stomach.

"I've been meaning to ask you if you've heard anything about that William McLean from any of the inmates in here."

Ed wipes sauce from his lips with his napkin, "No man, I haven't," he says, "but why are you asking now?"

"I don't know," Condry says, eyeing Ed, "just got a feeling in my stomach."

"You sure it wasn't something you ate?" Ed jokes.

"No, man, it's that same feeling I got when Miranda died," he explains.

"Oh, man," sighs Ed, "I hear that."

"Maybe your people…you know," says Condry, "can inquire and tell my people if they know of anything."

"Who are *our people*?" says Ed, his lazy left eye squinting earnestly.

"Ask the tier upstairs and they'll pass it along to get back to me," Condry explains, peering sternly at Ed.

"No problem man, I'll see what I can do," he stands and pushes away from the table, leaving half a sandwich on his plate.

"Looking like time is up already," Condry glances at the clock.

"I know man," Ed says, "but I do love the night shift – except its got its problems, too."

"All the shifts do," Condry says.

"Just some more than others," says Ed as he tosses peppers onto his plate, and Condry steps out the door.

Kristi cocks her head to the side, "William," she says, "what's your last name?"

"It's McLean," he says.

Kristi nods, amused by the coincidence and mildly curious. "The same William McLean who was driving a different car last year," she says, "the one…"

"Yeah," he pipes in, "traded it for the truck."

"So, then, you are…"

"Yes," he interjects, "Marissa's friend, William. You do know that she worked here, right?"

"No," stutters Kristi, "I didn't exactly know that, I mean, my father and I don't talk a lot – just about normal stuff."

"Normal stuff?" he asks.

"Well, he makes an effort to ask about the store I have in Bedford – I sell angels and a hodgepodge of other trinkets."

"Well, maybe you'd like to tell me more about that hodgepodge sometime," he says.

"Maybe," she responds.

"Well, for now we can get out of this parking lot," he says.

"That sounds like a plan," she jokes.

"Well, it's only eleven on a Friday night...what do you normally do after work?" he asks.

"Planned on heading home," she yawns, "I just worked a double. Maybe some other time," Kristi shrugs.

"How about tomorrow night?"

Kristi turns toward the restaurant, "I'll be getting off at eleven," she says.

"Great, then I'll pick you up tomorrow," he smiles.

"Alright. Bye."

The evening brings on a steady pace at The Hub. Kristi rounds the bar wondering why Will isn't working that evening, but she didn't think to ask during their conversation outside. She's glad she brought her favorite sundress to wear. The day is bright and hot. The evening will still be humid. She wonders too where they will be heading out, she forgot to ask. She smiles to herself contemplating something romantic – a passion that has died in her for Rick.

She had planned to attend a women's retreat at a local spa and stay at a hotel where there was an outdoor bar, a large pool on the roof and live bands. Kristi, however, canceled her plans and received her deposit; which still sits in her savings. She's hoping to venture somewhere remote in August–

perhaps a cruise or a retreat to Florida – as long as it has a beach and solitude. Kristi hopes, too, that she can begin writing again.

Kristi knows that telling Rick her work hours will extend until 2 AM is untruthful, but she also knows that work is currently her only excuse to get away from their relationship. Rick, a loans officer, works long hours, often before the sun comes up, which makes him tired and groggy– unmotivated to do anything with Kristi. Separate work hours makes quality time feel stagnant and boring. The bank, Rick mentioned often, needs to hire more employees – but that has yet to happen and he often finds himself having to cover the role of missing employees on days they call off.

After her shift, Kristi changes in the largest stall of the facility, having nowhere else to get undressed. She stands in front of the mirror and fixes her make-up, removes a perfume bottle from her purse and dabs it lightly to her wrist and neckline. Her long black and white sundress shows off her small curves. Kristi exits the restroom and heads toward the front door to look for a large black Chevy Silverado. As she turns the corner, she and Will nearly bump into each other as he catches her by the waist.

"Oh," says Kristi, "I was just about to look for your truck."

"Looks like I found you before you did," he laughs.

"Well," she says, "you found me, so now what's the plan?"

"Just cut right to the chase," he smiles.

Kristi laughs and brushes the hair from her face. Rick puts his hand to the small of her back and guides her toward the door. The female bartender suspiciously watches their exit.

"Who was the bartender?" Kristi asks as they step into the July humid air.

"Oh," says Will, "that's Mila."

"She was looking right at you," Kristi says.

"Well, I guess I was distracted," Will smiles, "I didn't notice."

"Do you two work together often?"

"About every Friday night," he says and anchors her toward the truck.

"Please excuse all the tools on the back seat," he says, "I've been meaning to get a tool box for my cab."

"No problem," Kristi says, and hoists herself onto the seat, grabbing the *oh-shit* bar. As Will drives away, their eyes meet as he checks over his right shoulder for traffic.

"So, where to?" she asks.

"I know of this great little pub downtown," he offers.

"You must be talking about Baltimore Street," she says.

"That's the place," he says, "are you hungry?"

"I could eat," she says, and he makes a right turn, The Hub disappearing behind them.

Pat's Pub is alive with a live band playing at the back of the bar. There is seating to the front of the restaurant: one table left and a sign that reads *please seat yourself.* Will takes a seat after Kristi is situated and a waitress places a laminated menu onto the table.

"Can I get you two something to drink?" she asks.

"I'll take an ice water and a Miller Lite," says Kristi.

"Bottle or draft?"

"Bottle," Kristi responds.

"Okay, and for you sir?"

"Give me the house lager," he says.

"I'll get those right out to you," she says, "Do you two need a minute to look over the menu?"

"I do," Kristi says, smiling at the waitress as she leaves.

"I've had the best bruschetta here," Kristi says.

Will looks up from his menu, "So you've been here before?"

"Yes, I have," Kristi responds, not mentioning Rick.

"I like the honey barbecue," he says.

"Think I'm going to have the salad with grilled chicken," Kristi says.

"Looks good then," says Will, "think we're ready to order."

"Yes, we are."

"You ever heard of this band?" asks Will, pointing over his shoulder.

"Not sure, who are they?"

"They're called Wrecking Ball."

"Nope, can't say I've heard of them."

The waitress returns, placing their drinks onto the table and takes down an order of grilled chicken salad and honey barbecue chicken.

"The band mostly does cover songs," he shouts over the loud music, "but they also do some original stuff. What's your favorite type of music?" he asks.

"I like classic rock and classical," she explains, and takes a sip of beer.

Twenty minutes later, the food is delivered to the table and Kristi is about to eat when Ed, with a few of his drinking buddies, enters the door. Ed steps into the restaurant, nods a quick hello then turns away to speak with one of his buddies. Kristi looks down to eat, when there is a sharp rap on the table.

"You gotta' be careful," he nods toward William before he proceeds to the front of the bar closer to the band.

"Who's that?" Will asks, smearing barbecue from his plate with the swipe of a finger.

"That must be about my Dad," she says.

"What is?" Will asks quizzically.

"That's Ed," says Kristi as she rests her fork onto her plate and leans back in the booth.

"He's my Dad's work buddy."

"Okay," Will stabs at a piece of poultry with his fork.

"Well," she hesitates, "all my Dad ever said was he nearly ran over Peaches."

Will's eyes dart upward from his plate, "ran over Peaches," he repeats.

"Yeah," responds Kristi, "You have to understand my Dad, the only way he knows is honest and blunt."

"That was your dad?" Will says, dumbfounded.

"That was my dad," she explains.

Will looks above Kristi's head toward the front of the bar – Ed, hand on hip, nodding while a buddy talks, peering at Will.

"Well, what's Ed mean by that?" he asks.

"Nothing, but to be careful, I guess," she says, and lifts her fork from her plate.

"Well, I hope they don't think I had anything to do with…"

"You have to understand," she says again, "you have to understand my dad defends his family, even my brother who has been on drugs and alcohol since he was sixteen – but it's mostly because my mom died."

Will adjusts slightly in his seat, getting closer to Kristi across the table, speaking louder than the music, but not loud enough for others to hear.

"Well, what's that have to do with me?"

"Nothin'," she says, pulling an onion from her fork, "it's not you, it's my dad."

"Look," Will says, defensive but softly, "there's a lot people who don't know about Peaches…"

"Where she'd get that name, Peaches?" Kristi interjects.

"Marissa's favorite scent was peaches since high school, she got her name from…" he pauses.

"From who?" Kristi asks.

"From her boyfriend."

"I thought you were her boyfriend?"

"That's what a lot of people thought…"

"Well, why weren't you?" she asks.

"She thought her boyfriend could kill her…kill her and I both."

"So what did you all do?"

"We tried to be just friends, without him knowing it."

"Well why? He's insecure or something?"

"He was a real jock – popular with all the girls in high school and Marissa was a cheerleader…"

"Typical drama right there," Kristi snorts.

"I guess classic," Will agrees, "but not really typical at all."

"Why is that?"

"He started to smother her – had to see her every day and she wanted her space…"

"I know how that is," Kristi mutters, looking away.

"What do you mean by that?" Will questions.

"I just mean that all people need space," she shrugs. "So, what were the two of you then?"

"Well, I just explained that," he says.

"No, you didn't," she snickers, "because you two were not just friends."

Will examines her face, "What makes you say that?"

"Because no one normal jumps out of a car over a friend," she explains.

"She wasn't exactly normal," Will tosses his napkin onto his plate as Kristi takes a swig from her Miller Lite.

"You all need anything else?" The waitress removes the plate.

"No," Will shakes his head, "we're ready for the check."

Kristi smiles at the waitress who turns to leave, "Alright then," the waitress says, "I'll be right back with that."

Kristi eyes Will, "Are we in a hurry?"

"He's making me uncomfortable," Will nods over her head.

"Oh," Kristi says, and looks over her shoulder; Ed stands at the front of the bar, eyes on Kristi.

"He's just observant," she shrugs, and takes another swig.

"He's not taking his eyes off me," he responds.

"Here you go," the waitress lays a folded check onto the table. Will reaches into his back pocket and removes a single bill, placing it over the check.

"Let's go," he says, standing to leave.

Outside, the night sky is gray; the air is humid and thick.

"Well, where do you want to go from here?" Kristi chirps.

"What," Will smirks, "you don't want to go home yet?"

"I can if ..."

"No," Will interjects, "I didn't mean it like that..."

"Then what do you mean?" Kristi asks.

"I mean, would you like to come over to my place?"

"And where would that be?" Kristi digs her keys from her purse.

"It's by the lake, in a place called Lakewood, about fifteen minutes from here," he says.

"Okay," she says, "take me to my car and I'll follow you there."

Will smiles, looking in Kristi's hazel eyes, "Not a problem."

Kristi pulls into the driveway of a dark, well paved road. A solitary house light shines on a door of a rough exterior. The wooden house has been freshly treated, stained dark mahogany. They enter the front door and an alarm sounds, voice activated, the speaker stating "code off" making Kristi jump.

"Wow," she says, "pretty extravagant for bartending wages."

"Yeah, I know, but…"

"But what," she asks

"But this is my father's place," he says. "He got hurt in a work-related accident," he continues at the look on Kristi's face, "broke his neck and back in several places, a rib punctured his lung."

"Oh, my god," gasps Kristi.

"He stayed in the hospital on tubes," Will says, "But couldn't make it."

"What did your father do?" she asks.

"He owned a construction business," he explains, "he left me the house, the company, all that he had – but I had to sell off his business."

"I'm so sorry to hear that…"

"Now, I just pay the utilities here and tending bar covers it," Will explains.

"How old was your father?"

"Only fifty-three…"

"My mother was only fifty-one," she says, her eyes glistening.

"Hey, but uh, do you want something to drink?" She nods and follows him into the kitchen.

Will flicks the switch to pendant lights that illuminate the interior kitchen. Marble tables decorate the kitchen and living space. Hard wood floors shine like maple and the curtains adorn venetian blinds. The double wall oven and gas top stove gleam from the pendant lighting.

"How long ago was the accident?" she leans against the counter.

"It was five years ago," he explains as he rummages through the stainless-steel refrigerator.

Kristi inhales deeply, slowly, through her nose and looks down at her feet, "It's been five years ago since my mother died," she says.

"Hey, I got some aged California wine here, a little sparkling cider if you're wanting non-alcoholic beverages…" he says, head bent in the fridge.

"I'll take a glass of the sweetest red wine you have in the house," she says, smiling.

"Alright," he closes the door, wine in hand. "I got that coming right up," and pops the cork. Then Will removes wine glasses from a glass cabinet and pours sweet red Roscato for two.

"Do you like to toast?" he asks as he dims the light holding both glasses. He hands Kristi a filled glass. "To being…" she says.

"To being alive," he responds, and their glasses *ting* …

"To being young, I was thinking," she says.

"And alive," he smiles, "to enjoy this moment." Their eyes meet.

Chapter Four

Lips slightly parted, William cranks his neck and Kristi leans in closer. They embrace passionately, holding wine glasses in one hand and each other in the other. Slowly, William leans her toward the sofa and she takes him by the hand, taking his wine glass from his delicate fingers and places both glasses on the glass-top coffee table.

"Show me to your room," she says.

William's eyes peer down the slit in her dress, at her short, petite frame, to the small of her back as he kisses her shoulder.

"Sure," he whispers.

They take each other by the hand and move toward the bedroom. Kristi smiles radiantly and they embrace, finding one another's lips, and they fall gently to the bed. Kristi on top of William, she removes a strap to her dress. William places his hands onto her waist.

"This is hard for me," he says.

Kristi leans closer to him and presses her lips to his neck, then to his ear lobe. "Why is that," she says softly.

William takes a deep breath, "Because I haven't had sex since…"

"Since what," she places both hands to his shoulders, laying her body onto his.

"Since Marissa," he says.

Kristi lays her head upon his chest. "It's going to be okay," she says.

"But it's not okay," he puts both arms around her.

"What's wrong?"

William rolls over onto his side, turning Kristi to face him.

"She…she liked it rough," William explains.

"She liked what rough?" Kristi raises an eyebrow.

"Sex," he says, taking a deep breath.

Kristi frowns, "I don't think I want to hear this."

"But I need you to," he responds astutely.

"Okay," she whispers.

He lays his head into her chest, pushing her on her back. "She liked domination. She used to ask me to do things to her…"

"Like what?"

"Like grab her by the arms and twist them behind her back…"

"While you have sex from the back," Kristi shrugged, playing with his hair, "that's not that weird."

"She asked me to grab her by the throat, slap her across the face… she wanted aggression and domination…it turned her on to be the submissive," he finishes.

"Still not weird," Kristi wraps a strand of hair around her fingers.

"When she jumped," a tear falls from Will's eye, wetting the front of her dress, "I ran her over with my car. I broke her spine with my car or maybe she wouldn't have died," he heaves into her chest.

"I'm so sorry," she says softly.

"When they found her, there were cigarette burns on her back. They think I have something to do with it," he says, "but I don't even smoke" he covers his mouth with his hand.

"Then you weren't the only one," she concludes and taps him on the top of the head.

"Look me in the eyes…it's not your fault," she says, "She jumped from your car."

"But I told her that it was over and that I was done. I said it knowing that she was a manic depressive, that she stopped taking her pills and stopped seeing her counselor."

"But you did not push her out of the car. She did that on her own, it is not your fault," she repeats, sternly.

Condry walks into the restaurant thirty minutes too late; the bar is at full capacity and Ed is buried in the crowd. He approaches the crowd to the back of the bar and motions for Ed to exit the back door; once outside, the tables are crowded with smokers and boozers. Condry finds a corner tucked away from the crowd and Ed gathers beneath dim lighting.

"What you find out?" Condry asks.

Ed inhales and sighs, "It's not what I found out," he says.

"Then what is it?" Condry asks impatiently.

"Well," Ed says, "they were here together tonight."

"Who was?"

"Kristi," Ed pauses, "and McLean."

"You don't really mean William McLean do you?" He pinches the bridge of his nose.

"Yes I do," Ed says.

"Over my dead body," Condry growls and walks away, "I've gotta get back to work," he says and darts around the corner.

Monday morning, Kristi arises from the bed, William sleeps soundly next to her. Quietly, she makes her way to the front of the house.

"Where are you off to?" She hears from the room.

"I've gotta get to the store," she explains, putting on her shoes.

"Don't you have employees for that" he yawns as he enters the kitchen. "Do you have time for breakfast?"

Kristi chuckles, "Sure," she says, and tosses her purse onto the sofa.

"I've got eggs," he says, "might be out of pancake mix."

"You cook?" She asks, taking her shoes off again.

"I worked the restaurant business since I was seventeen," he explains, "started out as a dishwasher, bus boy, a cook – and now I tend bar," he says, removing two mugs from the cupboard. "Do you drink coffee?"

"What do you have?"
"Got the handy Keurig right here," he pats the machine.

"I'll take the cappuccino," she says.
"Vanilla?"
"Sounds good," she says.

Kristi removes a stool from the center island and takes a seat. Across the kitchen, on the wall beside the mantle, she notices a photo of a man in his fire suit.

"Who is that?" She points toward the wall.

"That's my dad," he says.
"Oh was he a fireman, too?"

"That's right," he fires up the gas stove and removes a pan from the drawer, "a volunteer fireman at night."

"Well, juggling two jobs has become common place," she says.

"You do it," he says.

"On occasion," Kristi shrugs, "like you said, I've got an employee for that."

"Alright," he holds out a pan, "what are we having for breakfast?"

"Surprise me," she says, "I'll eat almost anything."

"Okay, how about an omelet?"
"I'm not surprised," she laughs.

"Hmm, alright then, an omelet it is and the rest is a surprise." He hands her a hot mug filled with coffee. "Let me know how you like it," he says.

"It's good," she says, taking a sip, "tastes like vanilla."

"Well I hope so," William laughs, cracking an egg over the frying pan.

Kristi jumps, spilling some of her drink on her chest, as glass shatters across the front living-room.

"Oh, God," William groans, dropping an onion on the floor "Not again."

"Not again?" Kristi grabs a hand towel from the counter, wiping cappuccino from her chest, as William races to the front door.

46

Swinging the front door open, William sees the tail end of a red pick-up truck peeling out down the street.

"It's got to be Flint," he says. "Marissa's ex."

"Are you going to call the police?" She asks, approaching the door.

"I'm not sure," he sighs. "It's complicated," William shuts the door. Turning, he opens the hallway closet; he removes a broom and a dustpan.

"Here," Kristi says, "let me help you with that."

"I've got it," William tosses the dust pan onto the floor, "You've got bare feet. Stay away from here."

Kristi walks away into the kitchen, "At least let me check on the eggs."

"Appreciate it," William sweeps shards of glass into the pan.

Candace Meredith

Chapter Five

"What's complicated?" Kristi asks as Will enters the kitchen. "And where are the plates?"

"Cabinet to the right," he nods.

Kristi removes two porcelain plates from the cupboard and scoops eggs onto the plate. "I hope cheese is enough," she says.

"That'll be more than fine," he sighs, "I'm sorry about breakfast."

"It's not a problem," she says, "but I still want to know what is complicated."

"Flint," he says, shoveling shards of glass into the garbage can, "Flint's father is a deputy at the local police station."

"It doesn't mean he gets away with destruction of property," she says.

"Well, he is," says William.

"My father might know someone," Kristi offers.

"My father was acquainted with the police chief. That's why it's complicated," he explains and tosses the broom back into the closet and turns to the front door, "and now I have to replace another damn window."

Kristi faces the window as she stuffs single bills into the drawer.

"Covering for Kim today?"

"Oh, hello June," she says, looking up from her task. "I'll have your earnings on Friday if that's okay."

June, dressed in a floral sundress and hat, smiles happily, "I see someone bought my landscape."

"Sure did," Kristi responds, "That meadow was gorgeous."

"Painted that meadow in Ireland," she explains as she tosses her hand bag on the counter. "My father's Irish and my mother was from Wales."

"I didn't know you're European," Kristi closes her drawer.

"Well, I guess I'm not," she says, "I was born in Pennsylvania then we transferred to the Appalachia when my father began business for the railroad," she explains as the bell above the door chimes as it opens.

"Where have you been?" Kristi sighs as Rick storms through the door.

"I was with a friend," she says.

"I guess I should get going," June picks up her purse and touches Kristi's shoulder, "let me know about lunch sometime."

"I'll text you soon, June," Kristi walks June to the door. Ignoring Rick, they hug briefly, June's cherry red hair swirling in the breeze.

"You do that dear," she waves, walking away.

Not wasting time, Rick, who stands six feet tall, thin as a rail, wearing a blue button down polo and blue jeans, steps aside, runs his hand through his hair.

"What friend?" he stammers, "Where the hell have you been Kristi?" Beads of sweat form on his receding hairline. Kristi sidesteps Rick, returning to her counter, and brushes her hair from her face.

"I was with a friend," she says, grabbing some cleaning supplies

"Who?" He demands.

"A guy," she responds, spraying chemicals on some paper towels.

"A guy?" He stutters, "Do you like this guy?"

"I think I do like him," she says.

"What does that say about us then, Kristi," he says, one hand on his hip, the other flying through the air.

"It means that I still need a break."

"What?" He narrows his eyes.

"Look, we had this conversation. I thought this conversation was over?" she says buffing the counter.

"Maybe for you, but not for me," he sighs. "What exactly do you want?"

"I want space and separation…" she says, scrubbing at a cloudy spot.

"After two years together?"

"Yes."

"Well, you don't love me or what?"

"Yes, I do …"

"Then, what is it?" he slams his palms on the counter.

"Love just isn't enough," she shrugs.

"You want more then. What, like a ring? There isn't anything that I can't give you…"

Kristi covers her mouth, inhaling the faint scent of cleaner. "I just want time and space, Rick."

"I don't know if I can do that," he says.

"But you'll have to," she says, "There just isn't anything else."

"The hell with this shit," he growls. "Did you…did you sleep with this guy?"

"Yes… I … did." The words come out in a rush. "Yes, I slept with another man, in his bed, in his house, and it wasn't out of love. But it was genuine…"

"Stop, Kristi, I don't need to hear this shit."

"You asked," she shrugs.

"I don't know what the fuck is wrong with you."

Kristi puts on her business face as a lean woman wearing a coral tank and jean shorts walks through the door.

"You coming, Rick?"

"Who is this?" Kristi raises an eyebrow at him.

"It doesn't fucking matter now, does it," Rick growls.

The other woman rolls her eyes, "Are we leaving now?" She asks, one hand on her hip, the other clutching a hand bag.

"Yes, we're leaving now," he says, and opens the door. As they walk out, Kristi steps through the door.

"Well, then it doesn't fucking matter does it," she hollers, pedestrians stop to look, and Kristi slams the door, bells clanging against her. Just then, Kim walks in from the employee exit, putting her cell in her pocket.

"Who was that?" she asks, adjusting her skirt.

Kristi turns around, headed towards her office. "That," she says, "is now my ex."

"Oh," says Kim who is merely twenty and flighty. "I'm off break," she says. Her sheen blond hair and pink lips sparkle against the sun that illuminates the foreground.

"Well," says Kristi, "just be sure to lock up, I'm not coming back tonight. I will be in my office, going over inventory for a while."

"Will do," Kim stands behind the counter.

Halfway through her inventory check, she hears Kim greet someone and footsteps come closer to the door. There is a knock on her open door.

"Dad…" she greets, surprised.

"Kristi…"

"What are you doing here?"

"I've come to see you…"

"Well, obviously…"

He leans against the door, arms folded. "Look, Kristi, I just worked twelve damn hours, but I came here because Ed told me."

"Stop right there Dad, I'm twenty-four."

"I know you are an adult, sugar, but you don't know this guy…"

"Dad, you don't know him…"

"And neither do you." Kristi sighs, grabs some paperwork and stands from her desk. She pushes past her father and walks to the front. Placing paper in front of Kim to sign, she ignores her father who follows anxiously.

"Do you all want me to leave?" Kim asks, apprehensively, signing the paper.

"No. I am leaving." She idles past her father, opening the door, ushering him out.

"But I know the law," he says, one hand on her shoulder, "and I know convicts."

"Well, he's not a convict," she says, removing her father's hand from her shoulder. "Don't try being a parent now, Dad."

"Look Kristi…." His face sags a little.

"Look, nothing, Dad, you have to stop this."

"Stop what? Stop caring?"

"Stop smothering me," she pauses, "like Rick." Shrugging him off, she starts off for the parking lot, picking up the pace and darting around pedestrians. "June is expecting me," she says, "and you're not invited." She turns and stops dead in the street, "Mom would get to know him first," she says, "so stay out of it." Kristi holds up her palm to his chest, re-directing his intention to follow her.

"I knew your mother," he mutters after her retreating form, "and I know this guy. What about Rick?"

Chapter Six

Kristi, a voice says, startling Kristi from her sleep. She peers at the alarm clock: 5:40 a.m., and wonders why the voice of her mother would be so clear, so audible, and earthy. She stopped hallucinating about her mother in the hallway, in the street, in the shower, behind the car, hovering over the oven, showing her how to prepare the bird for Thanksgiving and aside the Christmas tree.

She even saw her mother on campus. It startled her so much that Kristi dropped her books to the ground, kneeling over papers filled with stories of how families were broken by the unexpected death of someone they loved. Kristi knew she stopped writing to preserve her mother's life. The hallucinations were warmer than her account of the past; her absent father, her distant brother, and a mother who tried to keep it all together under one roof.

"At least he puts the bread on the table," she remembered her mother saying. She owed her father that much; his warmth missing like his spot at the dinner table – but the bread was abundant, at times. Perhaps, she thinks, that she just didn't get close to her father, like her brother, because she was closest with her mother – an irreplaceable love that cannot be tapped: not by Rick, not by Jake, Dad or men. It was the reason sex could be so casual, so brief, so physical because relationally she was inept.

Kristi rolls over in bed, dragging the sheet to her face, smelling in the scent of lavender – like the scent of her mother's garden. Kristi jolts upright at the sound of the fist to the front door. She quickly grabs the robe draped over her vanity chair and heads down the stairs, flicking on the light, peering through the peep hole at Will.

"What the fuck?" She says through a slit in the door.

"I'm sorry," he shivers, water dripping from his clothes.

"Don't you know how to use a cell phone and why are you so soaked?" She asks.

"I got up at about four this morning."

"Doing what?"

"Visiting my father's grave…"

"At four?"

"I couldn't sleep," he says as Kristi opens the door and he enters, wet down to his boxer briefs.

"Mind if I take these off?" he asks, stripping off his shirt.

Kristi nods holding out a hand for his wet clothes, "You called me?"

"I sent you a text," he says.

"I was sleeping."

"I know, I'm sorry," he says.

"How do you know where I live?" She asks over her shoulder as she heads toward the dryer. Will removes his shoes, "I had to follow you home, Kristi, to make sure you wouldn't be followed by Flint, or any of his macho jock friends."

"But why would I be followed?" she asks returning with a dry towel.

"I don't know, I just don't want anything to happen to you."

"Okay," she takes his shoes and walks toward the kitchen, "I can make some coffee, and do you want me to find a shirt?"

"I'm fine without the shirt," he says, "but I'll take the coffee."

"Have you decided to notify the police?" She asks, removing two coffee mugs from the cupboard and filling the pot with water.

"No," he responds sitting on a dry part of the towel, "I just don't think it's going to matter."

"It matters."

"It does, you're right, but it's my problem – not the police."

"It's their job."

"It's my house and my problem."

"I know, but I'm just saying …"

"I know you are sweetheart, but some things matter and some don't." William stands and paces about the room. Stopping, he sees a photograph of Kristi and her mother on the end table.

"You look a lot like your mother," he says.

"That's what my father has always said. You like hazelnut?"

William nods as Kristi pours creamer into both the mugs and swirls hazelnut around the rim.

"What's your plans today?"

"Taking the day off…"

"Any particular reason? Holiday?"

"Today is my dad's birthday, he would have been fifty-eight."

"What about your mother?"

"She lives in North Carolina. I used to see her about once a year on Christmas mostly – she's re-married to an alright guy, named Mike, but she kinda moved on with her new family."

"So, you two get along?" Kristi sips from a pink butterfly mug.

"Yeah, we do," he says, "like I said, he's an alright guy – but you know, he's just not my dad."

"They're irreplaceable."

"Well, it's not alright, you know, it's not alright that our parents died."

"It never will be alright."

"But how about today, what are you doing? "He asks, finally sipping from his blue and white mug.

"I'm off today," she shrugs, "but I have nothing planned."

"You're not going to the store?"

"No, Kim can handle the store."

"Want to meet some of my friends?"

"And do what?"

"A barbecue, at my place…let's say around noon."

"Sure," she says, placing her mug onto the coffee table.

"Alright, then it's a date. I have some of my buddies coming over. We do it every year to honor my Pops. You're lucky because girls aren't usually invited – but I'll make an exception this time," he laughs.

Kristi smiles, pulls back her hair into a ponytail, "Alright Mr. McLean, I'll be there." He leans closer into her, his bare chest to hers as they kiss.

Candace Meredith

Chapter Seven

Kristi pulls into the driveway. Large trucks align the street, a flashy Dodge blocks her view from the house. Kristi steps out of the car and locks it. The window has been repaired in the front door. She walks onto the porch step and raises her knuckles to the door, forgetting the door bell and alarm system. But the music is loud and no one comes to the door. She steps to the side and peers through the window, inside, an average-built brunette with a short bobbed hair cut waves her in. Kristi moves through the front door.

"You must be Kristi," the brunette says, extending her hand. I am Kelly. Will told us about you."

"Yes, nice to meet you," says Kristi walking through the door. Notices everyone holding red plastic cups, alcohol bottles on the tables and an array of food.

"Am I late?" She asks.

"Oh, no," says the brunette, "we got here from Virginia last night. Come, we can go and find Will." Kelly takes Kristi through the crowd, heading toward a large male wearing Wrangler jeans and boots.

"This is my boyfriend, Brody," she says. "This is Will's girl, Kristi."

"Hi, Brody," says Kristi, playing with her necklace, suddenly embarrassed.

"Hi, how you do'n?" He asks, clenching a bottle of Sam Adams. His friends nod with beers in their hands.

She is saved from further small talk by a tap on her shoulder.

"Hey, girl," Will greets her enfolding her in a huge bear hug. "Glad you made it." Will, dressed in khaki shorts, Hawaiian shirt and flops, takes a sip of his draft brew.

"Would you like a drink?" He asks.

"You got a Miller Lite?"

"Got bottles in the cooler right over there," Brody points.

"Here, let me get it for you," Will says and turns past the stereo speakers and into the kitchen. He lifts the lid of the cooler and withdraws a Miller Lite. A David Bowie song fills the air and the crowd of about twenty holler and crank up the volume.

William cracks open the bottle top and hands it to Kristi, he raises his draft, and proposes a toast, before the music gets loud again.

"Hey, uh," he stammers, "you know I have you all here to commemorate my dad, Charles McLean, everyone called him Chuck – so here's to my dad," he says.

"Chuck," raises Brody, "we love you man, you were like a father to me."

"We can all drink to that," a voice calls out.

"Thank you, Ricky," Will says, and takes another drink.

After a moment of silence, the group go back to socializing when a horn blows from outside.

"Looks like Flint Richard, and his whole damn family," Brody says, peering through the drapes.

"Holy shit. You have got to be kidding me, man," sighs Will.

"You ladies stay in the house," Brody picks up an empty beer bottle from the table.

"What's that going to do," Ricky asks, a hefty 5'9", grabbing a knife from his back pocket.

"Get outta here man, you won't need that," Will waves him off.

"The hell we won't," Brody says.

"Will ..." says Kristi, as Will throws open the front door; Rick, Brody and ten other friends clamber outside.

"What you doing at my damn house?" Will hollers out the door.

"You think you're tough with all your little friends," a voice hollers back.

Kristi moves toward the door, peering out a slit in the door as some laughter filters through.

"I told you all to stay inside," Brody yells over his shoulder.

"We ain't coming out," Kelly hollers next to Kristi.

Flint, still built like the high school football player he once was jumps out the back of a red pick-up truck followed by five buddies and two from the front seat.

"Who's that?" Flint huffs, "You got a new girl in there ..."

"None of your damn business," says Will, who takes a step forward.

From behind Flint, a well-cut buddy, leans over to pick up a rock. He heaves it toward the front door, which Kristi quickly closes with a thud.

"Son-of-a-mother-fucker," Brody growls as he charges Flint and his friend. Flint charges back, knuckles hit Brody square against the jaw. Brody raises a fist to hit back, but gets an upper cut in the gut. Brody staggers, and a few heavy bodies jump him from the back. Ricky rushes past the pick-up truck, followed by Will, becoming a free-for-all in the front yard of Will's father's house in broad daylight. Kelly runs out the door, as fifteen hefty bodies leaning to-and-fro, upper-cutting and dodging, fists swinging and hitting, getting hit back and blood spurting – littering the front driveway. Will, pressed up against Brody's Dodge, receives a direct blow to the face from Flint.

"Stop," yells Kelly, chucking her bottle at Flint's head, hitting him in the neck.

Flint turns around, looking at the blood on his hand from the back of his neck. "You little bitch."

"You mother fucker," Brody yells back, being double teamed by blows to the face.

Flint hits Will against the face, blood careens across the Dodge window. Will collapses to the ground.

"I'm calling the police," Kelly yells, as her and Kristi run back into the house. Flint grabs Kelly by the back of the hair, making her fall to the ground.

"You asshole," Kristi says, kneeling beside Kelly.

Suddenly Flint drops to his knees and falls forward, Ricky is standing over him, his knuckles bloody and raw. Brody staggers up to them blood dripping from a cut in the lip, "Honey," he says, "Kelly, you alright?"

"Yeah," she responds, getting to her feet, she wipes a cut from her elbow.

"I'm going in," Kristi says, running for the door, she reaches for her purse from the marble table and calls 9-1-1.

Chapter Eight

When Will wakes in the hospital, Kristi smiles with relief. She leans over his prone body, her cool hand stroking his forehead.

"Hello," she manages with a small smile.

"Where am I?" Will asks, removing the oxygen mask to the side.

"You're in Sacred Heart," she says, "you're in the hospital."

"I bet I look like hell," he says.

Kristi smiles lightly and cocks her head at an angle to kiss him softly on the lips, then leans back, adjusting the pillow beneath his head.

"No," she says, "you look like shit."

He chuckles, then whimpers, noticing a bandage around his head, his face, his chest and his right arm.

"Damn, did I break anything?" He tugs at the oxygen mask, "Why am I wearing this?"

"You were choking up blood, so your bed is at an incline, and you got hit hard when Flint wouldn't stop smashing your face," she whispers compassionately. "He wouldn't stop until the police arrived."

"Damn, my face does hurt," he winces, gently touching his cheek.

"He broke bones in your face," she says, pulling at the blanket, tucking it into one side, "you're on morphine so you shouldn't feel too much pain."

"No, just a tightness in my face," he says, resting his head back into the pillow.

There is a knock and they both look up as Officer Mingolelli walks in.

"I'm here to find out if you want to press any charges," he says, hand on his belt, his elbow nudging his revolver.

"No," Will says, "but I'll take a bullet in the head."

"Now you don't want to talk like that," the officer says, "I knew your father–he'd tell you the same thing."

Will manages a quick smile before the morphine takes over and pulls him under again. Kristi, checking to make sure he is indeed asleep stands to face the officer, "Shouldn't he press charges?"

"Not if he don't want to."

"But look at his face." she gestures to the sleeping man behind her.

"I know," says the officer, "but Flint's a good kid, a tough young fellow who takes losing his girlfriend real hard."

"But that doesn't give him an excuse to…"

"I stay out of it, miss," he says, and with a nod, he excuses himself out of the room and slowly closes the door behind him. Kristi sits beside Will and removes the oxygen mask from below his chin and places it gently to his mouth when she hears the door slowly open again. This time it's Kelly, whom Kristi motions to come in.

"Hey," Kelly leans against the window. "How's he doing?"

"He woke up for a few minutes."

"Did he say anything?"

"Yeah, he could talk, despite the swelling."

"That's great," Kelly moves closer to Kristi and stares at Will.

"How's Brody?" Kristi asks. "Anything broken?"

"Just a few fingers," Kelly sighs, "but they're all bandaged up."

"Will told the officer he wasn't going to press charges…"

"Neither would Brody," Kelly rolls her eyes, "that's how men are."

"Where is Brody?"

"Still here but getting ready to leave the ER… he wasn't admitted like Will."

"And how about Ricky?"

"He's cut up, like on the lips and stuff but, he's been released."

"Anyone else still here?"

"Brody will be coming up to see Will once they let him go, but the rest had to get back home."

"How about you?" Kristi squeezes Will's hand without realizing she is doing it. "How are you holding up?"

"Oh, I'm fine," Kelly says, "and how about yourself?"

"I'm doing alright," Kristi shrugs. "Tired."

"It's been a long couple of hours."

"It's been a long couple of years" Kristi counters.

"Why do you say that?"

"Will and I both lost someone – me, my mother, and Will, his dad…"

"That's made it hard then."

"Yes, yes, it has."

"Well, if you ever need anything, I'm only a ninety-minute drive to VA so you can stop by at any time," she smiles. "Just get the directions from Will."

"I will do that," Kristi says as they hug. A sob escapes Kristi and Kelly looks at her. Kristi wipes away a tear.

"I just bet that Carl has both his parents."

"Who's Carl?" Kelly asks, taking Kristi's hand into hers.

"The boy who hit my mother, with his car – he just drove into her head-on. And she died right there, in the car."

"I'm so sorry. You must miss her every day. Kelly gives her hand a squeeze. "I can't imagine what you and Will have gone through."
"I just wish she could have been here…"

The girls jump as a nurse walks in the door. Silently she checks the fluids of the IV and inserts a needle into the port before heading back out the door.

"Well, I better get back to Brody down there…I wanted to be sure to check on the two of you."

"I will let Will know you were here."

"I'm sure Brody will be up," she says, and makes her way toward the door.

Kristi turns to Will, gazing at the tubes and the machines, remembering them trying to save her mother. They tried everything to bring her back to life: tubes, CPR, life support. But it was too late. Her mother was dead; now, Will clings to consciousness. The heart monitors, the oxygen levels, the iv fluids and the catheter, all signs that he is alive and stable, but her mother didn't make it that far.

Kristi clings to the thought of her mother, to her hopes and her dreams that her mother could be there, to help her understand how men could be so vile. Memories of her father come to her too. She remembers her father's painful words at the courthouse: he didn't care how sorry he was, Carl had no right being in that car; he had no right defending his own careless judgement. The judge and jury took his words to heart and Carl was sentenced.

Chapter Nine

Condry steps into the corrections facility at 10 p.m. to begin his night shift. He busily paces the corridor of tier four, checking that the inmates are quiet. Its lights out after ten and do not come on again until 4:30 a.m. for morning chow. He is on duty until five and is in charge of first morning call. Condry knew the inmates liked to stay up through the night, many of them sporting fresh ink in the morning, tattooed by a cell buddy, and tonight was no exception.

Tier four consisted of high risk inmates that were serving longer sentences and had nothing better to do with their time but to fabricate ink pens into tattoo guns or some sort. To Condry, that was better than any shank they would otherwise make. The process went unnoticed since the inmates waited until after lights out. Satisfied that all is quiet and without incident on tier four, Condry finds himself at the end of the hallway where a well-known inmate peers through the bars in his direction.

"I heard you was looking for something on that Grand Avenue fellow," he says, with his chin resting on one hand, feet hanging off the cot.

Condry stops, turns slightly facing the scrawny, tatted up inmate. The inmate sits up, placing one hand to his knee. "I might know something about him," he says, pretending to yawn.

"And how is that?" Condry asks.

"Went to school together," he snickers, "had detention a time or two together, too."

"Oh, yeah," says Condry, "for what?"

"Dunno but he liked to smoke the reefer."

"What's that got to do with anything?" Condry asks, squinting.

"Might have had something to do with that girl's back," the inmate leans back into the cot, both knees bent, propped against his chest.

"What about her back?" Condry asks, nonchalantly.

"You didn't hear? Someone put cigarettes out on her back. Coroner found her all scarred-up with holes on her back…"

"You know William did it?" Condry let his curiosity get the best of him.

"Can't say for sure, just know he was with her. Also, know her boyfriend didn't know about him either, not until they found her, well, until you found her – all laid out in the street like that."

"Well, if it wasn't Will, you know if it could have been anybody else?"

"Nope. No one's ever said she was with anybody else."

"Alright, let me know if you get anything else."

"What's in it for me?"

"I won't say anything about that new tattoo you got on your arm," Condry scoffs and steps through the tier door. In his office he finds Ed, sipping coffee with a newspaper laid out on the table.

"Looking for a new job?" Condry asks.

"No," says Ed, looking up from his paper, "but they got a job posted for a clerk at the courthouse – if you're looking." he chuckles.

"Hey, uh, have you heard anything from the inmates in here?" Condry asks.

"No, man," says Ed, tossing the paper aside, "haven't heard a thing. You?"

"No," responds Condry, "but let me know if you hear anything."

"I'll let you know the moment I have anything on him, but I am wondering what was Kristi doing with him?"

"She got a job at The Hub serving tables," Condry says, "don't know anything other than that."

"Not enough money at the store?"

"She never stopped waiting tables," Condry shrugs. "Not since her mother died."

"Whatever happened to the other guy?"

"Rick? I don't know man, she seemed to like him enough, but maybe not for long enough."

"Mingo might know something for you," Ed sips from his coffee mug.

"Mingo?"

"Mingolelli, from the station."

"Oh, what's he know?"

"There was a fight."

"A fight?"

"That girl's boyfriend got a hold of William again."

"Again?"

"Evidently, but you should talk to him. Apparently, Flint got a hold of Will, took a beating to the face, got all banged up."

Condry grins slightly as he pours his own cup of coffee. "Thought you said you didn't know nothing?"

"Well, not from any of the inmates in here," he shrugs.

"Alright, I'll check into it," Condry grins at the thought of Will, face full of blood, taking a beating from Flint.

"How bad was it?"

"I don't know exactly, only know it was bad enough to put him in Sacred Heart Hospital."

"Don't know what good showing up there will do."

"Well, by what I hear, Kristi can tell you more than I can."

"You-gotta-be-shitten-me," Condry groans, "she's taking a liking to that guy?"

"By the sound of it," says Ed.

Condry made his rounds every hour, checking the cells. When morning finally rolls around, the bright lights flicker on. The inmates, right on cue, roar awake, ready for breakfast and roll call.

Thompson, Condry's connection on the inside, skin fresh with seeping black ink and body art consisting of skulls and crosses, made his way down tier four, past the guard shack, where the inmates convene for chow in the common area. Earlier, Condry pulled his file, learning that Thompson was incarcerated for four years for armed robbery and a slew of drug charges, mostly consisting of possession of narcotics including marijuana and cocaine. Thompson, knowing about William McLean, echoed his discontentment and disdain for Will, despite his connections with a father who volunteered at the local fire department.

Condry was convinced that Will could not be trusted. Will's past in juvenile detention mirrored his personality. Someone who could break the law, could potentially assault someone else, like another woman, a woman who had a boyfriend, who had a life she was trying to protect, to defend, to honor.

Condry felt that she must be trying to do something right by Flint, whose father is a deputy and is the leading football athlete for the local state college. Condry felt severe dislike and almost pure hatred for a punk like Will, who was no doubt responsible for burning holes into her flesh. She must have been trying to flee for her safety but couldn't get away fast enough before he somehow put his hands on her.

Chapter Ten

Kristi wake up, her mother's voice says as Kristi's eyes flutter open. The morning sunlight illuminates the bedroom, peeping through the part in the curtains. Kristi's thoughts turn to Will. How long he'll be in the hospital, why no one will file charges, and when it will happen again. Kristi steps outside her covers, placing her feet into her soft, pink slippers and heads downstairs from her loft apartment.

The summer heat penetrates the window, a glint-like prism casts across the wall, filling the room with geometric shapes. The clock reads 7 and the automatic timer on the coffee pot has turned on – filling the room with its aroma. Kristi is due to work that evening and Kim should be opening the store right about now, she thinks, planning to visit the store after the hospital.

Kristi pours herself a cup of coffee, adding hazelnut cream before she heads back upstairs to shower. *It's Thursday*, she thinks, the start of a long weekend, working the busiest shifts at The Hub. Kristi also hopes to see June and Lisa today, hoping Kim can handle the hours at the store. Stepping into the shower, Kristi hits the on-button to her portable radio player; the radio voice announces that it's going to be near 100 degrees today, no rain, but dry and humid.

Great, Kristi thinks. The Hub will be especially busy: the outdoor seating will be slammed with reservations, but its good money. She was still hoping to make plans for her vacation–dreaming of the beach as she lathers her body with the scent of apple blossoms.

"The bones in your face will heal," the doctor says, "they're not broken, but fractured, and we were able to straighten your dislodged nose."

"My nose," Will says, touching his face.

"Your nose is broken," explains the doctor, "the reason why you're wearing metal on your face."

"Yeah, I can see that," says Will, shifting uncomfortably in the bed and pulls off the itchy blanket

"The bruising and swelling will also go down," the doctor flips the pages attached to his clipboard. "You can use these records to file charges, if you choose to do so."

"Okay," says Will, "thank you." He leans over the side of the hospital bed and stretches his legs; his face hurts but so does his ribs, and his back is stiff.

"I'll be sending you home with Percocet," says the doctor.

"I'll take what I can get," Will, twists his back, then in the opposite direction, trying to crack it.

"Okay, you will be discharged now," the doctor says, "You can get dressed."

"Thanks." Will slides out of the bed, watching the nurse follow the doctor out the door.

"I'll have your discharge papers ready for you," she says, as she exists the door.

Will scan's the room for his clothes. There is a partially open linen closet and when he opens the door all the way, he finds his personal belongings wrapped inside a plastic bag. Removing his gown, he pulls his tank over his head when there is a knock on the door.

"Hello," he says, as Kristi pokes her head through the opening.

"Oh, sorry," she says, "didn't realize you were undressing."

"It's not like you haven't seen me naked," he laughs pulling her into the room. Kristi can feel the weight of his penis pressed to her thigh.

"This is awkward," she laughs.

"I know," he sighs, "why didn't you tell me about the broken nose?"

"Because you had enough to worry about," she throws her arms around him, "you should put on your pants."

Will rolls his eyes and continues to dress. "It's good to see you've come back," he says.

"Oh," she says, "Kelly wanted me to tell you they were here."

"I'm not surprised I don't remember. Too much morphine," he explains, "but Brody is like a brother to me. He better have been here," he laughs. "How are they doing?"

"Brody has some busted fingers," she says.

"Probably from busting out the glass to the Dodge," he says, "the last thing I can remember. I would be dead if it wasn't for Brody."

"He had a lot of Flint's friends on his back," she says.

"Carried that weight to take care of my ass," he says, pulling up his pants, fastening his zipper; his Hawaiian shirt stained with blood.

"Better get a new shirt," he says. "Does work know where I am?"

"Yes, I told them you were here," Kristi hands him his cell phone.

"Shit," he says, "my phone's busted."

"But you're alive," she says.

"Yeah," he says, placing his phone into his pocket.

Together, they exit the room and head down the hallway. Will is greeted by the receptionist, who hands him discharge papers, a medical note for work, and a prescription.

"Try to have a good day," she says. "Thanks," says Will, signing the paper.

Outside, the day is bright, dry and hot. The heat instantly penetrates their skin, sweat beads on their foreheads. Will, escorted in a chair, holds his head to the sky, the porter bringing him his vehicle.

"Can you drive?" Kristi asks.

"Of course I can drive," says Will, stepping out of the wheel chair. "I got this," he says, leaning forward, kissing Kristi on her lips, getting into his truck, "I gotta get home and shower," he says.

"I'm heading to the store before work," she says, "then to the coffee shop – meeting Lisa and June for lunch today."

"Tell Kim I say hello," he says, and gives her another kiss to the cheek.

"I sure will," Kristi says, and makes her way toward the parking garage.

"How about Costa Rica?" Kristi asks, sitting beside June at the Bedford Coffee House.

"Central America," says June, "a very beautiful place."

"Have you been there?" Kristi asks.

"Yes, I have," says June, "I have been to Peru and Monteverde and Arenal in Costa Rica on retreats. I did some photography, zip-lines, and visited the tropical areas. Also went on a horseback tour, toured Tortuga Island and went snorkeling," she says, "I highly recommend it."

"How long ago did you go there?" Kristi asks.

"Fourteen years ago in 2002," June says, "when I was still in my twenties. I stayed in a hostel. It was only seven dollars a night to stay in a dorm room. We stayed in a private room with a queen bed at a hostel in Monteverde, but stayed in an expensive hotel in Arenal – it had a hot tub that was much needed from all the bruising caused by a four hour horseback ride."

"And who were you there with?"

"My ex-husband," she sips on an iced latte as Lisa plops her purse onto the chair beside Kristi.

"Ah," she says, "time for lunch," she huffs, wearing khaki pants and a green apron.

"We were just talking about Costa Rica," Kristi says.

"Sorry girls," Lisa pulls an elastic band from her ponytail, letting down her long, black curls. "This band has been pulling at my head all morning."

"It's okay," June says, fluffing her silver cropped hair, "at least you have hair, I got all mine cut off."

"Glad you could make it out today, June," Lisa sips her sweetened iced tea.

"I'm glad to be here," says June, "I have a few hours to do nothing today. I can't garden – it's too hot for that."

"I have a small garden they designated at my loft," Kristi adds, "it's their effort to promote going green, like we can plant our own vegetables out there."

"It's a good initiative," June says.

"I don't garden," Lisa says, "never had much of a green thumb."

"Well, I'd really like it if I went where there's a good beach," Kristi looks at Lisa, then back to June.

"Well, then you can check out the beach at Montezuma," June says, "that's where I ended my tour in Costa Rica, it's where I found a two-hundred-foot waterfall, and from there I took a ferry to snorkel at Tortuga Island."

"A waterfall," Lisa sighs dreamily, stirring her drink idly, "sounds stunning."

"It was," June says, "got the pictures to prove it. And that's where I met Pedro."

"Pedro?" Kristi asks.

"That's right. He was one of the only English speakers there, I happened to ask him if he spoke English, and he did. He has a brother who lived in Chicago who taught him English. Anyway, I found him stooped over his Volkswagen Bus, which had broken down – it was Easter, and the locals in Costa Rica were all on a vacation. Venues were set up and they were selling all kinds of trinkets, necklaces, beads and so on. It is initially what inspired me to make my creations. So I asked Pedro if he could help me speak to the artists. Then he guided me and David up the trail to the waterfall with a large group of his friends. We all hung out there at that waterfall for the rest of the day."

"Sounds like a beautiful place," Kristi says.

"It was. We spent twelve days there, used our tax return money and a single paycheck to make the trip. I was a counselor then at the local animal shelter helping people adopt pets into their forever homes."

"Well, June," Kristi lightly hit the table with the palm of her hand, "I think you have me sold on going to Costa Rica."

"But not during this time of year," she says, "this time of year is their rainy season; you'll want to go around March before the rainy season begins."

"I think I'll consider doing that June, thank you."

"You are very welcome, Kristi, and thank you for helping me sell my product– my hobby enables me to consider taking a vacation myself, alongside working." June sips her tea. "By the way, how's the angels coming along – made anything new?"

"Sales are pretty good. People seem to like them to use for decorating around Christmas and as gifts."

"Well then that's good – your mother would be so proud to see them."

"I'm glad you two could come by here for lunch today," Lisa cuts in, looking at her phone, "but my break is about over."

"And mine as well," June says checking her phone as well, "I've got a showing scheduled in twenty minutes."

"My job starts at five," Kristi laughs and yawns. "Think I'll go home to my cat and maybe take a nap before my shift starts."

"You do just that," June says, sliding her chair beneath the table. Lisa stands and hugs them goodbye, before she heads back to the counter.

"Have a good day, girls," Lisa says.

"You do the same," June and Kristi say in unison, laughing.

Outside, nearly visible heat waves emanate off the pavement. Kristi enters her car at a slow gallop. Breathing a sigh of relief when the air conditioning hits her at full blast, she turns the dial on the radio up and speeds away from Pitt Street.

Chapter Eleven

Kristi places a fresh bowl of water onto the floor for Tuly: her female muted tortoiseshell. She removes a plastic pouch from the cupboard and unzips it, startling Tuly from her nap on the sofa. Kristi drops three to the floor and Tuly eagerly swallows and devours them.

Tuly purrs, licks her face and nudges her nose against her hand. In the middle of rubbing her head, there is a knock on the front door. Peeking through the peep hole, Jake stares back at her. Jake hasn't been by her apartment all year and is barely around to begin with. Kristi opens the door and peers at Jake, tall and thin, wearing a chained belt around skinny jeans and a form-fitting tee.

"Jake," Kristi greets him, "What are you doing here?"

"I came to see my sister," he mumbles, stoned.

"For what?" She asks, stepping into the hallway.

"Well, can I come in?"

"I guess," Kristi shrugs, "I've got to be at work soon."

"I won't take long." Jake pushes past her, leaving a boozy smelling trail behind him as he heads into the kitchen. "I came to talk to you about your boyfriend."

"What are you talking about?" Kristi folds her arms, leaning against the counter as Jake opens the refrigerator door.

"I'm trying to say that Will might not be a good guy for you."

"And what would you know about him?" Kristi asks defensively.

"Look," he says, grabbing two apples, "my supplier...we both know him."

"Your supplier?"

"Yeah."

"Who supplies what?"

"Weed mostly."

"And what else?"

"Look Kristy," he mumbles through a bite of apple. "What I'm saying is that we both know the same supplier."

"And what else?"

"I don't know much else about the guy."

"Did Dad put you up to this?"

"No, I don't even talk to him. But people are talking about the fight. My supplier heard he got busted up. We was talking about him, then he mentioned your name."

"And who is your supplier?"

"I can't talk about that," he said, starting on the other apple.

"Then you obviously can't help me."

"Maybe not. But I'm your brother and I'm here to look out for you."

"Look out for me? You can't even look out for yourself."

"Well I'm twenty-one now."

"You think that gives you the right to reek of alcohol and it's not even five yet? Let alone when most people get drunk."

"When do most people get drunk?"

"Like happy hour, something like that," Kristi cocks her head to the side.

"Alright, listen," Jake says, removing a piece of paper from his wallet, "here's my new cell number. If you need anything at all, you can call me. Or text me." Kristi doesn't move as Jake lays the paper on the counter.

"I'm just saying I'm here for you," he says, making his way toward the door.

"Go get sober," Kristi rolls her eyes as she follows him to the door.

"I love you, sis," he says as he steps into the hallway.

"We barely know each other," she whispers.

"We know each other by blood," he says.

"Yeah, like Mom's blood," angry tears start to form in her eyes. "Who you never even try to visit."

"Visit? Like what, her grave?"

"How about at the hospital?"

"When she was on tubes, and her body was a vegetable. She was brain dead, not even alive," he shouts.

"But you could have been there," she growls angrily, "but instead you were out getting drunk and stoned with all your friends."

"I told you Mom couldn't die."

"Well she is, and she did," Kristi yells, slamming the door on her brother, "but you're still getting trashed."

Leaning the back of her head against the door, she rubs her temples, chest heaving forcing back the tears she's shed many times over the brokenness of her family. Kristi grabs her purse from the chair, and her keys from the counter, looking around her apartment. Checking that things are where they should be, and not utterly displaced, like her heart and wrecked mind. She pats Tuly on the head and slams the door behind her, jabs the key into the door knob and locks the dead-bolt before she races down the stairs. She has an hour until her shift starts as she heads toward Will's house which is either her personal sanctuary or her personal hell.

Fifteen minutes later, she makes a left turn toward Lakewood and speeds up the driveway. She prayed the whole drive that her brother's problems, were not Will's too. Bounding up to the door, Kristi pounds on the wooden exterior.

"Alright, alright, I'm coming," he yells as he opens the door. He looks at Kristi in surprise.

"Who's your supplier?" She demands, impatiently.

"Whoa, whoa, what?" He gasps. "Who's my supplier? Come inside, please."

Kristi steps inside onto the foyer as Will closes the door behind them. She angrily turns on him.

"I know you do drugs. Who is your supplier?"

"Wait a minute, Kristi, I don't know who you have been talking to, but I don't do drugs…"

"Well my brother does, and he knows you."

"Okay, listen." Will runs a hand through his hair. "I have purchased weed a few times from a guy named Skinny Pimp."

"Skinny Pimp …" she huffs, "You get weed from a guy they call Skinny Pimp?"

"Yes, but he is in jail on a drug bust, possession, armed robbery, all kinds of charges were brought against him."

"Oh yeah, what he do, rob a convenience store?"

"Yes."

"Are you serious?"

"Yes."

"His actual name is Thompson."

"Wait, where is he incarcerated?"

"I think he's at WCI."

"The prison where my dad works," Kristi pinches the bridge of her nose and sighs. "Okay, well, that explains why my brother stopped by.

"What did he want?"

"To warn me about you."

"To warn you against what?"

"I don't know exactly, he just said you two know the same supplier."

"I only know Thompson…or Thomas, something like that," he says, a little relieved that he isn't being yelled at anymore, "Who they call Skinny Pimp."

"Well, and I bet my father knows him as well, probably even asked my brother about him."

"Well, what did your brother have to say?"

"Oh, he would lie for my dad," Kristi sighs, her anger deflating.

"That's in the blood, Kristi."

"I'm blood, too."

"I know, but what I mean is …"

"You mean camaraderie."

"Yeah, something like that."

"Just like the whole fight," she said, changing the subject, "and you not filing charges, because you are too proud," she punches his shoulder, wiping a tear from her eye.

"Don't say that." I don't want you to be upset. I want you to be happy," he wipes a tear from her cheek with his thumb.

"I want to be happy," she whispers.

"What can make you happy?"

"My mom not dying," she lowers her head, turning away from his eyes.

"But I can't bring her back."

"I know you can't."

"I wish that I could…"

"I wish you could, too." She tosses her purse on the floor and wraps her arms around him. Quickly taking his face into her hands, she kisses his lips, wedging his bottom lip between her teeth. She shoves her body into his, nudging his waist with her hip, leaning into him, he lifts her from the floor. Her feet dangling slightly; they fall to the floor as they rip each other's clothes off. Lying on her back, he braces himself, hovering over her body, bringing her arms above her head, wedged between her legs and she straddles her legs around his waist – not letting go.

Chapter Twelve

Will's pelvis thrusts repeatedly, softly at first as he cradles her head off the floor. Quickly adjusting, she brings her knees to his shoulders, as he puts his other hand around her neck. She gasps louder still, as he thrusts harder, penetrating deeply inside of her. When she tilts her head up, exposing her neck to his balled-up fist, he leans over sucking the exposed flesh. She tries to move, but he pins her there. Her legs parted, she moans harder, as he begins to thrust violently, bringing her hips off the floor, he holds onto her tighter, not letting go.

When she tries to moves her hand to his shoulder, he takes both of her hands into one of his and pins them above her head, the other to her neck still. She submits to his rage, gasping, yelling, pleading not to let go and to go harder still. He throws one leg into the air, holding onto her with a grasp to the inner thigh, parting her legs more, as he thrusts into her. She moans again, panting, both legs to his shoulders, both hands pinned above her head, his hand to her neck. Her naked breasts heave as they reach orgasm together and he lets go pushing away and off of her. Not satisfied, she reaches for him again, pulling him to her as her nails rake down his back. They kiss passionately, sweating, panting, and rubbing his hands down her naked thigh.

Condry steps into the station scanning the room for Mingolelli with the intention that he can bring more information to the table. The station is relatively quiet but for the clicking of keyboards and the hushed whispers of people on the phone. Mingolelli is diagonally across the room at a desk. Condry makes his way to the other side of the station; wearing his corrections uniform, he is tired after working all night, but he has decided to stop on his way home from work. Condry approaches the desk, as Mingolelli stretches out his hand, gesturing for him to sit down.

"I had the feeling I'd be seeing you," he shakes his hand.

"Well, then you might know why I'm here."

"I suppose it's to get some information on the fellow from the fight."

"Yes, that is correct."

"You know, professionally speaking, there isn't much we can do. Considering there hasn't been any charges filed."

Condry tilts his chair closer to the desk, "But is there anything you know about him?"

He shrugs. "Nothing that isn't on, or would be on public record."

"I've already looked into that," Condry waves his hand and brightens slightly, "but I hear he might be into some drugs."

"That might be the case, but nothing official that we have on him."

"And if there would be anything, official, you think you could let me know?"

"I could pass the word that we have something here." Mingo smiles.

"I have an inmate who says he knows him."

"Well, now, you know it takes one to know one. We'll see what we can do," Mingo says, resting back into his chair.

"I appreciate that, from one father to another."

"That's right. And from one law abiding official to another," he says, tapping his knuckles onto the desk.

"And that, too," Condry says, nodding, "I'll be looking forward to hearing from you." He rises from his chair.

"Likewise." Mingo replies, "I'll let you know what I hear."

Condry excuses himself from the station stepping into the light of day, putting on his sunglasses. He whistles as he drives away to his house.

Pulling into his driveway, he spots Jake, standing on the front stoop.

"What's going on, Jake?" Condry asks as he walks up to the porch.

"Nothin' just got back from seeing Kristi," he says.

"What she have to say?"

"Just that she didn't really care what I have to say."

"Well, if she knew what was good for her she'd care."

"I guess she doesn't know what's good for her," Jake shrugs, bored, "but I'm just saying that I did what you asked."

"I appreciate that," Condry says, punching the lock button, sounding the alarm to his four door Jeep Sahara. "And how about yourself, Jake?"

"I'm just fine."

"Yeah? Where are you working?"

"No one seems to need a journeyman," he spits into the dirt.

"No one can keep you around, if you're failing drug tests," Condry says, shoving the key to the door lock.

"I haven't failed any tests," he pouts.

"Are you coming in?" Condry asks, opening the door.

"Nah," Jake steps from the porch.

"Alright, then," Condry says. "I'm just getting back from work."

"I know, you've been working that shift forever now. Bye, Pops." Jake says, with the wave of his hand.

"Bye, son," Condry shuts the door as Jake starts the engine to his dated Volvo, and takes off, heading away from Yuma Street.

"You act like you've never smoked weed before," Will says, rolling over onto his back on the floor.

"Actually I haven't," Kristi turns to her side, places her hand to his chest.

"What, really?"

"Nope. I guess I leave that stuff to my brother."

"Well if it's any consolation, I haven't smoked in quite a while." He puts his arms behind his head.

"Well Mr. McLean, that's mighty proper of you," she laughs.

"Proper is my middle name," he jokes.

"I'm sure it is," she nudges him. "So you took that bandage off?"

"Hell yeah," he says, feeling his nose with his fingers, "I'm not wearing that thing."

"Doesn't it hurt?"

"No. Actually the doc gave me some Percocet that I haven't been taking since it doesn't feel too bad anymore," he says.

"I've got to get dressed for work," she says, looking at the watch on his wrist.

"You should call off, we can spend the day fishing by the lake," he pulls her closer to him.

"I can't."

"Sure you can."

"No, I really can't," she sighs, "in waitressing if you don't work, you don't get paid."

"Have you thought about finishing those college courses?"

"No," she replies, standing up and looking for her clothes.

"Well, you should," he looks up at her naked body. "You wanted to be a writer?"

"Creative Writing," she responds.

"Maybe now you can do that."

"I haven't thought about it in a while."

"If anything, you can think about it," he jumps up off the floor, looking for his clothes.

"I will," she says, sliding on her panties, and shoving one leg through the hole of her work jeans.

"It's too hot for jeans," he says, pulling his shirt over his head.

"I don't usually wear shorts to work," she says, "I'm used to working in fine dining."

"Now you're at The Hub," he says, smiling, "where you can wear shorts to work."

"I know," she says, and shoves her other leg through the pant leg, as Will pulls on the rest of his clothes.

"I have to wash up," she says, "then get to work."

"The room is all yours," he says.

"Thanks," she says, "I'll only be a minute."

Kristi closes the door to the washroom behind her and Will finishes dressing, staring at the bright sun outside. As the water runs in the bathroom, Will decides to use his boat while Kristi works.

Placing the electric-motorized boat into the water, Will spots several kayakers in the water, fisherman along the Lakeside Loop Trail, and swimmers across the lake at the small beach area of the state park. There are several hours of daylight left; the beach area lifeguard has left for the day, so the swimmers "swim at their own risk." Will hoists his fishing pole into the boat and pushes his way out into the wide-open water, with space to himself at the far end of the lake, where there are campers, and the small cove makes for a quiet site. Will hopes to get some trout to take home and prepare on the grill.

Chapter Thirteen

Condry lies in bed, staring at the ceiling, contemplating crushing Carl's skull like a small grape against the sole of combat boots. It is nearing Christmas, and he thinks about his wife, the broken shell of his family, and missing Miranda especially this time of year. He thinks about the desserts she made during the holidays and how much she liked egg nog, chocolate dipped strawberries, and how much she liked to bake and bring him desserts.

Now the house stands empty, knowing that he'd be working on Christmas as he always had, but he won't have Miranda and the kids to return home to. He sat at the foot of his bed on his days off, contemplating showing Carl his new gun he had stashed away in the locked safe along with his collection of revolvers. He thought about taking his own life, knowing he could never act on either one of his thoughts because they'd both be foolish to Miranda who he knew was stronger than he'd ever been.

Condry doesn't decorate during the holiday, keeping mostly to himself and filling in at work if someone needs to take the day off. He'd call Jake and Kristi if he could think of something to say – but often he couldn't so he would send a text stating something logical and to the point. He thinks of William, contemplating how he'd shoved that girl from his car, how she'd showed up at the coroner's with holes burned into her back. Then he'd get angry knowing his own daughter gave him the time of day – feeling, at the pit of his stomach, his disdain was not careless or brash.

Kristi sets the timer to 400 degrees, prepping the ham she's baking for Will, who is to show around seven. The television is on the food channel, and she is mentally taking notes on how to bake a five-layer macaroni that calls for gouda and goat cheese. She had made Thanksgiving dinner at her place and Will had shown with a bottle of sparkling wine. Over wine and turkey they talked about brokenness, divorce, and the family connections they have with their pets. Laughing, they shared fond memories of their deceased parents; how the past is bitter sweet.

Now, tonight, Kristi makes another dinner just for two with the intention of wearing something sexy, something to bring on the spontaneity – the spark she needs to fill the gaping hole that had been incomplete before she met Will. She found evening wear on sale at the Locked Door where she also purchased knee-high laced boots and fishnet stockings. The corset she wears beneath her striking-blue nightgown is laced in the front with strings she plans to ask him to untie with his teeth. She places candles at the dinner table, cloth napkins atop fine China and two sparkling wine glasses.

Tonight, she thinks, *he's going to get the surprise he's been waiting for*, as she adjusts the radio player to classical, she's hoping to dance to later in the evening. On the menu: hot, baked ham, five layer baked macaroni, green bean casserole and potatoes. She's hoping a home-cooked meal will entice his senses before she puts on the dessert: New York cheesecake with strawberry topping and whipped cream on top. *All this preparation better get him in the mood,* she thinks and starts the timer.

"Oh Tuly," Kristi says as Tuly rubs her face onto the edge of the center island in the kitchen meowing loudly, "I almost forgot about you, cupcake," and removes a can of salmon-flavored moist cat food from the cupboard. She cracks open the can and spoons food into a glass dish, sitting it onto the floor. Tuly laps the meaty morsels with her sandpaper tongue, purring as she eats. Kristi parks herself on the sofa, turning down the volume to the food network before she sees a text message from her father:

Calling for snow and ice. Be careful.

Kristi changes the channel to the weather, thankful that Will has a truck. It's December 2nd and the weather calls for their first snowstorm of the season: a potential of twenty inches of snow due to begin after midnight. *Perfect,* Kristi thinks, thinking Will has no other choice but to get snowed-in with her tonight, best to bring Dude, his six month old Siberian Husky, so she sends him a text.

Bringing Dude, he texts back, *not a problem, be there at 7.* She smiles, texts back: *see you then.*

Kristi removes her box of Christmas decorations from the closet. She hangs the wreath, the array of stockings across the mantle, places her artificial tree in the corner of the room, extending its branches, affixing gold and red balls from its limbs, hangs lights above the door and places mistletoe in the archway – leaving only the outdoor lights for Will to hang – possibly in the morning. Two hours later she is done. She scans the room for unkempt packaging and places the boxes back into the closet beneath the stairs.

Should be here any minute, she thinks, patting Tuly on the head, who is busy licking her paws.

Three familiar successive knocks on the door. She checks her clock. Right on time.

"Hi sexy," he comes in wearing a jersey and coat. He removes his hat and gloves, "its damn cold out there." He kisses Kristi before taking off his coat, placing it onto the chair by the door.

"Well, get in here and let me shut the door," she says, holding him by the waist.

"I've seen warmer days," he says, getting out of the way, as Dude bounds in next to him. "Just a day or two ago, when I took Dude to the lake."

"Here, Dude," she offers the happy puppy a piece of ham.

"You're spoiling this dog," he gives Tuly a rub behind the ear.

"How are things going?"

"Since I've seen you yesterday... not bad," he laughs.

"Okay, smarty-pants," she says, gesturing for him to sit down.

"Looks good in here Kris, did you do all this today?"

"I sure did."

"Not bad."

"I have some outdoor lights you can hang up on the balcony for me. Maybe after dinner, please?"

"I see you have the table all set up … you go through too much trouble for me," he takes her by the waist, bringing her in close, kissing her on the cheek.

"Well it is the holidays," she says.

"Yeah, maybe so." He says, eyeing the dessert.

"That's for later tonight – we're having ham."

"Damn, babe, all this just for the two of us?"

"Just for the two of us," she says, radiantly, bringing the salad bowl to the table, "I also added the salad," she places vinaigrette dressing on the table.

"Bon-Appétit," she says, as they take their seat at the table – the candles already lit, as classical music plays elegantly in the background.

Chapter Fourteen

"I can't take my eyes off you," Will says, watching Kristi rinse the dishes.

"Oh yeah," she drops the dish into the washing machine. "Then close your eyes," she demands, removing the bottle of vodka from the fridge, placing it atop the table, "and no peeking."

"What?" Will asks.

"I'm serious, close your eyes," she orders, taking him by the hand. His eyes shut, she guides him to the sofa and he lands gracefully with a flop.

Kristi runs to the radio, switching the dial to soft British pop music from the eighties era. Removing her dress, quickly rushing to grab the vodka, she darts back toward the sofa. Wearing the tight black corset, knee-high laced boots and fish net stockings, she places one high-heeled boot atop the center piece table aside the bottle of Vodka.

"Okay," she says, "you can open your eyes."

His green eyes flash open, and Kristi begins swaying her hips to the music rhythmically, raising her hands above her head, her shoulders shimmying.

"Damn," he whistles.

"Shut up," she picks up the vodka, approaching the sofa. She bends over, removes one strap and then the other, allowing them to fall from her shoulders. She opens the bottle, pours two small shot glasses, and places them onto the floor as she kneels, unzipping his pants, gripping onto the form-fitting briefs underneath with her teeth. She pulls lightly, then harder, dragging his jeans below his belt-line, and pours the bottle onto his naval, while salting the lemons she hid beneath the table. She parts her lips, sucking on one finger, then tongues his naval, peering into his green eyes, she winks, and he smirks, tilting his head back.

He moans as she digs her nails into his chest, removing his jeans. She stands, dropping the corset below her waist. Then she quickly straddles him, moving her pelvis to the sound of the music. Rubbing his shoulders, she throwing her hair back, as he grabs onto her and penetrates her deeply as she takes the shot glass, and pours, crisp, cool liquid into his mouth. Together, they suck on the lemon, until the next song begins to play. They finish together on the sofa, wanting to be in this moment – for eternity – but what could only last temporarily, suspending them.

"Oh … my … God, Kristi," he says, his arms flailing like a child at the toy store, and she cradles his head into her breasts.

"Do you want more," she whispers, and tongues his lobe.

He grunts and throws his arms around her. They claw at each other haphazardly, trying to become one body, trying to outdo the other one in heights of ecstasy, knocking the bottle on the floor. They lay there all night, beside the artificial light of the candles, burning the scent of vanilla cream whipped topping, like frosted cupcakes, until the morning light casts across the window sill, and the candles burn down, to a low, faint glare.

"Where the fuck did you go?" Kristi shouts when she opens her eyes. She rises from the floor where they once again, spent into the night. Wrapping herself in a blanket, she walks around the apartment for Will or Dude.

"Did you take the fucking dog for a walk," she mumbles, and checks the window. His truck is still parked before the alley, and Kristi closes the curtain.

Outside, Will rounds the corner with Dude in tow. A passerby stops to pet the black and white Siberian Husky.

"He's got those piercing ice blue eyes," the man says, patting Dude on the scruff of his neck. Dude makes the effort to jump, but Will takes him by leash, reeling him in.

"Yeah," is all he can say.

"He's beautiful."

"Thanks," As the man turns to leave and Will stares ahead at West Patrick Street. Condry, leans against a stop sign, wearing nothing more than a light jacket and faded blue jeans.

"Mr. Sullivan?" Will asks, cautiously approaching him.

"I'm going to be watching you, boy," Condry growls.

"What do you mean?"

"I'm not stupid, and I wasn't born yesterday," he huffs as Dude makes an effort to jump. Will forces him back down.

"Down boy," he says, looking at Dude.

"You heard me," Condry says, walking away, "I have my eye on you," and enters the Jeep parked at the curb.

Will slams the door to Kristi's apartment and is met with an envelope shoved in his face.

"Look what I have here," Kristi huffs.

"What is it?" Will asks.

"It's money," she says.

"Money," he repeats.

"Yeah, shoved beneath my door."

"Well, how much is it?"

"Six hundred dollars."

"What?" He grabs the envelope from her and peeks in it. "Any clue who it's from?"

"Not at all. There's no note–just six hundred bucks shoved under the door in all hundred dollar bills."

"Well maybe someone dropped it," Will says, removing the leash off Dude.

"I don't think so – someone shoved it under my door."

"When?"

"I don't know, it was there this morning. You didn't see it?"

"No, but uh, your father was outside."

"My father?" Kristi frowns. "Well, he didn't come by here."

"You sure? Maybe he had something to do with it…"

"I doubt it. He would have knocked."

"That's very strange."

"Yes it is," she places the money back into the envelope, "they didn't leave a card or anything."

"Well, maybe you should hold onto it in case someone lost it."

"Yeah, I guess I should do that," she shrugs, shoving the envelope into the drawer. "Well, I've got to get to the store today and I need to shower first though."

"You want to have lunch afterwards, or before work or something?" He asks, standing by the door.

"Sure, I guess so," she says, opening the door slightly.

"What, are you kicking me out?" He laughs, pretending to pout.

"Well, it's just that I have to get going," she says, as he kisses her. "You can tell me what my dad had to say over lunch," she says.

"Nah," says Will, "it was nothing."

"Not when it comes to my dad."

"Well then you already know," he says, stepping into the hall, "he said something about keeping an eye out for things, you know."

"I'm sure," she says, kissing him on the cheek. "Bye," she says, closing the door behind him.

What are you up to Dad, she huffs silently stepping into the kitchen. Putting the bottle back into the fridge, closing the door, she turns to make her way toward the shower thinking about the money, and where something like that would come from.

Chapter Fifteen

Carl, with his parents, siblings, aunts, uncles and cousins, reserved the back room at The Hub for eleven in honor of his grandmother's 80th birthday. It is Sunday after church, and Kristi isn't scheduled to work. Carl, seated at a table aside his girlfriend and her four-year-old son watch as the family takes photographs of Grandmother Jodie. Her four sisters, younger brother, and their children crowd the front of the room as flashes from digital cameras take their picture.

Nervously, Carl cocks his head to peer around the restaurant. The bar doesn't open until later and Kristi is nowhere in sight, but Carl knows who she is and what she looks like. He's been keeping tabs on the family through social media since he had been released from prison. The Sullivan's are familiar to Carl in more ways than one; Condry often visited tier three, seeking out Carl, inquiring from other Corrections Officers on his status, his condition, and anything they could find on him.

What the Sullivan's didn't know was how little Carl Anderson used to drink, or the jokes the fraternity played on him that night, or how uncool or unpopular he was in high school and college. They didn't know how he would have been initiated that night if he had stayed. How the fraternity would make him stick a cucumber up his ass and walk naked through campus while belting out the National Anthem, but instead, after rounds of beers and initiations he ran. He ran far and fast toward his car, toward home, and away from the personal hell he found at the initiation ceremony.

But Carl didn't make it home. Instead, Carl drove through a red light head on into a Jeep Liberty. Waking up in the hospital to tubes and machines that preserved his life, he found out that he passed out behind the wheel of his car, and killed a woman by the name of Miranda Sullivan who had been returning home with the groceries.

Carl remembering Kristi Sullivan and her brother Jake was mean to him. They were roughly the same age, and he lives with the fact that he ran because he was scared, bullied, humiliated and undignified – but none of that could make it okay. None of it could keep him from getting into his car, keep him from running – and if *he could have stayed* perhaps the cucumber and the beer would have been the last thing on his mind because he wished, and could have taken, his own life instead.

But Carl was alive, and he knew that in prison, no inmate would sympathize – and neither would the Sullivan's for that matter. He therefore knew that in a single night he became a killer and a coward, and could never add up to anything ever again. Carl contemplated taking his life as he sat in jail, he knew the fraternity that got him drunk and coerced him to initiate would never be responsible, and that responsibility resonates solely on his shoulders. He recognizes that hazing is a ritual the fraternity uses to initiate its members, and he deals with the fact that if he would have stayed he might have been initiated – but instead, he left confused, disoriented, and ultimately unwilling.

"Come on, Carl," Aunt Cindy says, "let's get a picture of all the grandkids," she ushers him to the front of the room as Carl forces a smile.

The picture of Carl, next to his grandmother and cousins, are posted in the paper, wishing their grandmother a happy eightieth and her husband – a happy eighty-first birthday. The next day, Kristi examines the paper, fresh from the shelf when she stops at the convenience store for a cup of coffee before she heads to the store to check on Kim, and to take inventory.

Kristi recognizes Carl's lean frame and hunched stature. She knows him from all the newspaper articles. His unkempt face is thin and his hair is a reddish-brown. His smile is crooked and his teeth are perfectly straight.

Kristi enters the store with the paper bound and tied, as if putting it together again could somehow mend it all. Concealing his face could only do so much, to tuck away the sight of his auto, crumbled like tin beneath her mother's SUV, wondering how he could survive and her mother could not – if only she didn't turn her wheel toward the tree.

"It's nearly Christmas," Kim says, examining the paper as Kristi tosses it on the counter.

"It sure is," Kristi forces a smile.

"Any big plans?" Kim asks.

"Not yet," says Kristi, "but I have been considering Saint Martin."

"Saint Martin? Really? That would be nice."

"I have the money put away but I haven't decided for sure yet."

"What would you do there?"

"I would write I think. Write on the beach, alongside a margarita."

"Well the store is doing great here," Kim says.

"Yeah, sales for the holiday are doing well. Glad people buy scarves and hats."

"And angels," Kim dusts the shelf, cocking her head over her shoulder.

"I wasn't really prepared this year," Kristi sighs, looking at the shelf, "but I think I have enough inventory."

"Hey, have you thought about finishing those two college courses?"

"Not really, why?"

"There's some pretty cool online programs, you could try them out. I'm looking at finishing my program through West Virginia at Wesleyan," Kim says, fumbling with some garments, straightening the shelf.

"That's great to hear, Kim," Kristi says, "what are you studying?"

"I'm taking up Liberal Arts and Women's Studies," she says, "and they offer writing courses online."

"I can consider that, Kim," Kristi removes the cash register, counting out change. "Are you planning on leaving sales?"

"Eventually, but I have about two more years of study before I can make any changes."

"I actually have to study a second language to earn my degree," Kristi sighs.

"Take up French. I know you can do it – you have it in you."

"You sure do have faith in me."

"Six credits away from your degree."

"That's right," Kristi says, closing the drawer, folding the cash, "maybe after Saint Martin," she smiles.

"Sounds like a good plan," Kim looks down at the paper on the counter, "who is this guy?"

"That is Carl," Kristi says, flatly.

"Carl? From the accident? Well, what's he doing in the paper?" Kim asks, hand on hip.

"His grandmother had a birthday party, at The Hub," Kristi says.

"Oh, man. What if you were at work yesterday? Would you have left?"

"I don't think so," Kristi shrugs. "But I doubt I would have been serving him either."

"I bet not," Kim huffs.

"I thought about writing him a few times."

"What would you say?"

"I guess to hear what he has to say."

"I'm not sure he knows that."

"Knows what?"

"What he would say."

Kristi shrugs her shoulders, "What could he say really?"

"A lot I guess. Or nothing at all."

"Only one way to find out."

"I haven't decided on that yet."

"I'm curious. If you do."

"Well I'm somewhat curious myself, but I'm not around this time of year. It's just one more holiday without her."

"I'm sorry, sweetie."

"I know you are. I know how much everyone is. But him."

"Well maybe make that trip," Kim says.

"I might do that," replies Kristi. "I really might do that."

Chapter Sixteen

Kristi enters The Hub with plane tickets in hand; rather, a ticket for one. "I got my ticket," she says, waving her hand in the air, cranking her neck across the bar. The Hub is thick with guests seated and standing at the bar. The room around them is also densely populated with the game on the television: college football, and West Virginia plays Oklahoma. Mountaineers' colors of gold and blue flashes across the screen for the home game. Will peers at Kristi as she begins her shift for the evening.

"Where am I in this plan of yours?" he asks, eyeing the ice for a Mimosa cocktail.

"A girl can think when she's alone," she says, tying her apron.

"A guy can be romantic when he's invited to stay," he counters quietly across the bar.

A guest seated at the bar snickers. "Where you going, sweetheart?" He asks nosily.

"Saint Martin," she says.

"Haven't been there, but it's the right season for the Caribbean, should be a good time. You going by yourself?"

"I intend to immerse myself in my first novel there," she clicks the top of her pen.

"Maybe you should immerse yourself then," he says, "whatever works for you."

Kristi smiles, excusing herself to begin working the long evening shift. It's Friday night and she plans to earn enough tips to splurge on her travels: shopping, touring, sun bathing, night life, golfing and relaxing – especially at the spa. She has already booked her stay at the beautiful Villa in a guest house at the Villa La Source in the area of Les Jardins d'Orient Bay that is known for its fine, white sandy beaches and turquoise tropical waters.

Kristi visits Saint Martin. Solo because she is not especially akin to romance, not that she is a sadist, but because she needs her time away from the burden of memory and the past. During the four hour flight, she enjoys peanuts, soda, and chicken salad.

Arriving at her destination, she hales a taxi that takes her to her Villa, tucked away at the majestic Orient Bay beach where she is greeted by a concierge and provided with a rental car for her week stay. She plans to be served by a private chef, bask in a relaxing massage and be provided a personal tour – all provided by the Villa. Her earnings from the

store, her tips, and her tax return, she has
enough money to venture out.

Kristi enjoys the private pool
provided by her villa that looks like a Tiki
hut, steps away from the Caribbean Sea. La
Source takes her to the local nature reserve
where she dines next to a butterfly garden on
the Route du Galion in a greenhouse
alongside waterfalls that spill into pools
occupied by Koi beneath running waters.
Kristi dines at the traditional huts at the
Village of Grand Case where she's served
lobster and Alaskan Snow Crab legs.

She strolls along the vendor tables
during the Harmony Night Festival,
purchasing local crafts and listening to
Caribbean jazz.

Kristi retires to her Villa, perfectly
content in her small corner of the world that
has so much to offer her. She falls
comfortably into her blanket and pillows,
succumbing to the night that turns to early
morning as she wakes to the light of a new
day.

Will has been calling but she doesn't
answer. Today, in this place, she doesn't care
– she soaks in her hot tub, and catches the
rays of the sun with her toes. Perfectly at
peace, she ponders what she can write,
thinking about the memoir of her mother that
would captivate her audience. She would

write about her mother's drunken state at her wedding and their honeymoon to nowhere special because the money was not enough – but they bought a home, bought a new state-of-the-art fridge and had moments to share, at the times when they were a family.

Kristi slips beneath the water, air bubbles protruding from her lips, she peers at the haze of a blue sky, submerged, and thinking that she too could have a family someday. But not now, she thinks, and comes up for her first breath of air.

Today, she says aloud, *I'm going shopping.* The luxury of fashion boutiques await her.

"*Damn-it*," Will yells as he paces the floor, the endless ringing in his ear ending and Kristi's voicemail box. He hangs up as engines rev outside. When he opens the door there are four pick-up trucks in his driveway. Condry steps first out of his truck, followed by Flint and his friends from the other trucks that block Will's Silverado.

"Where is my daughter?" Condry growls as he storms the driveway.

"She's in Saint Martin, you mean you don't know where she is?"

"No, I don't, you little asshole, don't lie to me," he stabs a finger into Will's chest. "Why hasn't she picked up the phone…"

"I don't know," Will steps backwards, "She won't answer for me either."

"She never said she was going anywhere,"

"She wanted to go alone."

"Alone," Condry repeats.

"Oh, bullshit," Flint says, stepping from his vehicle.

"I'm not lying," Will exhales.

"Oh, well, now you think I think you're lying. I know all about you, boy."

"You don't know anything Mr. Sullivan."

"Don't tell me what I do or do not know, boy." Condry nearly pushes Will off the porch.

"I'm sorry …"

"You better be," Flint pipes in as his friends howl in approval.

"You best let me know when you hear from her, that is, if she wants to talk to you again."

"I will, Mr. Sullivan."

"I know you will," Condry turns on his heel and saunters back to his truck, "I think we're done for tonight, boys," he says, as he starts the truck.

"Bet you anything I ain't done," Flint spits on the ground.

"Merry Christmas, mother fucker," says Flint's buddy, piling into the Dodge.

"That's right. Merry Christmas," Flint says, "and she better show up soon, or else," he threatens as he pulls a rifle causally out of his truck, "you'll get it."

"She comes back tomorrow," Will raises his palms, stepping from his porch, onto the frozen ground.

"We'll be seeing you again," Flint screams from his truck, window rolled down, screeching into the night.

Kristi stocks up on gifts for her friends, including Will. She spends the two remaining days writing in her journal that she plans to use to write her memoir, titled *Helen* - her mother's mother. Before her death, her mother told her stories that were about abuse, deprivation, famine, disease and grief – and how her mother survived it.

She would write about her mother's life, her struggle, her ability to deal with the pain. Her ability to deal with loss when her first pregnancy at 16 ended when the baby was born early at six months. Then how she married the man, and gave birth to another daughter, then a son, and how hard her mother worked as a cleaner at the hotel.

Kristi closes the pages to her journal, forcing herself to remember the stories told to her. She shuts her eyes, searching for the words to express the memories and awakens later in the day – forgetting that she has to be at the airport in the next hour.

Chapter Seventeen

Kristi walks through the door, tripping under the weight of bags, luggage and more luggage. She hopes that leaving Tuly for a week was not too long – thinking that perhaps she should have asked Will to pet sit. She texts Will *"I'm home"* and searches for Tuly – finding her curled into herself behind the curtain.

Kristi rubs her behind the ear and checks the laundry room which is a mess. She begins cleaning the floor when her phone vibrates on the kitchen table.

I think you should contact your father. Sighing, she types a text to her Dad, *I'm alive if that is what you are wondering* and tosses her phone onto the counter, before picking it up again, and typing in response, *done*.

She plops onto the couch, journal in hand, begins to turn the pages, thinking about Saint Martin: the crisp cool air, white sand, iridescent water, and her massage by the glass door that overlooked the Villa landscape, and the live jazz playing throughout the festivities. She huffs thinking about having to clean up after Tuly, and returns to her magazine, thinking about her mother and how much they would have enjoyed a women's retreat together. In her heart, she knew she didn't want to invite Will in place of her mother, but instead she had rather gone alone – and she's glad she did.

Kristi peeks behind her journal at the mess of luggage and bags still blocking the front door. Delaying the inevitable, she opens her tablet and types on a social media platform: *I'm home! Tomorrow I start a new chapter in my life.*

Then she skim-reads over other messages, tapping a few photo likes and responding to some messages from friends. Kristi has always shared her messages with the people she meets through work, often gaining some personal connections with peers or those who are a generation older.

She notices her phone vibrating on the table – an indication of texts and emails. As she retrieves her phone from the table, there are more messages from Will, her father, and an anonymous call but no voicemail. There is a knock on the door and Kristi tosses her magazine on the table to answer it

"You smell good," Will grumbles when he enters and hugs her.

"Thank you," Kristi says, wryly, "Are you okay?"

"You didn't bother picking up the phone. You didn't bother writing back…"

"I told you that I just needed some time to myself," she says bluntly.

"What's the new chapter in your life?" He asks, watching Dude and Tuly greet each other.

"Wow that was quick."

"I was in the area, when I got an email, with your message posted to the message board." He explains.

"You were in the area?" Kristi says, locking the bolt to the front door.
"Yes, I was, but I'll get to that in a minute. I have something for you," Will nervously rummages through his pocket, he takes out a small box, grasping it between his thumb and forefingers. "I'm still wondering about that new chapter," he says.

"I'm going to start, I mean finish, those two courses I'm missing," she stammers, "What is that you're holding?"

"It's for you Kris, but first I want to know about your classes."

"French and Writing about Literature," she says, "Kris, that's what my mother used to call me."

Will takes a knee, and Kristi's hand into his, opening the box, he looks serenely at Kristi, "I know that I can never replace your mother, and that's not what I'm trying to do."

"Will?" She whispers.

"Kristi, I'm asking you to marry me, and start a new chapter with me."

"Will," Kristi says again, "I don't think I'm ready for that yet."

He takes her gently by the hand, kisses below the wrist. Standing, he leans into her and closes her hand around the small box, and the one carat diamond inside, "Just hold onto this," he says, "until you're ready, until you think you want to put it on. I'm here for you Kristi," and kisses her gently.

"Thank you," she kisses him back, "maybe when I'm ready," She removes a cedar chest from the cupboard, "It was my mother's jewelry box," and places the diamond inside, closing the lid.

"I want you to have it, Kristi," Will says, calling for Dude.

"You don't have to go."

"You have to unpack, I didn't want to bother you."

"You're not bothering me," she says, "it's just that I'm getting back to the real world now and I wasn't prepared."

"I know," Will says, "I'd ask your father, but I'm afraid."

"He's just protective," she says.

"I know he is Kristi, and I wouldn't have it any other way."

"I'm sorry that I missed Christmas."

"Me and Dude had a good time."

"What about your mother? Any word from her?"

"No," he whispers, "she's moved to Florida. Re-married, and settled down. I guess with the grandkids. I don't know."

"I thought she was in North Carolina."

"She moves around a lot. We just don't speak much."

"Well I'm here for you too, Will, but I just can't."

"You don't have to explain anything to me, Kristi."

"I know I don't Will, I know that you understand but I still think it's hard."

"You don't have to be broken for me," he says, leashing Dude. "You'll be ready, when you're ready."

"I'll never have my mother to be there at my wedding, and my father…"

"I don't think he'd be there to walk you down the aisle. Not with me. But I want you to know that I'd take care of you. Of us, and our family, the way a man is supposed to."

"I'm not sure that's what I want either Will. That's what my father always promised, and he was never home. He was too busy taking care of us, so we never saw him, as ironic as that is."

"I'm going to be here, Kristi," he says gently, "I'm going to be here for as long as you need me."

"I know you will," she says, bracing herself at the counter, as Will turns to leave, before he steps out the door, with Dude in tow, "Good night," he says.

"Good night," she smiles.

Chapter Eighteen

Kristi discovers a bouquet of plush-colored roses on her front stoop as she steps outside her door on the morning of New Year's Eve. She picks up the arrangement and reads the card attached to a small butterfly clip: *Good Luck,* is all it says, and she takes the flowers inside noticing their thorns have been removed from the stem, and places them onto the table. Her college courses begin mid-January, as she has registered to study on-line, taking up French and Writing about Literature. She types a quick note into her social media platform, stating *"Thank you for the roses, if only I knew from whom,"* and pushes send.

When Kristi doesn't receive a response, she pushes on with her day thinking of how she will finally graduate college. She is a writer at heart, and feels deeply about sharing her mother's story of how she persevered. Kristi also thinks about Rick, remembering how he wanted her to finish her college education.

She had graduated high school a year early after skipping a grade in elementary school. Earning straight "A"'s earned her enough scholarships to pay for her education. She took college courses as a senior in high school, then she went to work at the mom and pop diner in town where she lived. Her mother and father would visit the upstairs bar on occasion and she worked the dining-room downstairs; adjacent from the dining room was a coffee shop where the truckers liked to stop at the restaurant for an early breakfast.

Kristi had become named *the hostess with the mostess* by some of the regulars. Kristi often left the dining room side to borrow sugar packets or syrup bottles when the dining room would run out of supplies. Her parents had got her the job there, by recommendation to the owner who they knew personally. His name was Tony: a balding man of about forty.

Kristi thinks too about Rick who grew tired of her absence and had met someone else. She regards his intrusion in the store as a misogynistic ploy to make her feel guilty, but she revels in the fact that their relationship wasn't working. His love of DC and his job as a banker just wasn't the right fit or the right attitude. He had carried the façade of being earnest when deeply he was a control freak who liked to organize his multitudes of women, and account for them the same way as he did in his math – always worried about the numbers as opposed to genuine affection. He was simply put, too proud, and evidently not just one woman could make him happy enough.

Kristi steps into the shower, wincing at a sharp, stabbing pain in the pit of her stomach – shrugging it off as the settling of her breakfast.

Will gets out of the bed at a knocking at his front door. As he opens the door, tired, groggy and shirtless, he finds Officer Mingolelli staring back at him, his police cruiser parked in the driveway.

"Hello, Officer," he yawns.

"I'm here to tell you that I got a noise complaint," he says curtly.

"There hasn't been any noise here Officer," Will says, widening the door.

"Well I got a call, and the caller says you were making noise here, starting last night, and until this morning."

"But there hasn't been any noise…"

"That's what the caller said, and now I'm here just doing my job."

"I appreciate that, Officer."

"Well, now, we appreciate if you keep the noise level down," Officer Mingolelli puts one hand on the door, the other on his belt. "What is that odor I smell coming from inside?"

"What odor, Officer?"

"Smells like skunk urine to me…"

"Then it probably is a skunk," Will stutters.

"I wasn't born yesterday," Officer Mingolelli stretches his neck to peer inside, "I know the smell of marijuana, and I'm telling you that that's what it smells like."

"Officer, I haven't been…"

"Well, now, maybe you haven't, but maybe one of your friends is…"

"There isn't anybody else here."

"I didn't see anything so I'll be on my way now, just doing my duty, to tell you to keep the noise down."

"Yes, Officer," Will says compliantly, "I will do that."

"The neighborhood here would appreciate that," he turns toward the police cruiser he left running in the driveway. Will shuts the door and shakes his head, wondering who or why someone would complain. He's been asleep all night and no one has been over to his residence since the party, aside from Kristi, who hasn't been around much since trying to make up for the money she spent on her personal retreat.

Will plops on the couch, picking up his cell phone he forgot to charge before he went to bed early. As his phone charges, he scrolls through social media. Noting that Kristi got flowers, he types in *who roses*. Laying the phone on the couch, he heads to the kitchen for some breakfast. As he butters his toast, his phone chimes. He glances at Kristi's message. *Of course, I thank you.*

Will looks quizzically at the text, "Thank me for what?"

"For the roses," she says.

"But I didn't send them."

"Oh, then idk who did."

"I thought someone responded on FB."

"No one did."

"Then idk who left them either."

"That makes two of us."

"Was there a card?"

"Yes. Just said Good Luck."

"For what?"

"Assuming from my last post."

"Which was…"

"About starting a new chapter."

"Right. You mean college?"

"Yes."

"When does that start?"

"January 15."

"Okay. Lol. See you at work tonight, babe."

"Yep. See you there."

Chapter Nineteen

Kristi and Will leave work at 11 on New Year's Eve and make their way to Will's house. Brody and Kelly, along with Rick and some mutual friends, have planned a party at his place. Four minutes later, Brody drags a keg through the front door, closing the door behind him.

"Anyone want to do some bong hits?" He yells across the room.

"Hey, uh, we can't do that here," Will stammers.

"What do you mean, man?" Brody huffs.

"I mean the cops have been showing up."

"What are you talking about man?"

"I mean like this morning."

"This morning?" Kristi asks, exasperated, "You didn't tell me this."

"I didn't want to worry you," he says back.

"Don't let those little mother fuckers get to you, Will," Brody pipes up, "They can't do nothing, especially when they don't know anything about us."

"They know plenty," Will says back.

"Like what?" Brody asks.

"Like the pot."

"Will, that's nothing more than a misdemeanor…"

"I don't need any charges…"

"Hey," Kelly, intrudes, "let's just leave the pot out for tonight."

"I guess…" Brody says.

"It's just best to do that," Kelly says, placing her hand to his shoulder.

"We can have us some beers though," Ricky says.

"Sounds good to me, man," Brody says, "I like drinking beer," he pulls the tab on a cold National Bohemian beer. "Let's drink," he says.

"But not for me," Kelly says, blushing.

"Why not, baby?" Brody asks, taking her by the waist.

"There's something I haven't told you yet. I'm pregnant…"

"What?" He stammers, "Are you serious?"

"Six weeks," she says. "Just found out this morning. I wanted to announce it with everybody."

"Congratulations," Ricky says, holding a beer to a toast, and Brody holds his beer, tapping against Ricky's.

"Hell yeah," he says, "Maybe it's a boy."

"Or maybe it's a girl," Kelly says, smiling, and they kiss. Ricky steps up to the radio player, turning the dial up, with Credence playing in the background.

"It's time for a celebration," Brody pounds his beer onto the table, then cracks open another can.

Kelly scoots close to Brody on the couch, leaning her head onto his shoulder.

"Anyone want to play a game of pool?" Ricky asks, and another friend darts in, moving his way through the group, picking out his pool stick. Ricky removes the cue ball from the wrack; he begins with a break, landing two solids in the pocket, and gets prepared to bank a shot when a knock on the door startles them and Will turns down the music.

"Not again," he says. He opens the front door to find Officer Mingolelli along with four police cruisers in the driveway.

"I told you to keep the noise level down," he says, snickering.

"The music isn't that loud, Officer," Will says, "no one should be able to hear."

"Oh, they hear it alright."

"Who can hear it?"

"We got a complaint for noise," another officer says from behind him.

"Now we're gonna come in," another says, "and search the premise."

"You can't do that without a warrant," Will says.

"Well we got one right here," Mingo says, "for suspicion of drug usage and trafficking." Officer Mingolelli bumps shoulders with Will as he enters the front door, along with another officer, as two policemen wait casually outside. Officer Mingolelli asks all if anyone is carrying a concealed weapon and requires everyone to put down their alcohol and stand in a line against the wall, as they perform the search for concealed weapons or contraband in their pockets. Mingolelli ruffles his hands across Brody's shoulders and down the sides of his arms. When he gets to his pocket, he withdraws a dime bag of pot.

"And what did you intend to do with this?" Officer Mingolelli asks.

"Smoke it," Brody replies.

"Don't you get smart with me, boy," Officer Mingo says, twisting Brody's hands behind his back, removing his cuffs from his belt, and escorts Brody from the residence.

"I'm not," he tries to explain.

"Brody…" Kelly says, eyeing him like a cat on a mouse.

"The rest of you can get on home now. It looks like this party is over," another officer says as Officer Mingolelli takes Brody outside.

"He got anything on him?" Mingo asks the officer who hovers over Will.

"Nah," he says, "he's empty."

"Well, today is your lucky day," Mingo says to Will.

"No one here was being loud," Will says.

"Then why we'd get complaints?"

"I just don't think anyone did," Will shrugs.

"Well now it just doesn't matter what you think now does it?" Mingo ushers Brody past Will.

"I guess not, sir," he says, lowering his head.

From inside the police cruiser, Brody extends his neck to speak to Kelly but the officer starts his engine, and with a loud thud, he crosses the rocks that line the driveway.

"You're lucky we're not arresting you for disturbing the peace," an officer says, with a sly grin, and walks casually to his police cruiser, dimming the lights before he heads off the property, followed by two more cruisers, before they turn out-of-sight.

Condry steps inside the corridor of tier three and eyes Brody from within his cell. Brody, lying on his bunk, sits up at the sight of him.

"You're out on bail," Condry hisses.

"Then I guess I won't be needing this beautiful uniform," Brody tugs at the sleeve of his orange jumper.

"We'll be seeing you back here again," Condry moves back from the cell as another officer enters the tier. Unlocking the gate, Brody steps outside, peering at Condry's baggy eyes.

"I won't be coming back," he says.

"You should've stayed in Virginia," Condry closes the gate behind him. The inmates holler loudly as Brody is ushered out of tier three and steps into the isolation room where he is told to strip out of his uniform and into his street clothes. Outside the jail, Kelly waits in their Dodge, picking him up from the side entrance.

"Now what are we going to do?" she asks, turning from the jail parking lot, past the courthouse and toward Will's.

"Get a lawyer," he responds matter-of-factly.

Chapter Twenty

Several Fridays later, Kristi steps out of her car and onto the asphalt of The Hub parking lot. Will is off, helping Brody and Kelly settle into the in-law suit that has been vacant since his father died. Brody decided to re-locate his landscaping business in Maryland due to Kelly's pregnancy. She can be closer to family, and has the opportunity to stay home with the baby.

Kristi approaches the front door of The Hub with a slight jab to her abdomen. She purchased a home pregnancy test at the dollar store on her way to work. She thought about being late, about calling off work because in two days it is her mother's birthday, Sunday, and she wants the weekend off to spend it at Deep Creek Lake in McHenry, Maryland where her mother used to take her and Jake without their father.

They used to drive around the lake, taking in the large and expensive homes, and they would stop at the park with access to the camp ground. Beside the camp area is an aviary that is situated before the playgrounds, picnic tables and beach access. The science center is also located near the park entrance where they would visit the aquatic life, and they only had to pay $4 to spend the day swimming the lake, eating lunch from picnic baskets and playing on the slides. If they had enough time, they would drive to Swallow Falls state park with three falls to explore at different elevations. Their mother would take photos of them standing in a shallow pool collected at the base of the fall. Kristi was twelve the last time they spent the day at the lake. Their mother would comment how she wanted to stay at the resort sometime, if the money would be enough. Their mother loved to travel and she wanted to be in the outdoors. On one occasion, they rented a canoe, and another they rented a paddle boat.

Kristi steps into the restroom of The Hub and enters the larger, more private stall, removing her home pregnancy test from her purse. Almost as soon she peed on the stick, a faint blue line appeared on the positive mark of the test strip. The door screeched opened and Kristi jammed the test tube into her purse along with the empty carton and stepped outside the door. Washing her hands, Mila steps out of the stall, eyeing Kristi; this is the first evening they work together, especially without Will.

"So," Mila turns on the water spigot, "you're dating Will?"

Kristi rinses the soap from her hands and shuts off the spigot, searching the rack for a hand towel. "We hang out," is all she would say.

Mila snickers, "Yeah, that's what Marissa used to say, too," she rubs the soap into her hands, "She was my best friend you know," shutting off the spigot, ripping at the hand towel.

"No, I didn't know that," Kristi says, rather shyly.

"They had an argument at the restaurant," she sneers. "They walked out the front door, arguing. All I know is she wouldn't claim they were more than friends, but we all knew better than that."

"Why would she lie?"

"To save herself the trouble from telling Flint."

"Well, why didn't she just break it off with him?"

"You don't know Flint."

"Maybe you don't know Will."

"I don't have to know him," Mila shakes her head, "because I knew Marissa."

"Meaning what?" Kristi tosses the strap of her purse over her shoulder.

"She wouldn't jump from his car," she states.

Kristi reaches for the handle of the door, opening it, turning away from Mila, "I have to clock in," she says, stepping through the door.

"You might want to watch your back," Mila calls after her, as Kristi steps through the door, and into The Hub, tables already filled.

Kristi works the rest of the evening without incident. The Hub is too busy for another run-in from Mila. Kristi cannot help but to think that if they were best friends, she should have known Marissa was a manic depressive – or was she?

Who am I to believe, is all she could think – *how well do I know Will?* Kristi's mind began to fill with doubt. She was somewhat confused before, but now she felt her stomach turn at the thought of Will. She hated to think that he had killed Marissa Shaw.

Kristi wants her mother now more than ever. She wonders about the health of the baby growing inside of her, her own personal well-being, and the thought of Mila, who said she ought to watch her back – *but from who?*

She enters her apartment to the sound of Tuly at her feet, purring, rubbing on her legs. She picks up Tuly, cradling her into her chest. Kristi removes the apron she is still wearing with the wad of bills she made in tips. She isn't sure how much more doubles she'll be working to earn the wages she needs to make up for Saint Martin, but she is sure she has enough to spend a day at the lake for her mother's birthday.

The lake should be frozen over, she thinks. She can stay at The Inn, where she can write again in her journal, that will be the makings of her first book – but after she completes college. Her New Year's resolution was to earn an A in her courses and so far she excels the way she had before her mother had died. She wonders if her mother would think she should keep the baby – or if she is making the right decision if she decides not to.

Condry enters tier three and into the cell of Thompson, known as Skinny Pimp to his friends and enemies. He clangs on the bars, startling a sleeping Thompson. The prison had a shakedown that morning, in search of contraband, and Skinny Pimp came up empty. He sits up on a spare metal bunk. The prison has inmates who have to sleep on the floor due to overcrowding, but Skinny Pimp earned his place by himself in the cell for complying with the duties and chores he's assigned within the prison.

"I thought you told me Will was a junkie," Condry says.

"Yeah, he is," Thompson groggily stands from the bunk.

"Sit down," Condry growls. "His place came up empty, but that friend of his."

"Yeah, they both smoke weed," Thompson shrugs, sitting on the bunk.

"I thought you said they do more than smoke weed?" He asks sternly.

"They did," he says, "they used to buy all kinds of stuff…"

"Like what?" Condry asks.

"Like acid, heroin and even roofies."

"Roofies?"

"Yeah, that's what I said. Getting *roached out* you know?"

"No, I don't know. But, what I do know is you were supposed to see to it. He came up clean."

"Hey man, there's only so much I can do."

"Then do more," Condry says, stepping out of the cell, closing the gate behind him. He peers at Thompson, then makes his way down the catwalk of tier three.

Asshole, Thompson mumbles under his breath, *what the fuck can I do, in this mother fucking jail cell,* he thinks, laying back onto his bunk and closing his eyes.

Chapter Twenty-One

Kristi taps the ice at the edge of the lake with her foot, staring ahead at the frozen tundra before her. The lake is desolate and the summer activities she enjoyed with her mother and her brother are closed for the season. Kristi turns in the direction of the trail she walked with her mother and follows their steps back toward the car. It is merely twenty degrees outside on what would be her fifty-seventh birthday.

Kristi watches as the chipmunks and the squirrels scatter by the sight of her presence; the birds at the aviary huddle in the corners for warmth and the only other visible being is the park ranger who watches as the workers remove the snow from the parking lot. She tilts her head to look up at the opaque sky when she hears the voice of her mother: *just go back.*

Just go back where, she thinks, then the immediate response occurs to her at the same time: *home.*

Nearly an hour later, she enters her apartment building. She stops by the mail box on her way to the elevator to the second floor. She finds only a single envelope inside the box that has the shape and dimensions of a card – what would be a birthday card if her mother would be alive. She fumbles with the edges of the envelope until her fingers make a slit in the opening and she tears at the seam; she withdraws a card that reads: Thank You.

Thank you for what? Kristi thinks, as she opens the card to find a small letter inserted inside, without a signature. Wondering who the card is from, she opens the tiny letter:

Dear Kristi,

I am sending this letter because I want you to know how much you mean to me. I want you to know how much I care for you and for your family. I'd like to think that you know how much I want to take it all back, to go back and start all over again, but I can't. I don't know how else I can make it up to you, but to be here for you, to watch over you, to be sure that you are safe and that no one can ever hurt you or your family ever again. Through you Kristi I have learned how important this life is, that all life is valuable, meaningful and utterly precious. I want to make it up to you. I care deeply and earnestly about you and your well-being and feel personally responsible to you from within my heart. I am so sorry, Kristi.

Wishing you the Best,
Always

Always, she says aloud, and peers out the window – as if the person who wrote the letter would be standing there somewhere for her to reach, for her to know who and why they sent the letter.

*It can't be...*Kristi mumbles, as she slides down into her chair. Tuly jumps into her lap, purring loudly like a motor. She crumbles the paper gently as she begins to cry, ever so gently into Tuly's fur, as she rubs her palm down her sleek coat.

"Mom, I miss you," she says, and lowers her head. *All life is precious,* she thinks about her mother. Wondering if her mother's voice was a sign, to spread the message she needed to hear in the precise moment she needed to her it, when she has been thinking about abortion. But now she can't get past the voice of her mother who called to her, who told her to go back home, as if her mother knew the mail would be waiting there for her when she returned.

Then, Kristi thinks, that her mother would want her to celebrate life in the same way Will celebrates his father's by hosting a party on the day he was born. And Kristi thinks that she too will celebrate life, to live on in the New Year, in the new chapter that is her life. She would write again, she would finish college – she would do all this and more because all life is precious and meaningful.

Kristi knocks on the front door to Will's house, and is greeted immediately by Kelly who moves swiftly outside, hugging her.

"I heard the good news," Kelly says, opening the door for Kristi to step inside.

"Why didn't you tell us sooner?" Kelly asks dancing on her tippy-toe.

"Well, I wanted to wait," Kristi says.

"Wait for what?" Kelly takes a seat at the island stool.

"I needed time to believe it myself," she says, removing her coat. "Where is Will?"

"He's taking a shower. Tell me, how far are you?"

"I'm four months."

"Oh, that's great! And you're not even showing yet."

"Thanks," Kristi drapes her coat across the back of the chair.

"I'm already six months," Kelly says, resting her chin on one hand. "Have you picked out a name? Do you know the sex?"

Kristi sits across from Kelly, "It's a girl," she says.

"That's wonderful! I'm having a boy. Brody wants to name him Colton."

"That's a nice name," Kristi places both hands to her belly.

"How about you?" Kelly asks.

"I want to name her Delilah Rain McLean... after my mother's middle name."

"That's beautiful. Brody likes Colton Harvey, but I'm not big on the Harvey part."

"It's not bad," Kristi says, smiling.

"Has anyone planned a shower yet?"

"No, not yet," Kristi says.

"Well, then we can plan one together," Kelly says, tossing her arms around Kristi's neck, hugging her. "I'll plan one about a month before my due date, then you'll be around seven months."

"That's good timing," Kristi says, as Will walks around the corner.

"Hi babe," he says, smelling like soap and after-shave. He hugs her gently and kisses her on the cheek. "How's my baby doing?" He asks.

"Me or this baby?" She says, laughing.

"Both my babies then," he places his hand to her abdomen.

"I'm sure she's doing good tucked away in there," Kristi says, "but remember we have a doctor appointment tomorrow."

"Ah, got it," he says, pulling his arms through his shirt sleeves.

"Getting ready for work already?" Kelly asks.

"Yes," says Will, "gotta be at work by three."

"That's only an hour," Kristi says, "I wanted to go over things for the living arrangements."

"Yeah, no problem," Will says, "while Kelly here," he places an arm around Kelly, "and Brody rent out the basement– we have three bedrooms up here we can use."

"Okay," Kristi says, "sounds like you already have it figured out."

"Just have to get some of the rooms cleaned out and maybe put things into storage."

"That's what I was concerned about, your father's things."

"Yeah, well, it's no problem. We can use a bedroom for Delilah and put the rest of the stuff into the third bedroom."

"That works," Kristi says, "I'm going to miss my apartment though."

"That two bedroom shack?" Will laughs.

"It's not a shack," Kristi grins.

"No, you're right," he says, "It's just small and quaint."

"Cozy," Kristi says as Kelly laughs.

Chapter Twenty-Two

Condry makes his way down tier four as he completes his rounds. It is 3 AM and the corrections officers had to intervene in a fight that took place in the cell. One large inmate pinned a smaller, newer, inmate against the wall – one who didn't have the time to learn the ranks and positions about the prison system. The younger, smaller inmate was being shown how to respect his cell-mate before he could use the latrine. The senior inmate was sent to isolation for disturbing the entire tier during his outbursts.

"That puny punk has my daughter pregnant," Condry mutters at Ed on his way to the office to prepare the paperwork.

"Oh, man," Ed sighs, "I didn't know it was that serious."

"She's not telling me much."

"Well, what else do you know?"

"There's a baby shower posted online, she's having a girl."

"That says a lot," Ed shifts papers on his desk.

"It says enough."

"What can you do about it?"

"He's supposed to be a junkie."

"We tried that route," Ed interjects, "he came up clean."

"Supposedly he's been into more than drugs. Maybe something more sadistic."

"Sadistic," Ed says, "like what?"

"Pleasure from inflicting pain, they found that girl with burns in her back, appeared to be cigarette burns."

"Well, I'm sure Kristi wouldn't."

"Not my daughter," Condry says.

"I really don't think so man," Ed says, peering above the rim of his glasses.

"Well, I still want more on him."

"Not sure there is more to know."

"Kristi needs to open her eyes and smell the roses," he growls.

"She's smelling the roses with her eyes closed?"

"That's right."

"You might be right, but how can you prove?" Ed asks.

"Thinking about hiring a private detective on this one. Have him followed, see where he's going, what he's doing and who he's doing it with."

"That may work. It could even prove you wrong," Ed says bluntly.

"Then it'll prove me wrong either way, I'm want to get to the bottom of this. He's just a young punk," Condry growls.

As the months pass, Kristi cleans out her apartment to move into Will's house. Together they decorate the baby's room in yellow and white. The wall is adorned with small stuffed animals on shelves, pictures, and her sonogram photo on the dresser. They purchased a bassinet, crib, dresser, changing table, a bouncy-chair, a special dual car-seat and jogging stroller she intends to take to the parks, the canal, and the lakes where she can jog with Dude.

Etched on the wall is the phrase *Happiness is a Warm Yellow,* since yellow roses were her mother's favorite. Kristi opens the remaining closet in the den of the apartment where she stitches her mother's fabric into the angels she sells at the store. She removes a box her mother had packed away for her. The closet still smells of her mother – a blend of spring fabric and earth or wood. Kristi inhales deeply, breathing in the scent of her mother.

Inside the box are baby girl clothes, mostly white, pink, yellow and pale green colors, and blankets, rattles, two small bottles, a teething ring, bonnets and cloth diapers – all the baby items her mother had for Kristi. Her mother made the box of items and told her that it should always remain packed away, that one day she could open the box when she'd have her own children.

Kristi sits against the wall, holding the bits of clothing in her hands – thinking about her own daughter – the daughter that her mother would never meet, but would be part of her.

"Delilah's Grandma bought these for me," Kristi says to Tuly – rubbing the sides of her face on the edge of the walls. Kristi puts her face to a cloth blanket, inhales deeply, taking in her mother's scent one last time, before closing the lid to the box, ushering Tuly from the room, and closing the door to the empty room behind her.

In May, Kristi plucks a butter-colored tulip from the small garden she has planted in the green space outside her apartment. She sniffs at the delicate petals, thinking about how Delilah will be born in a month. Her baby shower is next week and she is nearly finished moving into Will's father's home.

Kristi places tulips in a vase to take to her mother's grave. The indigenous mountain flower was planted by her mother – enjoying that the spring plant brought a sense of happiness to the home, with money being short, they often spent time in the yard. Wages at the hotel where her mother was a housekeeper was tight and her father worked extra-long and hard to provide for the family.

Her mother would pick flowers and arrange them the dinner table, or place them onto the mantle above the fireplace. Her mother would also spread wild flower seed in various areas, preferring a more natural landscape as opposed to a manicured yard. She loved tall grasslands and wanted her home to resemble a prairie. Kristi wanted her grave to resemble their old home, so she chooses to plant as many flowers around her mother as possible without encroaching on the stones of others.

Kristi thinks about the store and its productivity during the spring months – wondering if her inventory of angels and glass pendants will suffice, or if she should add to the selection; maybe taking up needlepoint to make baby sweaters and bonnets. She even thinks about replicating her mother's scent, infusing the fabric with a blend of patchouli and musk, or cedar and eucalyptus.

Kristi walks barefoot, pregnant, and with tulips in hand when she sees Carl, idling, his arm out the window. She glances worriedly, wondering if he is leaving another note beneath the door, if he'll try to make contact, or if he'll keep his distance. He does not wave or make eye contact, and she wonders if he saw her at all. Kristi stops by the mailbox, finding it empty, but spots a package from UPS.

Opening it, she finds a stuffed bear holding carnations, with a note that says, *Congratulations*. Kristi doesn't know whether to scream, or to hug the bear, she thinks that perhaps her mother wants her forgiveness, to forgive him for his stupidity, or to forgive her mother, for the simple fact that she went out on that rainy evening in July when a storm was settling in, claiming that she would be okay, to her father who didn't want her to go. But she went anyway – and she died.

Kristi recognizes her father's wishes were for her mother's best interest. Being ignored, she left them there in the house while she went out anyway. She wonders if she should hate them both, that perhaps they were both equally careless and reckless, but Kristi will never know why her mother had to go out so late, other than the supper was not enough - but *didn't she know it could wait*, she thinks, slamming the stuffed bear onto the floor, *damn them both*.

Chapter Twenty-Three

Kristi walks to the end of the kitchen, removing the jewelry case from the top drawer. She takes the one carat diamond, beset in white gold, in her fingers and turns it slightly toward the sun. The diamond forms a prism on the wall.

"Well, mom," Kristi says aloud, "I guess you give us your blessing." A gust of wind blows the window, followed by a soft, gray dove that lands in the window sill, pecking its beak at the glass. She slides the ring on her finger. Then, she ever-so-lightly makes her way toward the window, as the dove flies away, she looks out into the daylight, where the cherry blossoms have bloomed across the landscape, and there is a large truck parked out front with a decal that reads: Getting Married is a Bliss Away.

She laughs "Mom," she mumbles, as she widens the crack in the window. She feels the warmth of the sun on her cheek and smiles, standing there, peering at the truck – thinking that in the moment, it was surely a sign from her mother.

Will makes his way home after working the day shift at The Hub. Signaling, he proceeds to turn toward his driveway when he glances at the rear-view mirror. There are flashing of police lights, followed by sirens, pulling him over. He pulls to the right side of the road, just before his exit on Halfway Boulevard. Officer Mingolelli appears, tapping on the glass. Will sighs, letting down his window.

"Hello, Officer," Will says, nonchalantly as possible.

"I need to see registration and your driver's license," Officer Mingolelli orders.

Digging into the glove compartment, Will extracts the vehicle registration, and removes his license from his wallet, handing them both to the officer.

"Do you know why I have pulled you over?" he asks.

"No, I don't officer," Will shifts in his seat.

"You were going seventy-eight in a sixty-five," he says, "I clocked you in back there. I'm going to ask you to get out of the car and come around to the back of the vehicle."

Will inhales, removing his seatbelt. Exiting the car, he makes his way around the back of the vehicle as two more officers' show up, lights flashing.

"Who is the owner of the vehicle," begins Mingolelli.

"That would be me," Will says.

"You'll need to renew your registration by next month," he says.

"I haven't received anything in the mail yet," Will explains.

"If you don't get it in the mail, be sure to stop by the DMV," he says, as the two officer's approach, standing with hands on belts.

"I will do that, Officer," Will says.

"Now I have to ask you if you have any contraband or illegal substances in the car."

"No officer, I'm not carrying anything like that," he says.

"The reason I'm going to look in the vehicle, is suspicion of illegal substances."

"Officer, I don't have anything."

"Then you don't mind if the dog does a search of the vehicle, then."

"No, Officer, I don't."

"Well then, these two officers are going to take the canine here around the outside of your vehicle."

As the officer with the large German Shepherd approaches the vehicle, another officer approaches Will, "We'll have you stand over here out of the way," he motions to the side of the police cruiser with his hand. Will steps to the far side of the road, just as Kristi drives by. She turns down Halfway Boulevard, and toward home.

Kristi reaches Will's driveway, parking and shutting off the engine. She is approached by Jake, with their father. Exiting the car, she shuts the door, perplexed and annoyed.

"What are you doing here?" She asks, hands placed on her rotund stomach.

Jake strolls over, hands in pockets, stuttering and mumbling at the same time, "I'm here for you, sis," he says.

"He's here to tell you that this guy isn't right for you," Condry interjects.

"Right for me?" Kristi asks.

"That's right," her father says.

"Look, Kristi," Jakes slurs, "he's not a real, great guy, like you think he is."

"So you say," Kristi huffs, "look at you, Jake," tossing her hands into the air, "What, are you drunk or stoned?"

"He's agreed to rehab," her father says, "and I gave my word to get him a car, to get him on his feet."

"That's just great, Dad," she says, folding her arms, sneering, "You think he's going to get clean, and what happened to the car you had anyway?"

"It's not run'n no more," Jake stammers.

"You're a heroin junkie, Jake."

"Making him knowledgeable about your boy," her father says, stepping next to Jake, "he knows the same friends as your boyfriend does."

"To buy pot, Dad, that's a little different."

"That's how I started," Jake says.

"That's why they call it a gateway drug," Kristi says.

"Exactly," Jake half grins.

"Doesn't prove anything."

"His dealer knows your boyfriend."

"I got it, Dad," Kristi yells, "because he used to buy some pot."

"That's just not what the supplier says Kristi."

"Hearsay, Dad, nothing but hearsay."
"I heard it right from the source, Kristi."

"You heard it from one of your inmate friends, Dad, that's not exactly reliable," she pushes her way past her father and brother, to get to the front porch, "It doesn't mean shit" she says, slamming the door. Opening the door again to yell one last time, "You both need to go home. And you need to go get clean," then slams the door again.

Candace Meredith

Kelly looks up over the sofas as Krisi plops next to her. "Will's been pulled over."

"Don't get yourself stressed, sweetie," she says, "You're pregnant."

"I know. It's my dad and my brother."

"Speaking of being pulled over, Brody got one-hundred-twenty hours of community service and probation."

"I'm sure he can handle that," Kristi says.

"Yes," Kelly snickers, "he's expected to plant flowers in the downtown district," she laughs again, "I mean, he does landscaping for a living."

"Then he's in familiar territory," Kristi smiles, and jumps when the front door opens. Will walks in and flops on the couch aside Kristi, placing his head to her chest, then to her abdomen,

"Is my princess kicking around in there," he says.

"Not today," Kristi says, stroking his hair, "What was all that about?"

"Oh, you saw that huh?"

"Of course, I drove right past you."

"He pulled me over for speeding. Then searched my car, but they didn't find anything."

"Why did they search your car?"

"Suspicion of drugs."

"Well I know that much."

"There's nothing else to tell."

"What did you do to piss off the cops?" Kelly asks.

"Marissa," he says lowly, "Flint Richard's girlfriend…"

"Whose father is a cop," Kristi says.

"That's right," Will says.

"But that doesn't mean they can search your car," Kelly says.

"They can do what they want," Will says, rolling over on his back, his head on Kristi's abdomen, feet hanging off the couch.

"When is this going to end?" Kristi asks.

"When they find something," Will says.

Chapter Twenty-Four

Kelly decorates for the baby shower she is hosting for Kristi, who is now eight months along and due within the next three weeks. Kristi has fully moved in, along with Tuly who shares her space with Dude. Kelly and Brody moved into their own home after renting the in-law suite, in the Western region of Maryland, close to the Pennsylvania line, and Brody has expanded his business – now that his community service has finished.

Kristi takes a seat at the front of the room as the guest of honor. Lisa and June arrive two hours early to help Kelly and to catch up. Kristi tells June that inventory at the store is sparse and they talk about starting a new line of baby clothing together. Lisa chats about her college and Kristi explains that she has finished her courses – earning an A in Writing about Literature and a B in French – and she's a college graduate. Her diploma is due to come in the mail, but she explains that she didn't attend graduation because she wanted to be home, nestling beside Tuly, rejoicing in her own private way.

As the shower goes on Lisa makes notes about what gifts were received and by who: Clifford the dog, story books, monitors, photo frames, diapers, diaper bags, wipes, socks, lotions, snacks, bowls, blankets and towels. Her guest laugh and talk about what it is to be a mother. Finally, after the last guest leaves, Kristi throws the last plate away and heads up to bed.

"You have my ring on," Will smiles at a tired Kristi.

"Yes," she says, changing into her gown, pulling back the sheets to the bed.

Downstairs, Dude howls, as Kristi settles into bed.

"I saw Carl, I think, drive past today," Kristi says.

"Be quiet," Will hollers down at Dude, who is barking.

"You know it's strange, but I saw that guy, Thompson, driving on the highway today. Leaving the gas station there on the boulevard."

"Did he see you?"

"No. I just saw him pulling out of the station, but I'm pretty sure it was Flint in the passenger seat."

"They know each other?"

"Yeah, I guess they do," he says.

Will opens the door, preparing to yell down at Dude, again, but inhales deeply.

"Do you smell that?" He asks.

"Smell what?" Kristi says.

"The hallway smells like smoke," Will says. "I'm going down to check on Dude, I want you to stay here."

"Okay," Kristi sits up in the bed, "but you're scaring me."

"Just stay here," he says, pulling up his jeans. Will opens the door, heading down the stairs, his feet hitting the hardwood as he goes down, yelling for Dude.

The house is quiet. Then there is faint yelling from downstairs, or outside, she cannot tell. She opens the door to the bedroom a mere crack. Smoke comes seeping in, she waves the smoke from her face, gasping.

"Will! Will!" she yells. Not hearing a sound, she realizes she is stuck on the second level of the home – the only way out being the window on the second story. She opens the window, bringing in the draft,

"Mom," Kristi yells, *"Mom, talk to me, tell me what to do."* Her words seem to drift like a faraway abyss as there is clambering downstairs, yelling, thrashing, Dude barking, then yelping, but she cannot reach them.

"Will! "She cries, searching the room for his cell, but it's downstairs, she hadn't thought about her phone all day. Suddenly the smoke seeps through the floor, and the room becomes hot. She reaches out the

window, trying to grasp the branch of a near tree, when smoke from the bedroom downstairs comes through the window. She chokes when she feels herself being pulled down the window.

On the ground, she gasps, trying to take breaths, fading out of consciousness as the smoke inhalation burns her lungs. She reaches for her belly, when she feels the tug at her gown, and a face peers above her. Carl, is giving Will CPR, filling his lungs with air, with deep compressions, then blowing into him – his chest rising with each blow.

"I couldn't get the dog," *he* yells in between blows.

Kristi gasps, coughing up dry phlegm when she loses consciousness. Then, fading into the light, she finds her mother, young again and smiling at her.

"*Kristi, go back,*" she says, "*it is not your time…*" She opens her eyes, watching as Carl's face comes into hers, using his thumb to part her lids.

"Kristi," he says, "stay with me. Help is on the way." Then she fades into the light again. When the contractions begin, she screams in agonizing pain. Carl holds her to his chest. The EMT arrive, taking Kristi onto the gurney away from the home that is engulfed in flames. And the new chapter begins, with the cry of the baby.

Epilogue

"Kristi swears her mother speaks to her," Condry told Ed one day.

Perhaps she speaks to Carl too, Condry thought. He learned that Carl had entered that burning house, severely burning his left arm. He carried Will's body from the ashes, grabbing him off the stairs where he had been trying to get back to Kristi.

Will had been hit hard in the back of the head, with a crowbar that, no doubt, Flint Richard had taken from his father's locked closet. Will, gasping for life, tried to get back to her. Upon entry into the home, Flint had busted the back door with the crowbar, Dude and Tuly had gotten out the door he left hanging open. Flint took a swing and busted Dude's jaw when Will jumped on his back from the stairwell.

They fought as Dude howled from a busted jaw. Carl, who never let the house out of his sight that day, possibly as penance for Miranda, had ushered Kristi out of the home, and laid her out next to Will.

Flint Richard started the fire with kerosene, but the fire department could not discern the fire was a result of arson. That night was Will's word alone.

They went to the hospital together, breathing from oxygen tanks, clinging to life. At the birth of their new baby, they re-gained consciousness. Delilah smiled, unfazed by the reality that was her birth, instead of her death. Condry went to visit Miranda's grave, finding a marble vase, lush with butter-colored tulips, knowing Kristi never made it there that day. The wind blew softly against him, almost as if it kissed him.

Dear Caroline

Prologue

Dear Caroline is all he could write before breaking down at the state penitentiary in North Carolina. Jimmy stays in a single cell, comprised of a single bunk, sink and toilet where the watchman can keep an eye on him since he's a suicide case. He's been awaiting trial for nine months and none of his family or friends posted bail.

He peers through the bars at night, watching the television over the night watchman's desk and can occasionally hear the faint sounds of music playing from the mobile phone. His son and daughter mail him some money to purchase the notepad paper and pencil he uses to write his letters. They always start out the same, and he tries to finish a single sentence, but his tears and anguish won't let him concentrate. His navy blue uniform is heavily stained under his armpits from his night sweats and the nightmares keep him up at night – unable to sleep, and yet unable to write.

Jimmy will lie in bed at night, thinking about his wedding day when he saw Caroline in her white gown and how she swayed elegantly down the red carpet at the

Baptist church - that was in 1967, and they would have been married for fifty years.

They were married on a warm and breezy day in September, the same month they met a year prior, and they honey-mooned at the Outer Banks where Caroline's family owned a second home. Jimmy and Caroline had a boy in 1969, whom they named Charlie, and two years later they had a girl, whom they named Melody.

Jimmy thinks about Caroline from his cell, how she smelled, how she dressed, her home cooking, the laughter they shared, and all she did to take care of their two babies. He used to tell Caroline that she had the grace of any fancy feline and the charm of fine crystal. He used to smell her hair when she'd come in from the garden, the beads of sweat on her neckline would sparkle in the sun light and smelled like her essential oils that she would carry around in her purse. Jimmy rolls over in his bunker with the thought of Caroline on his mind every night, and every day he sits alone in the cell.

His children don't like to visit much; the prison system is overwhelming, and intimidating. Charlie has two daughters and two sons between the ages of eighteen and twenty-five: Charlie Jr., Evan, Sammy, and Julianna; Melody has two daughters of her own: Macy, twenty and Marlene, seventeen.

Jimmy learns in prison that he's going to be a great-granddad since Charlie's oldest son, Charlie Jr., has a girlfriend who is pregnant and expecting around the end of August; they both attend college at the state university where Charlie Jr. is studying for his Master's in Business Administration.

It is January, the incident occurred nine months prior in March. Jimmy staggered Duke Hospital with a loaded pistol – he held the six-gauge revolver in his right hand, and a bottle of hard whiskey in the other hand, after more than thirty years of sobriety. He opened fire, sending rounds down the halls that echoed from the ricochet off the metal doorframe and another that shattered the nurses' cart that was carrying bed linens and water pitchers.

You sons of bitches, Jimmy hollered down the stairwell, as he staggered out into the hall, toward the room where Caroline had been staying, where Caroline should have woken up, but hadn't. Jimmy wrestled with the fact that she was never coming back. He went to the liquor store for the first time in forty years, his pistol tucked into his coat sleeve.

Chapter One

Jimmy staggers with a high gate and a left-sided gimp into the state penitentiary where he is greeted by the corrections officer and shown to his single cell. He flops heavily onto his bunker, licking at his lips to savor the last drops of whiskey he guzzled prior to sending off two shots.

"Should have killed him before he had the chance," he spats at the wall and collapses into a rather awkward lump against the wall. Unable to walk, he leans forward, heaving from dry mouth and coughs continuously, making the night guard angry.

"Keep it down in there," the night guard hollers as the sounds of late night television can be heard from around the corner – a scene from "I Love Lucy" bounces from the concrete wall, followed by "The Andy Griffith Show."

Jimmy lets go of his stance just enough to collapse onto the floor in a hard plop, rolling over onto his back, staring at a laden interior with the room spinning. In a daze, he drifts off to sleep – his dreams taking him into the night. In the morning, he awakens to chow being shoved through a small opening in the heavy metal door.

"Good to see you sobering up," the corrections officer says as he pulls his hand from the tray, "you're lucky enough that you didn't kill anyone," he says, shaking his head, walking away from the single cell.

Jimmy pushes himself up from the floor, resting on one arm, he grabs ahold of the bunk and hoists himself onto the bunker, ignoring the plate on the tray that is covered in thick gravy and two slices of bread. He tugs at his shirt that is wedged into his pants; his belt and shoelaces have been removed.

It is the first day of Jimmy's time in jail where he is facing charges on account of attempted murder. He is seventy-four years old and his head dangles from his lifeless shoulders, disinterested in food, and clinging to life, because his sole reason to exist was his beloved Caroline.

Jimmy met Caroline when he had checked into the mental health clinic at Duke's hospital in 1966 while Caroline began studying in medical school. She intended on achieving her medical doctorate, but became a nurse instead. Life with Jimmy changed her mind and she became a proud mother of two beautiful children. Their first year of marriage was rocky, until Jimmy became sober.

Jimmy's father, Earl Hedrick, was an alcoholic who committed suicide by the time Jimmy was seven years old; the incident sent Jimmy's life careening down a torturous path. He was placed in a school that was built for orphaned boys. Jimmy's mother, Priscilla Noel, was a beautiful woman in her day, who had Jimmy at a young age. After her husband's death her parents took her in, asking her to give Jimmy up for adoption, which she did rather than to deal with the problems that were imposed on her from an alcoholic husband. She had reasons to start a new life, and leaving Jimmy in the hands of the system allowed her to move on.

Jimmy became the school bully and sought attention by inflicting bad behavior; tripping students in the hallway, causing boys to spill their books all over the floor, being dominant on the field by stealing the ball, tackling, punching and kicking at any opportunity. At night, Jimmy would sneak out the window and smoke; often, he would venture to the all-girls school where the girls would congregate with the boys by the boat dock, lighting up cigarettes, telling stories into the night. Then, they would sneak back to their dorm rooms, hoping not to get caught, and serve detention or be given cleaning chores for being out of their quarters after dark.

Caroline was interning at Duke where Jimmy checked in at the age of twenty-four to get sober after a bar fight sent a boy to the hospital with a broken nose. It was his first night as a patient when Caroline began passing out medications in the company of a nurse. She was a gorgeous young woman with glossy lips, peach-colored cheeks and fine auburn hair that was held back by a headband.

Jimmy was prescribed medication for acute depression and was assigned a psychiatrist. The mental health clinic within the hospital had been re-modeled and Jimmy marveled with the fact that he could take showers independent of other patients. He was also served three hot meals a day, and the food was better than the ramen noodles he had been surviving on. The hospital linen was fresh and although the mattresses were firm, he slept well beneath the army green wool blankets.

Jimmy had taken a job working for the Union on a dredging rig that also took him to work in Iraq; upon his return, his managers recommended some time off since the bar incident broke out as gossip across the union workers. Jimmy's pension enabled him to pay for the costs of in-patient housing, depending on his recovery and diagnosis from his psychiatrist.

His first month was spent watching Caroline from the nurse's station, wishing he could speak with her quietly and discreetly – wanting to go unnoticed by the other staff who worked there.

He was asked by the psychiatrist, Doctor Hazel, to speak about his and if there were other close friends to talk about. Jimmy avoided talking about his father and his mother, and there were no close friends, as far as he was concerned. The boys at the dormitory often came and went, many were adopted by foster parents, growing too old to stay in the orphan house, or were transferred for whatever reason.

Jimmy didn't have friends among the union because work was intensive and down time had been infrequent – so getting to know anyone was rare. Jimmy lived alone in a small city apartment in Virginia before he bought a small two-bedroom home in Winchester; he had never taken to pets, let alone not having siblings to discuss – to avoid the conversation he would re-direct the topic. The psychiatrist however wasn't fazed and wanted to discuss his relationship with his mother and how his father's death affected him. Jimmy would explain that he barely remembered his mother, and hinted at his father's constant abuse toward his mother under the influence of alcohol.

"Let's start there," the counselor says with the first mention of Earl Hedrick. "Was it physical abuse or was it primarily verbal abuse?" Doctor Vivian Hazel asks, as she flips through pages of notes on her desk.

"It was all kinds of abuse," Jimmy says quietly, turning his gaze toward the second-floor window. The sun is dim over the horizon.

"Can you describe what it was like, what your father would do in front of you or your mother?" She asks, clicking the top of her pen.

"I can some other time," Jimmy replies, lowering his head.

"I'm afraid we have to discuss this now, Jimmy," she says, "your trial is going to depend on this."

"He cut her face once," he sighs, "he cut her face across the cheek, he hit her so hard, her lips swelled from time to time."

"What did your mother do, Jimmy?"

"She bled," he says.

"Yes, but how did she react?" the doctor prodded. "Did she do anything?"

"No."

A knock on the door startles the two of them as Doctor Muse shouts a minute warning.

"I'll need to discuss this with you next time, Jimmy. I'm afraid our time is up for today," she says, closing the file on her desk. Jimmy stands slowly from the chair, his back had been injured at the dredging company.

He loved the years he spent working for the union and he had a special affinity for the Florida Bay. He even asked Caroline if she would spread his ashes for him across the bay, that is, if they did not die together, as Jimmy always hoped they would, but he never foresaw that she would go before him.

It started with roses, Jimmy thinks as he lies back in the bunker, scanning the high ceiling before he closes his eyes to find her scent. *You smelled so good,* he thinks, and rolls onto his side.

His pencil, sharpened, lies on the empty tablet upon a small cement block – a makeshift desk. Jimmy, with his eyes closed, remembers when Duke's Hospital was a refuge for escaping the brawls he'd find on the streets.

He took solace in looking into Caroline's eyes when she'd appear at his door, med cup in hand. One time, he showed up with a bouquet of fresh cut roses he pulled from the garden. The thorns dug beneath his fingernails, and he bled slightly. He had found a small cup at the nurses' station which he used to place the roses and tied them off with a bit of ribbon he confiscated from the arts and crafts room. He stood at the foot of his bed, waiting for her with a Cheshire cat grin. Caroline strolled in behind a metal cart that contained medicine bottles and a pitcher of water. The fragrance of the roses overpowered the smell of the hospital room.

"Hello," Jimmy said, as she pulled the cart to the side of the bed.

"Oh, good morning, Mr. Hedrick," she said brightly.

"Please, call me Jimmy."

"Well then," she smiles, "good morning to you, Jimmy. Where did you find those flowers?"

"Went for a walk this morning."

"And you found them?"

"Yes. There's a garden in the back, and a small pond."

"Oh, well," she says, removing the pills with gloved hands, "I don't get outside much. I'm usually here tending to the patients."

"These are for you," he says, reaching toward her as he takes a step toward the side of the bed.

"How sweet," she says shyly, "but you know I can't take gifts from the patients."

"Well, I'm no longer a patient," he says, as she eyes a duffle bag at the foot of the bed.

"Why not, Jimmy?"

"I checked myself out this morning," he replies, "I'm going to do some outpatient care – they want to discuss my father."

"Then, that would be good for you, I suppose?"

"Yes, the job let me off for three months…"

"Where is it that you work, Mr. Hedrick …Jimmy?"

"I work all along the Florida Bay in a dredging rig."

"You'll have to tell me about it sometime," she says. "But how have you found yourself here in North Carolina?"

"I move all around in my job. I've even been to Iraq and Saudi Arabia."

"Lucky you?" she asked with a raised eyebrow.

"The pay is very good when working abroad," he says, placing the cup of roses upon her cart.

"Then thank you, Jimmy."

"How can I tell you about it sometime?"

"I suppose you know where to find me," she says, handing him a cup of water, and placing three white pills into the center of his palm.

"My doctor here says I should talk about it more…"

"Talk about what?"

"My father and my mother."

"I'm a good listener," she says. "But were they, you know, bad to you?"

"Well," Jimmy says, taking in a cool sip of liquid, "my father wasn't good to my mother."

"I'm sorry to hear that. Did your mother take you away from that?"

"My mother gave me up for adoption," he shrugs.

"Oh, I'm so sorry."

"It's alright. You don't have to be sorry …I grew up in an all boy's home. Got a pretty decent education out of it I guess."

"Any word about your mother?"

"I heard she had been living in Virginia and that's where I stayed throughout my childhood, too, but she hadn't tried to make any contact, not that I know of."

"Maybe one day…"

"Perhaps," Jimmy says. "I'm sure she did the best she could after what my father did to her."

"And you did as well," she smiles.

"Thank you," Jimmy says, "but I've had some difficulty."

"That you're trying to improve," she says, warmly. "All you can do is keep trying, so don't give up."

Chapter Two

Don't give up, Jimmy thinks as he rolls over in the bed, thinking about Caroline's last words as he packed to leave the in-patient ward at Duke Hospital.

"I didn't give up on you Caroline," he says softly and shuts his eyes again, and breathes deeply to find her scent, somewhere in his memory of Caroline among the roses. He sighs at the thought of her sweet breath, leaning over his hospital bed to give him the cup of pills he had to take every morning for his time there. He decided to leave to respect the patient and employee boundaries.

Jimmy returned to Virginia and sold his home to move closer to Duke Hospital, and continued his out-patient appointments there – he had only to visit the hospital every three months to renew his medication and see a counselor every month in a near-by clinic.

Jimmy and Caroline's life began in North Carolina in 1966 when he left the dredging company. He no longer wished to travel abroad and instead, took up electrical work after paying two-thousand dollars to be trained in a new trade. Jimmy worked in-state and later took up more trade in construction and masonry as side jobs, working feverishly to save money.

Caroline's family owned acreage near Raleigh where she always wanted to build a home, and Jimmy wanted to give her everything she dreamed of. She finished her internship in nursing and had a full-time job position at Duke Hospital by 1967. Jimmy would visit her during breaks when they could have lunch at the hospital cafeteria. He would tell her about his progress in counseling and how his first year in sobriety was the best year of his life.

He took up photography as a hobby, and showed her photographs of the rivers and lakes he would visit on the weekends when Caroline worked twelve hour shifts. He would return on Monday to show her his photos of falcons and other birds-of-prey, like the red-tailed hawk he photographed in the Western Appalachia of Maryland. He told her of the state park that housed injured birds like the Great Horned Owl and an Eagle.

It was his fondness of birds and the lakes and rivers that Caroline adored, and she became his reason for achieving sobriety, for not fighting his way out of the bar, and into the sooty streets where he would have landed himself in jail.

It was with Caroline where he found himself immersed in good conversation and splendid company. He enjoyed looking into her caramel-toasted eyes and he listened to her, too – about the boy that was saved in the ER who had been in a car accident but was revitalized during CPR. How she had the opportunity to bring warmth to his bedside, with the heated blankets she used to cover his legs. How the doctors were friendly and compassionate when discussing his recovery and how brave he had been. He was seven years old, which was the same age Jimmy had been when he left his mother and found himself in the boy's home. He recalled, too, how Mrs. Davenport at the home had been caring and warm toward him, like Caroline, and felt deeply that they were angels in his eyes.

In 1968, after spending two years in Caroline's company at the hospital during the times she wasn't working, Jimmy brought an engagement ring with him during his visit. He presented her with a ring and the idea that they could be married and spend their lives together in North Carolina among her family and friends – they could build a house together with the money he saved from his electrical work and the construction side jobs.

The ring was a beautiful white gold with a one carat diamond that shone bright like her smile, and the tears that traced her jawbone as she said yes and held onto him.

The embrace celebrated sobriety, life and the future, all in one hug. They began making wedding plans and plans to construct a home on farmland outside of Duke Hospital. One year later, their home was built in a Colonial construction style and Charlie was born; now, Charlie's own son was bound to have a son of his own – three generations bound to give life to the next. A life that is, without Caroline.

Caroline entered Duke Hospital on March in 2015 for a simple procedure to remove stones from her gallbladder. She was perfectly healthy and showed no signs of complications in her blood work or examinations. She was to undergo anesthesia and have her gallbladder removed – but Caroline didn't come back from surgery. She died on the operating table after the surgeons spent twenty minutes trying to resuscitate her lifeless body. But Caroline joined her late parents in the ever after, leaving behind Jimmy, their son and their daughter, and their six grandkids.

Jimmy took up the bottle of whiskey and the six-gauge revolver and entered Duke Hospital staggering, half from his gate from the years of work, and half under the influence and sent off two rounds – one aimed at the nursing cart and another haphazardly to the wind that came through the front door in a gentle breeze, nudging his cheek, but it went unnoticed at the glance of the medicine cart, and the face of his youthful Caroline pushing past the hall was all he could see.

"Dad what are you doing?" he heard his son ask, who never left the hospital. Their mother was still in the morgue as they were making arrangements with the funeral home – but Jimmy wasn't having any of it.

"You sons of bitches," he said, waving the revolver, his family standing behind him. "It's all your fault," he yelled to the surgeons and the doctors. "She died because you killed her," he cried out before firing, dropping most of the whiskey to the ground.

When security responded to the devastating scene before them, Jimmy was planted onto the ground face first into the tiled linoleum floor, knocking his lights out. When he found himself staggering back into the light – he woke on the hard surface of the jail cell floor, cold, stone sober.

On the third day as he awaited a pending trial after the funeral he missed – not because he was in jail but because she would not be there, he explained to his son and daughter on their visit – he simply asked that they give him only enough money to write a letter. He vowed in the prison system to write a letter to Caroline for every day he had to be alive without her, but every time he tried, he could not get words to paper. So he prayed. And the voice of Caroline spoke to him, finally, a month into waiting for trial.

"*Jimmy I'm here,*" the voice said, and a breeze blew past his cheek again, like the opening of the hospital doors, "*Jimmy I am here with you.*" Jimmy crawled from his rack on hands and knees, standing, leaning onto the wall, picking up his pencil, beginning with *Dear Caroline.*

"Dear Caroline," Melody says, her fingers trembling while unfolding the college-ruled notebook paper. "I cannot believe he actually sends these letters," she says with her voice half shaking. Charlie leans against the wall.

"I'm sure Dad knows she's not actually here to read them," he says, shifting his weight. His auburn-red hair shines bright against the sun in the back window of Melody's kitchen – a reddish brown like their mother's.

"Then why is he sending them?" Melody asks, taking a seat at the kitchen table alongside her two daughters, Macy and Marlene.

"It makes him feel better I guess,"
Charlie says, staring at the floor.

"Feel better?" Melody gasps, "How
can he feel better – after what he did in the
hospital…and missing Mom's funeral. I've
never seen Dad so drunk," tears roll down her
cheeks, "In fact, he's never acted so hostile
that I've ever seen."

"Yes," Charlie sighs, "but Dad has a
history of alcohol abuse, according to Mom,
and his own father…"

"But not around us," she interrupts.

"Alcoholism runs in the family, is all
I'm saying.

"We've never even met Grandpa
Earl," she says, as Macy places one
hand upon her shoulder.

"But we know the stories Mom told
us not that long ago…about why Dad never
had a family."

"But Dad has a family now," she
wails, "a family that he's ruined."

"Dad's going to get better," Charlie
says, taking a step toward Melody. "What
else does the letter say?"

"What does Grampy say in the letter,
Mom?" Marlene asks, waving her jet-black
hair from her face.

"Remember when," Melody says,
crying into her hands, handing the letter over
to Charlie who takes the neatly folded letter

from her hand and begins…. "Remember when…"

"Tell me more about Caroline," Doctor Muse says from behind her desk as she writes in her notepad. Jimmy explains how the boys' home had been like a large dormitory; where the showers were taken in open gymnasium-type stalls, privacy was rare, and how the boys would sneak out from their bunks at night to visit the all-girls home. None of the girls he would visit could match the beauty of his Caroline.

"She's a former prom queen," he says, his voice shaking slightly, "and she had the most beautiful long red hair – when it wasn't all tied up while she was working".

"Tell me more about the time you met."

"Well, we met at the Duke Hospital…"

"Did you tell Caroline about your life at the all-boy's home?"

"I told her everything she wanted to know," Jimmy sighs.

"And that didn't scare her away?"

"Not at all," he says. "She was a good listener. We spent a year telling one another about our life story…the years before we met."

"What did you learn about Caroline?"

"She had it all," he says, wedging his hands into his sides, arms folded.

"Such as, what?"

"She was Catholic, beautiful, and athletic."

"She played sports?"

"She was a runner."

"Tell me more about that."

"She ran just about ten miles every morning before work."

"That's a lot," Doctor Vivian Muse says, writing into her notepad.

"But it wasn't anything to Caroline," he says, "she could run for miles…I could never keep up with those slender legs…she was like a gazelle," huffing lightly, "and I was the one behind her the whole way…dying to keep up." He laughs.

"What was her life like before the two of you met?"

"She came from money. Her father owned a dental practice and put Caroline through private school and college. She was set up for someone unlike myself."

"And did her family welcome you?"

"No," he says faintly, "they tolerated me. But they respected me. Respected the fact that their Caroline was happy, and we always had enough money at least to get by."

"What was your life like, together?"

"We built a house on her family's farm. Her father's side of the family had a good bit of land in North Carolina, owned land around Raleigh and a second house at the beach in the Outer Banks."

"And that's where you went to honeymoon?"

"That's right. Wouldn't have had much I guess…"

"What do you mean?"

"Without her family."

"But you said you could provide …"

"I could provide just enough," Jimmy says, wiping his face with his shirt sleeve.

As the clock chimes from the desk, Doctor Vivian Muse stencils into her notepad, "I'm afraid we are up for today," closing her notes into a file.

Jimmy stands with a sideways gate and exits her office with two corrections officers standing aside the door out into the hall.

Chapter Three

Remember when, Jimmy writes on his paper after the session with Doctor Muse. Memories are coming back to him: the year he met Caroline, the year they spent getting to know one another – before their marriage, and before the birth of Charlie. He recalls of the time he met Mr. and Mrs. Stanton at their home in Raleigh, North Carolina – and of how he spent every month communicating his childhood to Doctor Hazel, and how he wondered if he'd have to make up a completely different life to Mr. Victor Stanton when he inquired about his own parents.

"Remember when your father threatened to take the college money away," Charlie reads from the notepad. *"Remember when I thought I'd lose you,"* he says, as he begins to stutter. Charlie sighs and leans forward into his chair.

"Why was he going to lose Grammy?" Marlene asks, shifting in her seat.

Melody places one hand around her youngest daughter and the other folds the bit of tissue paper to her cheek to wipe the tears away.

"Because Grampy was from a troubled past," Melody says.

"And they thought Grampy wasn't going to be able to care of her," Charlie says.

"So what happened?" Macy interjects.

"Grampy paid for all of Mom's tuition," Melody says.

"Working two jobs," Charlie says.

"And built Mom's house," Melody nods.

"Before Grampy could prove himself to Great Grandma and Grandpa Stanton."

"Why is Grampy in jail?" Marlene asks, turning her attention to Charlie.

"Didn't you see him at the hospital, with that gun?" Macy says, rising from her chair.

"Yeah, but," Marlene whines, "but Grampy is going to get better right?"

"Yes," Charlie says, folding the paper in his hand, standing to embrace Macy, "Grampy is going to get better."

"Dad's going through a rough time right now," Melody says, taking the letter from Charlie. And they all embrace, sharing their tears, holding onto the memory of their beloved grandmother and grandfather who shared nearly fifty years together. Melody and Charlie know their father hadn't been the only one for their mother.

I first had to change my job, and somehow earn enough money as an electrician before I could share my life with you, Jimmy writes, with a neat hand, despite his seventy-four years. *And after that year you spent with another man – who you were to marry. Not knowing you were already engaged when I handed you those roses-wanting to be more than we were, but you were always there to listen, and I had done the same.*

Jimmy shifts in his bunk as the guard yells *lights out.* Jimmy can no longer read his notepad paper, so instead, he lays back, his head resting on the hard stone of a bunk, and envisions the first time he met up for lunch with Caroline in the hospital cafeteria.

"I have to tell you something," Caroline sighs, "I am engaged to be married."

"To who, may I ask?" He takes a seat in front Caroline, staggering with a slight left-sided gimp.

"To a Mr. Edmondson," she says. "My Daddy introduced us. And he's approved of the engagement."

"But you are every bit worth those roses," Jimmy says, extending his hand to shake hers.

"You are very generous, Mr. Hedrick," she says shyly.

"And do you mind if we have lunch today?" He asks, shaking hands.

"I don't mind at all," she smiles.

"Then I can tell you more about the Florida Bay," he says, sliding his tray toward her, pointing at the fresh fruit, "Care for any fruit?"

"Oh, no thank you," she says, sipping her soda. "But I want to hear more about dredging for the Florida Bay."

"The water is beautiful out there," Jimmy says, slicing a strawberry. "And if you'd like – perhaps we could go sailing out there sometime."

"Perhaps," she says, her eyes meeting Jimmy's. "My fiancé, Henry, should come, too."

"I wouldn't have it any other way," he says, tossing a strawberry in his mouth.

"You surprise me, Mr. Hedrick."

"Why is that? And please, call me Jimmy."

"Jimmy," she says lightly, "I thought you wouldn't stay …"

"I want to meet him," he says.

"I thought you'd want to turn away."

"It doesn't matter what I think. Only that you are happy."

"Thank you," she says, "I'm happy to have your blessings."

"Blessings are God's work," he says, removing the rind from an orange. "But you have this shoulder to lean on."

"Well, thank you for that too, Jimmy," she says, taking the last sip.

"You are welcome, ma'am," he says, with a wry face.

"Please," she says, "call me Caroline."

"Caroline," he says, smiling radiantly.

"My beloved Caroline," Jimmy says from his bunk, staring at the blankness before him. *"I didn't know how hard falling in love could be."* He says gently to a soft breeze coming from somewhere, *"How hard loving a married woman would be."*

Jimmy packed his belongings in Virginia and moved to North Carolina, where he took up another trade in electrical work. Caroline got married to Henry Edmondson in that year they would meet for lunch – and where Jimmy would share his stories about growing up in a boy's home, how he took up alcohol as a means to cope with the stress of his father's suicide, how the boys home had to let him go out on his own as an adult at eighteen, and how working for the union has its benefits – but Jimmy wanted to leave all that. He wanted to leave it all to spend the day with Caroline, and hear her stories about performing CPR within the ER for a heart attack patient who had stopped breathing – and how twenty minutes of resuscitation brought him back to life. Jimmy was there to hear her stories about being the hero (in his eyes) within the hospital. Jimmy would never want Caroline to lose her internship within the Duke Hospital in which her residency was being paid for through her father.

"Caroline," he says, one afternoon during their lunch meeting, and after her marriage, "I want you to know how in love with you I am."

"Jimmy," she says quietly.

"I don't want you to say anything," he says, "I just want you to know, and for you to think about it."

"But what can I do, Jimmy?" She asks, picking up her nursing bag of supplies.

"You can just think about it," he says, taking her hand.

Caroline pulls away gently, "Jimmy."

"What's it going to hurt?"

"You know that marriage is for life."

"But not in the wrong one," he says.

"This one was arranged."

"Arranged by your father."

"But he's also …"

"Your father is paying for your residency."

"That's right."

"But what if he wasn't?"

"What do you mean?"

"What if he wasn't paying?"

"But that's not the only reason."

"Caroline, I understand your dilemma. I'm saying that I have the money that could pay for your tuition."

"But my father would never approve."

"Do you approve, Caroline?"

"What?"

"Do you approve?"

"I …"

"Tell me how you feel."

"I don't know."

"You don't know how you feel?"

"No, I…"

"Please tell me."

"I don't know that I really thought about it…"

"You did what you felt you had to do."

"I did as my father approved, and I cannot…"

"You cannot what, Caroline?"

"I cannot disapprove."

"Sure you can."

"But can you promise …"

"What?"

"Can you promise that you can raise a family?"

"I can Caroline, and I have the money to finish your residency."

"My father is going to reject…"

"He won't Caroline, not if he approves of your happiness."

"But a divorce is an abomination."

"God approves of your happiness, too, Caroline."

"I'm a bit overwhelmed…"

"That's why I asked if you could consider…"

"I don't know what to do," she whispers.

"Do what you feel is in your heart."

"I can't."

"You can't what?"

"I cannot get a divorce…defy my father's wishes…"

"You can follow your heart Caroline."

"I am married, Jimmy."

"But do you love him?"

"He is a good man."

"But do you love him?"

"Yes, I mean…"

"Do you love him?"

"I do care for him, Jimmy."

"But you also care for me?"

"I do," she whispers again.

"Then just think about it, for me," he says, taking her hand. "I will," she says, standing from the table, "I will," she says again, and disappears into the hallway, and Jimmy would not see Caroline again for another six months.

Six months later, Caroline emerges from the hall to meet Jimmy – where he had stopped for lunch every day, without her.

"You are back."

"Yes, Jimmy."

"I have missed you."

"I needed time."

"I can wait even more…"

"No need to," she says.

"You have a decision?"

"Yes."

"Caroline …" he says quietly.

"I can be with you."

"You have my heart, Caroline."

"But you have to promise me that we can have a family."

"I can promise you."

"And that your love for me is strong."

"It is, most certainly…"

"Because the man my father chose for me…"

"What?"

"He doesn't have my heart."

"He cannot give you all that I can."

"No," she says lightly, walking away into the distance. Turning her head over her shoulder, smiling radiantly. "I will see you again," she says.

Caroline returned the next day holding her signed divorce papers. Her husband did not disapprove on account that they were not intimate – and he was unable to provide her with children on the fact that a childhood injury left him sterile. Henry felt that it was best to re-marry and have the family she longed for. That she could do with a husband who could provide for her.

Caroline's father disapproved of the divorce and threatened to take away the money that was to pay for the final year of her residency – but Jimmy put up the money from his full-time work as an electrician and from the side jobs he worked every weekend. Jimmy became a jack-of-all-trades and worked feverishly to raise a family. Caroline finished her residency in the same year that they married and was pregnant with Charlie a year later – and two years later they had Melody.

Chapter Four

Charlie unfolds the paper his father used to write the letter to his mother and reads, again, *Remember when*, but scans the lines to find the part he didn't already know – how they spent the first year dirt poor despite his father's long hours at work and because their mother quit her job to stay at home. How her own father stopped speaking to her – and how they struggled in the first years to make it.

Charlie learns their father couldn't pay for it all alone, that they didn't build the house on her family's farm until long after Melody was born, and that they stayed in a tiny apartment for the first five years. Then his grandfather finally recognized Jimmy as the hard-working man he was, the loving and adoring husband, and the family man that wanted to give his two children more than he had growing up.

Melody paces the floor as the mailman delivers the mail, and inside her mailbox she finds another letter addressed: *Dear Caroline.* Within the pages, she finds a small note tucked inside with the number three and the pass code to their safe deposit box where Charlie stored the revolver that his grandfather had used to commit suicide.

I had kept the gun that my father used after finding him face down on the kitchen table, and the gun beneath a pool of blood. The gun was kept in my old hunting bag I used when my father would take me on weekend trips without my mother—the few times he was a decent man and wasn't hitting her. I stored the gun in the basement of the church I used to attend as a school boy, tucked away up in a dirty cellar where I knew no one would find it.

I kept that gun for reasons unknown and I later stored it in the safe deposit box that I have recorded here. I am giving it to you perhaps so that I don't try to use it since its past is with my father. Perhaps I don't know what I would do with it, but I wanted to keep it, being my fathers who used it on himself as opposed to my mother, and for that I suppose I thank him.

So I am leaving it onto you so that you may do with it what you wish, and so that I can let go of the memories of my father. But these damn psychiatrists think that by talking about him I can somehow make a reconciliation with the past, but I don't think that way. Talking about the man I found dead in the kitchen, face down in a bloody mess, isn't going to attest to the man that I am today. I am the man that I am, because I found you, my love.

Melody picks up the handheld receiver of her home telephone and jabs at the numbers to Charlie's cell. She leaves a voicemail message for him to call her.

"I think he's suffering from dementia," she says when Charlie returns her call. "He's delusional."

"What are you talking about?" Charlie asks, taken aback.

"Dad sent another letter," she says, shaking slightly, "he's given Mom a pass code to a security lock box."

"What lock box?"

"The letter says the one at home."

"Never knew he had one…"

"Neither did I, but in the letter he wrote Mom…"

"What's he saying?"

"He's giving her the pass code, stating she can do what she feels is necessary with the gun that's inside."

"The gun?"

"Yes …the one his father used," she cries, "the one he used for the suicide."

"The same one Dad used in the hospital?"

"That's what I think," she says, taking a seat at the kitchen table.

"Mel," Charlie says, "Dad can't identify with loss, he's going through denial."

"But perhaps it's more than that."

"I'm not saying it's not psychological, Mel, but I don't think it's dementia."

"Then what is it?"

"He has a psychiatrist he's seeing."

"In jail," she huffs.

"Jail doesn't mean the psychiatrist doesn't have credentials, or isn't reliable."

"We lost Mom," she says, tears falling down her cheeks, "now Dad is gone."

"He's not gone," Charlie says.

"But he might as well be."

"He's just absent," Charlie replies.

"He's not going to be around to see his own great-granddaughter born," she slams her hand on the table, loud enough for her brother to wince on the other end.

"By the New Year he might be home," Charlie counters.

"How? None of us have the money to post bail."

"And Dad doesn't want that."

"I'm not sure why …"

"Because Dad wants to write these letters to Mom," he says confidently.

"I know. I got one today."

"I finished reading the first letter today."

"What does it say?"

"Mom was married before Dad."

"What?" Melody takes the phone away from her ear and stares at it in disbelief.

"They never talked about it."

"No, they didn't. Not to me."

"Dad mentioned it once, but wouldn't say much."

"Well, tell me," she says, leaning forward on the table, rubbing the ever-growing crease in her forehead.

"Dad would visit Mom at the hospital where she worked, but she was married."

"Married to whom?"

"A Henry Edmondson."

"For how long?"

"Maybe a year it seems, but I'm not sure."

"Well, then what happened?" Melody stood and walked to the fridge to grab some iced tea and a glass.

"They divorced, and she married Dad."

"Then they built the house?"

"But not until you were about four or five."

"I'm not sure I remember," she says, pausing to take a sip of the sweet tea. "You?"

"Yeah. We lived in another place before the house, but I was about seven, but I didn't realize how hard it was for them."

"What was?"

"Their marriage. Mom stayed home and Dad worked, but it wasn't enough."

"I thought it was."

Charlie sighs and runs his hand through his hair. "Eventually Grandpa came around, but it took a while, and eventually he helped Dad build the house."

"I didn't know that."

"Mel, it means that Mom and Dad might not own the house."

"What?"

"Grandpa owns the house."

"But they are deceased."

"Mom and Dad don't own the home," Charlie repeats slowly.

"So what's going to happen?"

"We have to find the will," he says.

"Where?" Melody stands and grabs her glass to get some ice from the fridge.

"Maybe in that safe deposit box you're talking about."

"I'm not sure I want to look in that thing."

"I can do it," Charlie volunteers, "but why not?"

"The idea of that gun makes me uneasy."

"Mel," Charlie says, "he's already taken the gun out...when he used it inside the hospital."

"I know, I guess..." Melody taps the stem of her glass and put the tea back in the fridge.

"His mind is just creating a fantasy of the sort, I guess."

"He's writing letters like Mom isn't gone," she cries into the phone.

"But we need to find out if Grandpa Stanton left us the house in the will."

"Well, who else would he have left it to?"

Melody wipes an errant tear from her face.

"Maybe to Mom," he says.

"And Dad?"

"Perhaps not," Charlie says.

"But that's Dad's house, too."

"Well, what I'm saying is Grandpa might have bought the house for Mom, and for the grandkids, but left off Dad's name."

"Why would he do that?"

"Because Dad came from a troubled past," he says quietly into the phone.

"I'll give you the pass code," she says, "and you can look in the box."

"I'll be over tomorrow," Charlie says. "We'll figure this out."

Out the corner of his eye, Jimmy peers at the faint light of his cell; the light shimmers subtly into a roundish configuration before he closes his eyes tight and wishes for sleep.

"*My love,*" he whispers, "*good night sweetheart,*" as the faintest touch caresses his cheek and he rolls toward the wind. Startled by the heavy scratchiness of the green wool sheet, he tosses the blanket to the floor and sits up from his bunk.

"*I'm not there,*" a voice says faintly into his left ear, and Jimmy smiles, touching his cheek with a smooth palm and lays back, to take in her scent.

The next day, Charlie enters his childhood home, searching for a safe deposit box. He finally finds a metal safe tucked away behind tackle boxes in the dark corner of the basement. He punches in the code provided in the letter. There, in the lock box is a package. The heavy wood bench screeches across the floor as Charlie takes a seat and withdraws the documents.

At the bottom of an envelope he removes a letter addressed to Caroline from her mother; the document goes over the family's various properties, and in the faint penmanship that Charlie can barely read, it explains that his mother is the sole owner of the land that his father and mother shared and the home itself had been left to Caroline. Charlie sighs as he realizes his father knew, but had never told them.

The house will be auctioned by the state, he texts Melody, *Mom was left the house as well as the farmland.*

Charlie sighs as he neatly folds the documents back into the large manila envelope and closes the door to the safe. He pauses and takes another look inside. At the bottom of the safe is an empty case. A case that would be used to store a small pistol, lined with green felt fabric and a container of empty shells beneath it. Charlie removes the cases, shutting the safe deposit box. Standing, he walks heavily up the stairs and out the door where he finds a metal garbage can. He quickly empties the casings inside and walks away, his phone buzzing.

Chapter Five

Jimmy's eyes flicker open. Before him, is a panoramic swirl of various colors that stretches like a horizon. The spectrum of light shimmers and hovers, radiating a type of indescribable energy. The energy pulses brightly as a voice says *"I like her, Jimmy."* The aura spans the entire space before him, then moves seemingly up and backward like a vortex of colors before dissipating into a light stream of smoke, leaving behind sterility and concrete.

Jimmy sits up from his bunk, his mouth slightly parted as a single tear traces his cheekbone. *"Who,"* is all he can muster to say before he leans into the wall. *"Who could that be about,"* he says again to the empty sink in front of him.

Quickly, he picks up his pen to begin again: *Dear Caroline,* it says, as he starts his first line, *you won't believe this, but I've seen the shining light of God.*

Melody waits by the door of her mother's home, pacing until the mail arrives, but there are no letters that day, nor for the next four weeks. The letters from the bank, however, are abundant, and Melody and

Charlie deal with the fact that their parents' home and farmland are not going to be paid by the due date, and the bills are now nearing six months past due.

Melody's job as a veterinarian assistant won't be enough to pay her father's debts. Charlie's income is equally modest as debts were too large for even himself after he fell from a scaffold during a roof repair on his Victorian home. His neck and back injuries almost left him paralyzed and unable to return to work in civil engineering. Charlie had to abandon his own home, making a modest sale after the economy crashed in 2008, and in 2009, he and his wife settled in a smaller home. Charlie's wife Adele works as a librarian and wanted to put their own kids through college, but the money would never be enough. Charlie's son, Charlie Jr., was the first in the family to attend college followed by his three siblings, who all have college loan debt.

"We are a family lineage of debt and a modest income," Charlie explains into his cell phone as Melody's voice echoes in the background.

"What are we going to do?" She asks, her voice fading in and out of range.

"There's not much we can do," Charlie explains calmly.

"But I don't want to lose Mom and Dad's house," she says, shaking.

"I just don't know what else can be done," he sighs.

"There must be something."

"Not if we don't have any means to pay for the farm."

"Can't we rent it out?" Charlie rubs the back of his injured neck. "We should have thought of that months ago."

"I guess, if you think there could still be hope."

"We've got to think of something."

"How about we ask Dad?"

"Dad's gone delusional."

"He's just in denial."

"If that's what you call it."

"It's not fair to say Dad is ill."

"Then how do you explain the hospital?" Melody argues, as she runs the sink water lightly to start washing the dishes.

"It's part of his depression, and his denial."

"If you say denial one more time…"

"Perhaps he's not the only one."

"What are you saying?"

"You've got to take it easy on him."

"They posted his bail at a few thousand dollars," Charlie lightly taps the wooden doorjamb with his closed fist.

"Dad's managing."

"He's writing letters to Mom."

"He needs that."

"This family needs him."

"This is going to get worked out."

"How?"

"We will find a way."

"I'll hold you to that."

"Just trust me," Charlie grinds his knuckles into the door, causing the skin to crack slightly.

"Okay," Melody says.

"Alright. I'll talk to you soon."

"Alright," Melody sighs

"Bye," Charlie says.

"Bye."

A large five bedroom and three bath spacious country home sits on more than four acres of land; the bills are past due, and the money is tight. Charlie writes a modest check but doesn't feel it will do much good – but something might be better than nothing.

Jimmy hasn't left his single cell for months, but he continues meeting with the ward psychiatrist. He hasn't mentioned the perceptible aura that visited his room on the account that the voice sounded like his Caroline. His shaky left hand grips at the torn envelope the guard handed him through the small opening of the large metal door. He takes a seat at the make-shift table and examines the handwriting. He knows Caroline's lettering was cursive, but the writing on the envelope is written in print. He unfolds the stationary paper that looks like a little girl's letter aside from the handwriting. Inside, the letter begins, *Dear Jimmy Hedrick*. Caroline would call him by her pet name "Jimbo" or even James, but his last name would be irrelevant. Jimmy scans the page to the bottom finding the name *Priscilla Glass* and peers at her stationary letter written in fine print – wondering how old she could be.

Dear Jimmy Hedrick,

I do not know by what design your letters have arrived at my door, but I have been receiving your letters for every day that my husband Henry has passed away. Your letters are however, not addressed to me and I do feel that we most likely do not know one another nor do I know of the woman Caroline who you have been writing these letters. I tried to post the letters back to the sender unopened, but the last letter came back to me. So I decided to open the letter to address the sender.

I am writing in the best manner that I know how, to whom I do not know, with the intention to tell you that your letters have been finding their way to my mailbox. It is not my intention to be too personal here because I see that you are writing from the penitentiary. I, myself, live in Concord, North Carolina, which is about a two-hour drive from your location. I hope you do not mind if I say that you write beautifully to her and I wonder why it is that she is not receiving your letters, and I wanted to address the matter with you.

I hope this letter finds you and that it goes to the right place. Best of wishes to you, but I am sorry to say that I do not know how to get your letters to Caroline personally.

Best,
Priscilla Glass-Edmondson

Jimmy turns the letter over one more time before taking the letter he addressed to Caroline from his bunk. He scans the envelope and the letter and notices that nothing is wrong with the address he has written on the envelope. He sighs deeply and wonders how his letters have been directed to a town that is a two-hour drive away. He simply removes a sheet of ruled paper from his tablet and begins:

Dear Priscilla,

You have my mother's name, and I don't know how you have been receiving my letters that I have intended for my wife Caroline. I guess I ought to be frank here, but my beloved Caroline will never actually receive these letters because she never returned to me after her surgery. She has passed on to the heavens, but within your letter it appears that you are also experiencing loss. I don't have much to say at this time but I want to express that I hope you are well. Thank you for writing a very kind and generous letter.

Signed,
Jimmy

P.S. My friends call me Jimbo.

Jimmy sends the letter the following day. Weeks pass before a second letter arrives.

Dear Jimmy,

I think you may know my husband, but perhaps we can discuss this at a later date, when we may meet in person.

Signed,
Priscilla

After the letter, Jimmy returns to see his psychiatrist in ward nine before his trial or remediation. Jimmy learns that the doctors of Duke Hospital are especially understanding of his demise and are willing to accept his plea bargain without further punitive consequences – that is, if he continues counseling while undergoing care at the in-patient ward for a period of two years.

Instead, Jimmy vows to serve his term in the prison instead. There he can think of his wife without being reminded of her for every day they would want him to talk about his life. Instead of talking about his life within the hospital where they met, he could hold onto her.

Chapter Six

Removing the spare key from the rusted nail poking out the front stoop, Jimmy enters his residence at 206 Heide Cooper Road to find his home empty. He walks inside to the bedroom where he last spoke to Caroline about the up-coming surgery and all they had been through and experienced at Duke Hospital. He examines the stains on the wall – an imprint of their antique bedroom furniture that had been Caroline's Grandmother's and sighs, knowing that the country farm house never belonged to him anyway. That part he cared little about, but the rest – the years he spent within that space with the woman he loved settled deeply within him.

The nine additional months he spent in the penitentiary had been long, tiresome, and desolate, but Jimmy managed to work in the office, filing papers and within the library. His life became modest within the prison system where he ruminated over the past, rather than talk with anyone else about the orphanage and widowhood. He felt deeply about being widowed, but considered his Caroline if she had been widowed. God needed Caroline to come home, and he would also have to wait until it was his time.

The thought of Caroline under the bed sheets, her hair full of curlers, began to recede as the front door of his home opened slightly from its hinges, and a woman began to enter. Jimmy limps toward the front door when he glimpses at the face of a youthful, yet aged woman staring back at him. In that brief instant, the face of his Caroline morphed into focus as if juxtaposed on the woman. She gasps, and he taken aback, falls slightly into the wall, his chest heaving.

"Caroline," he calls, extending one arm to the front door as the light of day forces itself in and a breeze escapes past the door, nudging his cheek, and he calms. Wiping his eyes, he squints at the figure before him.

"Caroline?"

"Who...I mean, is that you, Jimmy?" She hunches slightly, and extends a hand to help him up. Her sleek, gray hair is fastened neatly into a bun and she wears lilac, her turquoise and silver jewelry sparkling in the streaming ray of light.

"Yes, I'm Jimmy," he says, accepting her outstretched hand.

"There's no one else out there," she says.

"But I saw her face," he huffs.

"I'm sure you did, Jimmy," she says calmly.

"My Caroline was right there a moment ago…"

"That's how they communicate with us, Jimmy."

"What do you mean?" Jimmy eyes the woman suspiciously.

"Spirit, Jimmy. Spirit is not of the flesh, but a celestial light."

"The light," he pants.

"Yes, Jimmy. The light of spirit makes its presence known in ways that are subtle yet endearing." The woman lets go of his hand as he gets his bearings.

"I'm sorry," he says, wiping dust from his pants. "But who …"

"I'm Priscilla, Jimmy. Priscilla Glass, wife of the late Henry Edmondson."

"Henry…" Jimmy stutters lightly.

"Yes, Jimmy."

"Well, how… who…"

"The belongings within the estate were taken by family to do with it as they needed, but the home, I'm sure you know they were unable to afford … but…"

"Yes. I know," he waves a trembling hand at her.

"Then you probably know that the house was left in a will, given to my late husband, Henry Edmondson."

Jimmy focuses on the lines of her cheekbones, and at the radiant jawline as if her age was significantly less than his own.

"No." he whispers. "I did not know that."

"Your children tried to put up the money for the home, but eventually they had asked if I could maintain and care for the home in place of their absence. I was hesitant at first, but then I decided to sell off my own home and with that money I could pay for this one in full."

Jimmy peers out the front window at the abundant sunlight on the hot August day, and back at Priscilla Glass.

"Did you say," He whispers, "Henry Edmondson."

"Yes, I did," she says with a radiant smile. "The home was left to him in a will written by Victor and Suzanne Stanton."

"Yes," he says, "My wife's mother and father." Jimmy sighs and turns toward the sunlight.

"Then, you do know my late husband," she says hesitantly.

"Hey, uh, did it get windy out there to you?" Jimmy looks at her, slightly bewildered.

"No, I can't say that it did," she says. "Why do you ask?"

"Nothing. No reason I guess."

"Certainly there must be a reason."
Jimmy sighs, a lost look on his face. "Well, you see, the wind felt chilly and then warm on my face. I had to re-think the weather," he explains.

"Perhaps you have read about the various ways in which spirit contacts loved ones," she says.

"No, I haven't," he says frankly.

"Well, I used to think that I had a visit from my father when I was a young girl. He used to smoke cigars, and there were times when there was a presence of cigar smoke, or the scent, and no one else would be home. I was very close to my father, and his death was unexpected."

"Do you mind if I ask what happened?"

"He died from clogged arteries by the age of fifty-five."

"I'm sorry to hear that," Jimmy says, turning his focus around the vast and empty room that used to house his wife's piano.

"Me, too." She says, "He was a good man."

"Things have been difficult," he says, "since Caroline passed."

"Yes. These things are certainly difficult for everyone."

"Yes, they are," he says, turning his attention to her again. "But may I also ask you…"

"Ask me anything."

"Why would you choose to leave the home you shared with your husband?"

"Well," she hesitates, fidgeting with a broach on her blouse, "the house was too much for me to take care of."

"And this one?" He sweeps his arm around. "This one isn't too much?"

"Your children and your grandkids, are interested in doing some work around the property."

"Have they agreed to that?"

"Yes, they are aware that the home has been left to my husband who left all our properties to me."

"How can they help you?"

"We are interested in building a bed and breakfast."

"A what?" Jimmy cocks his head, almost as if he didn't hear her correctly.

"And I need someone who can stay here on a regular basis."

"What are you saying?"

"We all want to do good for the community, to commemorate Henry and Caroline's life." She rushes, trying to explain it a little better.

"You've been discussing this?"

"I discovered that the address on your letters matched the residence that was inherited by my husband, so I reached out to them." She smiles sheepishly.

"Why do I know so little of this?" he demands.

"They wanted to wait."

"Wait for what?"

"Until you were better."

"Better?' he laughs. "There's nothing wrong with me."

"No Jimmy, but they might not know that."

"Why wouldn't they?"

"Perhaps it's best to discuss that with them."

"Perhaps," he says, quietly, scanning her face for a resemblance to his Caroline. Unable to find one, Jimmy, dragging his left leg slightly, makes his way toward the front door and opens it to the day's stagnant air before him. Ignoring Priscilla, Jimmy looks to the sky, thinking about Caroline, the day she entered the hospital, prepped on the table for surgery. Her hair was fully curled and she smelled fragrant like essential oils: lavender and jade.

Within the week, Jimmy settles into his home, taking refuge in the guest room alongside Priscilla as his roommate. They agree to use the home as a means of income so that the two of them can live there comfortably; with the house being paid for in full, they will have ample income to make the two of them comfortable.

Jimmy takes solace in the guest room, while not being the room he shared with his wife, it still reminds him of the way she had made the home comforting to her children when they'd visit for the weekend with the grandkids. The grandchildren often stayed awake into the night baking pies and homemade desserts Caroline had learned from her own grandmother.

Jimmy lies awake, thinking about Caroline's prominence within the home. She didn't just bake, but she also liked to plant vegetables in the garden and herbs inside in pots that bordered the screened-in porch. She crocheted quilts for the grandkids during holidays. She ironed their bedsheets and maintained their home in every proper way her up-bringing served her. Jimmy also thinks about the fact that he never had his father-in-law's heart or good graces.

Victor Stanton was raised by a prosperous man who had invested in the oil industry, educated in private schools and at home with a mother who also had been raised with the comforts of money. Jimmy fidgets as he thinks how Victor never forgave him for Caroline leaving her doctoral studies to be at home with her children–children that were Jimmy's and not that of Henry Edmondson. The irony does not escape him that his home is shared with the wife of Caroline's first husband and how strange to live in a place that no longer feels like home but more like the bed-and-breakfast it would become.

Jimmy flicks the light on to his guest room and removes the paper he has stashed in a large envelope with all the things he brought with him from the state penitentiary. He unfolds a single piece of ruled paper, and with his hand shaking he writes:

Dear sweet Caroline,

I have made it back home, but it no longer feels like home. Our home together was the place in which we raised our children, and the place where our grandchildren would come to visit on the weekends. Our home was the kind of place where you could perform magic, the kind of magic that never ceased to amaze me. Everything you did was incredibly beautiful and creatively sophisticated. I am honored to have stolen your heart and have you in my company for the fifty years. The work went unnoticed because I came home every day to a dedicated woman who had my soul in her reach. You my dear sweet Caroline, were my saving grace, for every time you met me at the hospital on your lunch break, I didn't think twice to drink, to being anything like my father had been to my mother, but a good man who could love you with all that I had.

I hope I did all that I could for you, and that there are no regrets for having taken my hand in marriage. I love you, dear sweet Caroline. May you rest in peace my beloved wife, but you will always be with me.

> *Love forever and ever,*
> *Jimmy James*

Jimmy folds the paper neatly in half and inserts the letter into the envelope, turning it over to address the letter he'd write once more to Caroline – this time addressed to Duke Hospital.

"Why there," he says out loud, to no one in particular, but the quiet serenity of his room. *"Because it's the last place she was alive,"* he says again, looking at the ceiling as if searching the heavens – and he lowers his head, licking the envelope to create a seal, and smooths the edges.

In the morning, Jimmy walks through the garden in his bare feet – the only place that still feels like Caroline. Depositing the letter, he cranks his neck to find the breeze, but all that he finds is the stillness of a new day in September. Realizing a new kind of life is upon him; the one without Caroline, he turns back toward the door, pulling it closed behind him.

Chapter Seven

Charlie and Melody enter their childhood home in the company of Charlie's wife Adele, their son, Charlie, Jr., who they call CJ, along with girlfriend Melissa and their baby daughter, Victoria. Victoria is three months, and today is the first time he'll meet his great-granddaughter. Melody and Charlie stopped visiting the prison on account that their father refused therapy and chose instead to fulfill his time within the prison. They were angry, and Jimmy felt then they had no right to be.

"You haven't had to talk about the things I've had to," he says, at the wall, sensing his two children standing behind him.

"We didn't know you were out," Melody says, shaking her head.

"How long have you been out?" Charlie asks.

Jimmy turns around ever-so-softly, heavy on one leg as he transfers his weight. "I've been here about a week," he says, turning his gaze to Victoria, in the arms of Cassie. "She's a pretty little thing," he says, stepping toward her.

"I'm sorry we couldn't bring her to see you," Melissa says, smiling with peach-colored lip gloss.

"Oh, it's alright," Jimmy says, reaching out toward her.

"Oh, here," Melissa moves Victoria to both arms, for Jimmy to hold her.

"She's already three months," her father says.

"CJ, she has your grandmother's hazel eyes," Jimmy says, smiling.

"Well, Mom isn't here Dad," Melody mutters, slightly annoyed.

"He knows that," Charlie says.

"Does he?" Melody interjects.

"Well, I do see your mother from time-to-time," Jimmy says, taking Victoria to the sofa, sitting gently with her clasping at his index finger, smiling and drooling.

"See, now I told you he's delusional."

"What do you mean by that?" Charlie asks.

"She came to me in my sleep."

"Where, Dad?"

"The correctional institution I visited for a while," he says.

"Mom died in the hospital, Dad," Melody says, brushing her long hair from her face with slender fingers. "She experienced serious complications and stopped breathing

– she was put on life support, then she died, in a medically induced coma."

"I know all this," Jimmy says softly.

"I know you know all that. But what you don't know…"

"Maybe not now Melody," Charlie says.

"Maybe what you don't know…," Melody continues, hunching above her father, pointing a finger at his chest, "is how the hospital staff responded immediately to her change in vital signs, her low blood pressure, her correctly administered aesthetic dosage – that her death wasn't from negligence – that the reason she suffered oxygen to her brain wasn't anyone's fault. She was resuscitated at the hospital, before she went into the coma, before you showed up…with your father's gun – might as well been his whiskey, too…"

"All they had to do was remove her gall bladder."

"But she experienced complications, Dad. She died. Mom is gone."

"Melody…" Charlie says, taking Victoria from their father and handing her to her mother.

"But she's alive now," he explains.

"Dad?"

"You're delusional, Dad. I'm the one who got your letters."

"But Caroline responded."

"Mom is gone…and you've gone gonzo!"

"Calm down, Melody," Charlie says, palms down to his sister.

"Mom can't respond to those letters, Charlie."

"But I could," Priscilla says, making an entrance in the living room, startling the family. "Not only that, but I can tell you that spirit manifests in subtle and creative or imaginative ways."

Melody stutters, "Spirit? What spirit?"

"As a young woman I used to smell the scent of my father within a room after he passed. Your father can see the aura of a brilliant white light that he attributes to being your mother," she says, crossing her arms.

"I don't believe in ghosts," Melody says.

"What is she talking about?" Charlie asks.

"I see things from time-to-time."

"A little less vague?"

"He's delusional, Priscilla. He's hallucinating."

"Hallucinations occur in the mind of the mentally ill and are often determined to have irrelevance to one's life."

"How does that matter?"

"Your father is experiencing manifestations from a spirit that he can recognize."

"I'm sorry, but I cannot believe any of this."

"He might see your mom," Melissa chimes in, with a youthful tilt of her head, cooing at her daughter.

"How?"

"Spirits manifest in numerous ways, perhaps through the mind of another person, through the voice of a medium, or through manifestations of a spirit body that people typically associate as a ghost. In your father's case, he sees a spectrum of light that is not describable in terms of physical existence, and through that light, he can sense the voice of your mother who communicates with him."

"What did she say?" Melody asks, eager.

"She said she likes her," Jimmy says, raising his head toward Priscilla, "which is the reason I stayed."

"Stayed where?"

"Stayed in this house."

"I don't understand."

"I assumed she was talking about Priscilla, it seemed to be a coincidence that her letter arrived the day after your mother's visit."

"So then what does all this mean?" Charlie asks, taking the baby from his wife.

"Your mother approves," he says.

"Approves what?"

"That's for us to find out," he says calmly.

"I've heard that the White House is known to have ghosts or spirits," Adele interjects quietly in the reclining chair. "People have reported having seen Abraham Lincoln there."

"But what does this have to do with Mom?" asked Charlie.

"Nothing, dear," Priscilla smiles gently. "I'm just saying that your father might be psychologically sound, and there are others who have seen people after they've passed on."

"But I think he should be seeing a psychiatrist about this."

"I've already been to psychiatrists," he says, resting his head into the palm of his hand.

"But you haven't talked about this," she says.

"Melody, I've been to the counselors and they all want to talk about my father."

"Can you even remember him?"

"Yes, of course I can."

"Then tell them what he was like."

"I have."

"Then do it again."

"Not any more, Melody."

"You weren't able to get proper help in jail, Dad."

"I served my time. Like an honorable man."

"Yelling at those doctors and nurses, drunk, and waving that gun wasn't honorable, Dad," Melody interjects.

"Neither was losing my wife."

"It's no one's fault, Dad."

"You don't know that."

"The investigation report says they did everything they were supposed to."

"These things happen, Dad," Charlie chimes in.

"I survived a heart transplant for God's sake!"

"And Mom survived breast cancer," Melody says.

"Alright everyone," CJ pipes up, "we're all getting upset at each other, and we know that Grandma wouldn't want this."

"You're right, son," Charlie says.

"But isn't all this a little odd? How is Mom's first husband in all this?"

"He was respected by her father," Jimmy says.

"He was a good man," Priscilla says, "But so is your father."

"Then why isn't this house Dad's anymore?" Melody asks, slamming an arm on the couch.

"Because that's not the way they wanted it."

"And you say that Mom approves?" Melody raises an eyebrow.

"Yes," Jimmy smiles softly, thinking about his wife. "It was her voice, I know her voice, and she told me *I like her, Jimmy.*"

"I like her, Jimmy," Charlie repeats.

"That's right," Jimmy says.

"Then Mom's got something in store for us," Charlie says, laughing slightly, "she always had something up her sleeve. Remember that time at the beach, at the Outer Banks? She wasn't very nautical but she winged it anyway, getting all us out there on that inner-tube, and she'd gun it–full speed, because she was always a thrill seeker."

"If she wasn't running, then she was running us," Jimmy laughs.

"I loved Mom's laugh," Melody wipes a tear from her eye.

"She won that pageant at seventeen," Charlie says.

"And she was so beautiful," Melody says.

"She is so missed, Mel, by all of us."

"She really is," CJ says, "I loved Grammy's pies, and hot roast beef sandwiches."

"Oh man, she could cook," Jimmy says.

"Sunday breakfast," Melody says, removing a tissue wrapped in colorful paper from her purse. "Well, I'm thankful that I can tend to her garden," she says dabbing her face, "I know Mom would like that."

"I believe she would too, Melody," Jimmy says.

"Mom, I love you," Melody says out loud, "if you can hear me," she laughs, then turns toward the door, "I have to go," she says, "I have to get back to work."

"We understand, Mel," Charlie says, hugging his sister.

"I miss Mom," she says, exiting through the door, turning to wave, "Goodbye."

Jimmy wakes from his reverie with a hard thud to the floor in the early morning hours. Jimmy leans into the side of his bed throwing one leg over and then the other. He climbs into his sheets, lays his back slowly inhaling and exhaling. He had a nightmare;

brought on terrors of the day he showed with the gun, but the gun was no longer his, but his father's again.

Jimmy was seven once more and found his father face down on the kitchen table, a butter knife on the floor in a pool of blood from a gunshot wound to his head. His father lost his job, likely to his own belligerence and constant patronizing of others to the point of fighting. His father fought his mother and turned once on Jimmy; he was thrown down the stairs violently while his mother lay unconscious on the floor – that was two days before his death.

Jimmy found himself not wanting to discuss it with anyone but Caroline. At night, he would lay awake talking to her image in his mind. He'd called to her, bellowing loud guffaws of excruciating agony. Suddenly the sheet had been ripped from his body, forcefully to the floor, and a kiss touched his forehead.

A vision of Caroline, alive, stood over his bedside, her face as stern, innocent, and kind as she had always been, stared back at him, and her lips parted to utter, *I love you Jimmy,* before she turned her back to him and walked a single step before she vanished entirely. Jimmy fell from the bed, his legs dangling from the side and his torso hanging on the edge. He lays awake, a solitary tear drop careening from a sharp cheekbone. Jimmy inhales again, deeply, letting out his breath into a hand, now clasped to his face. There was Caroline, and then there wasn't.

Candace Meredith

Chapter Eight

"It is very unusual for a spirit to manifest as a physical entity," Priscilla says, pouring hot tea from a pot on the stove. She stirs in the sugar while Jimmy sits casually in the kitchen chair and waits for her to proceed, but Priscilla carefully tends to her tea, removing ice cubes from the freezer and pours two glasses.

"What do you mean?" he asks.

"Well, to start," she responds, as she places a glass of tea before Jimmy.

"Thank you," he says.

"It's no problem at all."

"As you were saying," he says, sipping.

"Spirits use the energy source that is available around them to absorb it and make themselves present. It is not usual for a spirit to manifest as a physical entity, but instead they are typically blurry, or hazy, or may be somewhat transparent – but seeing directly through a ghostly spirit is also quite unusual. Others appear as orbs or swirling kinds of light energy."

"You use energy a lot to explain the phenomena."

"Well," she says, "look at it this way; energy is understood in physics as a kind of property that can be converted into a different form – spirit energy is therefore the appearance of an individual who has converted to a different form."

"Not dead, but different," Jimmy says, eyeing the ice in his glass.

"That's right. Energy has many forms. As we have discussed."

"Then how does one, I don't know, appear physical again?"

"That's a good question. But the only way I can explain it is by relating a story that I once read in a book. A medium, and one of the only ones able to make the deceased loved one appear as physical, was adept at communication with those who have passed on during a séance she conducted in her home. She used a silver cord to connect with the spirit and somehow used her own body as a spiritual cipher between the deceased and the loved one who was making the communication. She was heralded by her followers as an adept medium who could conduct a séance to the effect of physical communication with the deceased."

"That's extraordinary."

"It is indeed. Another medium I read about was Eileen Garrett from the 19th century. She was much like Edgar Cayce who was known as the sleeping prophet, in that in a sleep-like induced state she could uncover information that could not possibly be known by her. Some say she was a gifted medium."

"Can you tell me more?"

"I do know of another story."

"Please do."

"It's about the death of a friend's brother. He had died at seventeen, due to a drug overdose, and after his death strange things would happen within the home. My friend was home alone one day when her brother's bedroom door slammed shut. Another incident occurred when her stepfather was passing by the television screen and a picture frame flew off the wall as if to hit him – but they speculate the boy was very angry especially at his own step-father."

"I see," Jimmy sighs.

"I do know how it feels Jimmy," she says, "by our age we have experienced the deaths of those we love and many of them are hard to live without."

Jimmy inhales deeply. "You got that right," he says. "So what did they do?" He asks curiously.

"Who, Jimmy?"

"The family who lost a son."

"The family moved, Jimmy. They were renting and moved to another home.

Evidently, after the move the visits from the boy ceased."

"I suppose his rash behavior must have been hard for them."

"I'm sure it made his death that more difficult."

"Spirits must still have their own mind."

"I'm sure, but don't underestimate your own sensitivity."

"What do you mean?"

"What you have experienced is described as clairvoyance by mediums, or the ability to see those that are not physically present. You have experienced clear-seeing and mediums describe that a person has to be especially sensitive to communicate with spirits in the afterlife."

"Are you a sensitive?" Jimmy's fingers felt cold from the condensation on the glass.

"I've had sensitivity to spirits since the death of my father. I was twenty when he died."

"You smelled smoke?"

"Yes, he smoked cigars since I can remember. I smelled the smoke and knew that Daddy was making himself known to me. I'm not the only one in my family either." Priscilla smiles briefly. "My siblings and I all saw our Grandfather in spirit – he walked across the living room floor into the hall and vanished while the three of us sat on the sofa. It scared us because we were very little. Our mother said her father must have been protecting us."

"Well, my daughter believes none of this."

"She might come around."

"I doubt it," Jimmy shrugs. "But you never know I guess."

Priscilla turns her back at the sound of a knock on the back door. Charlie walks through the door, hands full of groceries. Grunting slightly, he places the full bags onto the counter.

"What's all this?" Priscilla asks.

"We're having a little get together," he says.

"A get together for what occasion?" Jimmy asks.

"It's Labor Day weekend, Pops." Charlie explains as he starts to unload the bags.

"Oh."

"What are you two talking about in here?"

"Discussing your mother."

"Anything in particular?"

"I still see her from time-to-time."

"Well, how is Mom doing Dad?" Charlies asks, more to the can of beans than to his father.

"Lovely woman," he says, "but we were also discussing your sister."

"Now you know that Mel is very logical, Dad."

"Stubborn. Always been stubborn."

"She's practical and everything has to be precise for her. Kind of like Mom," Charlie explains, removing some patties from the bag, "We're having grilled hot dogs and hamburgers."

"Who?" Jimmy asks.

"Mel is coming, then Macy and Mar, CJ and Melissa, baby Victoria, and Adele is on her way."

"I guess I better get changed," Jimmy sighs, slowly getting up from the table, "anyone else coming?"

"I think Mace might be bringing a boyfriend, and Mar might be bringing a friend. Not sure. How about you, Priscilla…you have anyone coming today?"

"I do have a younger brother," she says, "but I believe they're in Florida. They stay there through the fall and the winter, then they come back through the summer."

"The summer gets too hot," Charlie says.

"It sure does," Priscilla remarks, "and all the hurricanes. But I hope I'm not an intrusion."

"Nonsense," Charlie waves a dismissive hand. "Dad still has the house because you could be here for us."

Jimmy pushes away from the table. "I'm going to put some pants on," he says. Laughing, Charlie continues, "Dad needs a friend right now anyway."

"Well, he's got a friend," she says smiling, "and a good family, too."

Priscilla's silver hoops dangle from her neck, while stylish rings accentuate her long, slender fingers. Her silver hair hangs long at the sides of her face, and she favors pastels in her wardrobe. The years have been kind; her cheekbones are still prominent and rosy, and she has her own straight, white teeth that dazzle when she smiles.

She spent her time leisurely with photography as a hobby, and tended to her garden, like Caroline, but she did not have children of her own. Since Henry was sterile, they traveled instead, until he was diagnosed with clogged arteries and died three days later, leaving Priscilla with their three properties. She moved into the farmhouse on Heide Cooper Road after she learned that her husband inherited his first wife's home – knowing Henry could not give her any children.

She spoke to Melody in July while Jimmy had been in prison, stopping by the house where the letters were sent. Priscilla found Melody outside, coincidentally looking in the mailbox. There, Melody and Priscilla learned of one another and how the letters must have been re-routed to the original owner of the farmhouse.

They talked over Caroline's garden; Priscilla explaining how much she liked to garden in her own home, and Melody described the days she spent with her mother in the outdoors. She marveled at Priscilla's knowledge about various perennials and how to keep the garden fresh. A piece of Melody felt that her mother would like this woman, despite her marriage to her husband.

Melody learned of Priscilla's loneliness in widowhood, she was seventy years but didn't look a day over sixty, and how she didn't have anyone aside from her younger brother who often traveled with his wife Karin, and who would visit Priscilla mostly during the holidays. Priscilla explained that Henry worked as a banker and had come from a prosperous family, and that he and Priscilla had inherited several homes from his own parents.

However, Priscilla decided to sell them, as there was too much to care for on her own, and she instead, paid off the farmhouse. Melody thought that a bed-and-breakfast would bring life to her family's home, and Priscilla vowed to tend the garden, the way Caroline had done.

Melody and Priscilla began making plans for the farmhouse while Jimmy continued to write letters to Caroline, which found their way to Priscilla, and Priscilla would send them on to Melody, and she herself would write only one more letter until the day she could meet Jimmy in person.

So on the farmland outside of Raleigh, North Carolina, Priscilla Glass Edmondson and Melody Hedrick would commemorate Henry and Caroline by designing a bed-and-breakfast from a four bedroom farmhouse.

Chapter Nine

Jimmy enters the kitchen, dressed in blue jeans and a white-collared, button-down shirt. Opening the door to the backyard, he spots Priscilla in the garden, talking with Melissa, as CJ holds onto his daughter. Charlie stands over the grill, flipping burgers and smoking the hot dogs. As soon as Jimmy enters the backyard, a small breeze nudges his cheek, and he turns to see the trees, not blowing from the wind.

"I think your mother just came by for a visit," he says, one hand upon Charlie's shoulder, and together they share a wink, and a sideways smile. Behind Jimmy, Adele and Charlie's second son, Evan, closes the door behind him. Evan, 22, struts confidently aside his girlfriend Teri, 21, who is a bit shorter than his five-foot-nine frame as the top of her head nudges his shoulder.

"Hey, there," Charlie shouts above the grill, startling Jimmy.

"Oh, I didn't see you two come up behind me," he says, stepping to the side.

"Hello, Poppy," Evan says, giving his grandfather a giant bear-hug.

"Easy there," Jimmy laughs, "I'm an old man now."

"Hey, son," Charlie says, flipping a patty, knuckle-bumping with the other.

"Hello," Teri says, her dimples accentuating her round face.

"Hey girl," Charlie greets, "how the heck have you two been? Haven't seen the two of you since the beginning of the year."

"Doing good Dad."

"Did you go that graduation party?"

"There was one but we went to the beach early instead."

"Which beach?"

"Daytona Beach. Thinking about moving down there next year."

"You have a job?" Charlie flips one of his burgers.

"I don't right now but I'm applying, hoping to get someplace warm all year around."

"It's not that bad here in the Carolinas." Charlie grins.

"Yeah, but it's also not Florida," Evan laughs.

Echoing Evan's laugh are Charlie's fraternal 20-year-old twin daughters who arrive side-by-side, waving from the interior of the kitchen. Sammy the oldest, born just a minute before her sister Julianna. Sammy is average in height, petite and often referred to as "cute" by her friends. She has short, sharp, black hair that is tapered at the face, and hangs across her collar-bone to accentuate her neckline. Her twin, Julianna, is a slightly taller and fuller with long, curly vibrant red hair with freckles, but they both share deep, brown eyes and dark eyelashes.

"Well now, there's the rest of my kiddos," Charlie says, removing the slightly overdone patties from the grill. Jimmy shifts to greet the two girls who are making their way outdoors. Adele approaches and extends her arms as her two daughters push the sliding glass door to the side and step outside.

"We came in through the kitchen," Sammy laughs, darting her thumb across her shoulder.

"Hello, girls," Adele says, with a wide smile.

"Hi, Mom," they say in unison, sharing a hug with their mother.

"We were shopping," Julianna says.

"Shopping?" Charlie says, "Did you find anything good?"

"We got some new makeup."

"Yeah, and nail polish," Julianna adds.

"Where did you girls go?"

"The mall. Old Navy."

"And Target," Sammy says.

"Weren't one of you bringing a boyfriend?" Charlie asks.

"We both have a boyfriend, Dad," Sammy laughs.

"Well, what are their names?"

"Jared and Dylan." The girls answer in unison and giggle. "We all met at college," Julianna begins, "Jared and Dylan are both on the track team."

"You'll need to tell us more about them over dinner," Charlie adds, shutting the lid to the grill.

"Where is Mom?" Macy asks, approaching Charlie.

"You girls snuck in," Adele says, standing aside, allowing room for Marlene.

"We were talking with Melissa and CJ," Macy says as Melissa, holding Victoria, approaches the commotion.

"You came without your Mom?" Charlie asks.

"Yeah, I did turn eighteen," Marlene rolls her eyes and pouts.

"You're all growing up so fast," Jimmy says, straightening his back.

"Dad, have you heard from Mel?" Charlie asks, balancing the patties as he scans the driveway for her car.

"I haven't heard from Melody all morning," Jimmy says, wincing slightly.

"Alright Dad," Charlie says, nodding towards the bench, "let's all go have a seat, you must be tired from standing, and we'll wait to see if she gets here soon."

"You all told her to come, right?" Adele asks.

"I talked to her this morning," Macy says, "she was going to stop to pick up some wine or something."

"Well, why don't you try to text her," Adele says.

"I have," Macy responds, pulling her phone from her pocket.

"I hope everything is alright," Priscilla says as she helps Jimmy sit at the table and fixes him up a small plate of potato salad.

"I'm sure she's fine," Charlie puts the platter on the table, shooing off an errant fly. "She'll probably be here soon. She can't text while driving."

"I need Mom to help with my application," Macy says, reaching over to grab a dish.

"Thought you already entered college," Charlie responds.

"I did. But I'm in the process of transferring."

"Okay," Charlie says, "I was confused, thought it might be over a boy."

"That's why I'm transferring," Macy laughs.

"Over a boy," Adele chuckles.

"Yes," Macy says, blushing.

Suddenly a horn honks as a black SUV pulls into the driveway. The engine rattles and an arm waves from the driver side.

"I thought that might be Melody," Charlie says.

"Who is that?" Jimmy asks.

"That's Tom," Macy says, getting up, "my boyfriend. I invited him to meet everyone."

"Well the more the better," Adele says.

"I hope I like him," Charlie says.

"Mom already met him," Macy laughs, "and she likes him."

"And he's in the college you're transferring to?"

"Yes," Macy says, "but this will be his last year, he's a senior."

"It's a coincidence," Marlene grins, "our boyfriends go to the same college."

"Those little things always did intrigue me," Adele says. "Like it's God's plan."

"We were both pretty fascinated by it, too," Macy adds.

"Well, it's like Melody," Adele says, pulling a chair from the plastic fold-out table, filling her plate with a hot dog, baked beans and potato salad.

"What happened with Mom?" Marlene asks, taking a plate from the stack.

"She found out she was going to be a mother on Mother's Day."

"I don't think Mom ever told me that," Macy dips a spoon into the beans.

"Me either," Marlene says.

"That's because your mother doesn't believe in miracles," Charlie says in between bites of his hot dog.

"Well, I wouldn't say that she doesn't believe in miracles," Adele says, spooning baked beans onto her fork, "but she is very practical."

"Yeah," Charlie swallows, "she believes in science and modern medicine."

"With good reason," CJ says, accidentally spraying out bits of bread. "Pop survived a heart transplant."

"And your Grandmother survived breast cancer," Melissa says. "So she has reason to believe in the things that make a difference."

"I think God makes a difference too," Macy says, opening a water bottle.

"I think your mother believes that, too," Charlie says.

"I'm sure she's not atheist," Adele says.

"She just believes He has his place in the afterlife I guess," Jimmy says, tearing the bread on his hamburger.

"Speaking of Mom, I'm getting worried," Macy says, checking her phone.

"Let me check the home phone and see if anything comes in," Priscilla says as she stands from her chair to go inside.

"Haven't you been seeing Grandma?" Marlene asks, looking intently at her grandfather.

"I suppose you could say that," Jimmy says, his mouth full of candied yams.

"I've heard stories about kids seeing God," Marlene twists her macaroni salad with her fork. "A little girl fell from a tree and she said God told her she would be okay. And I heard of another story about a little boy who had surgery and he talked to some of his relatives who weren't even alive anymore."

"Do you know what they said?" Jimmy asks.

"His grandfather spoke to him. Told him he was his grandfather. He died before the little boy was even born."

"Maybe Mom should believe in little miracles," Macy says, wiping her hands on her napkin.

"Yeah, like God might have told her she was going to be a new mom, on Mother's Day," Marlene says.

"Stories coming from children must be pretty significant." Adele says, wiping her lip with a napkin

"It's profound," Jimmy says.

"That's a good way to put it," Charlie trails off as Priscilla emerges from the house, telephone in hand, exasperated.

"I've found her," she says, "They think this must be her."

"Who?" They all ask in unison.

"Melody. In the hospital. They think my description matches a woman they have in the hospital from a car accident," Priscilla says, her chest heaving.

Charlie grabs for the phone, listening as the receptionist describes his sister's accident, her black sedan hit a tree.

Chapter Ten

Single file, they slunk into room number 109 – the waiting room was not private, and they needed relief. For the last 20 minutes, the doctors and nurses perform CPR, unwilling to give up as the monitor beats, a slow, irregular rhythm.

Macy and Marlene peer down the hall, tears streaming their faces. The ER informed them that her sedan veered off the road from the highway and hit a tree. The paramedics speculate she swerved to avoid hitting a deer, because no other vehicles were involved. But her cell phone records were requested by the police.

"My mother never sent me a text," Macy explains to the doctor, "she would never use her phone while driving."

"It was hard to tell," He says, "medics say her belongings were hard to find."

"What do you mean?" Macy asks.

"Her car turned over on the side, and then rolled. It was bad. Your mother is very lucky to be alive." The doctor smiled clinically. "She is in stable condition."

"She's a tough woman, your mother," Charlie says, pacing.

"We will be sure to keep you informed of her condition," the doctor says, checking her vital signs on his chart.

"Thank you, doctor," Adele says, taking her husband by the arm.

Suddenly from behind them, a woman lets out a loud gasp, "Oh, no, no, no," she says, in an accent, "No, you cannot be in here," she says, waving her arms. "You are not allowed back in the hospital," she says, ushering a doctor toward the door.

"Nurse," the doctor says, "what is the problem?"

"That man is not allowed back in the hospital," she says.

"How do you know that?" He asks.

"He's the one...the one who came in here with that gun."

"Are you sure that's him?"

"Oh yes, he's the one," the nurse turns pale. "I am sure of it."

"Sir," the doctor says, approaching Jimmy, "I'm sorry, sir, but we have to ask you to leave..."

"My daughter is in here," he says, "and I'm not leaving."

"Dad," Charlie pleads, hands up, "just take it easy."

"I'm taking it easy Charlie, and I'm telling them my daughter is in here."

Jimmy gambols toward the vacant chair in the corner of the private room, and sits calmly in the chair, "I'll sit right here, not bothering anybody," he says, his head resting into his hand.

"I'll have to notify security," the doctor explains.

"Then you can do that now," Jimmy responds. "I'm not going anywhere."

Three minutes later, security arrives and informs Jimmy that they must be present for the duration that he is in the hospital. Jimmy accepts the compromise as they stand outside the waiting room door.

Melody's condition is severe as she continues to be connected to life support, but her brain is functioning and her vital signs are steady. The doctor has informed the family that her coma is due to her head injury, from hitting her head on the steering wheel as the windshield shattered on impact from the tree. Her broken legs have been placed into casts – the doctors are uncertain if she will walk again. The most immediate and pressing concern is her regaining consciousness, and so the family prays by her bedside when she is finally placed in her room with oxygen tubes in her mouth.

Weeks pass and the leaves change color outside of her hospital window. Her head is no longer wrapped in a bandage from the trauma she suffered to her left frontal lobe.

Macy and Marlene take turns visiting her bedside as they continue to pursue their college studies. Macy is due to graduate in December before the holiday and Marlene has begun her first year at the university, but studies are difficult as she struggles to concentrate. Charlie and Adele continue to visit each day, communicating with the doctors and nurses about his sister's progress, but she remains in the coma. Her vital signs are constant, but she fails to awaken at their presence. The bones in her legs are healing and her casts are due to come off in late October, but the doctors still speculate about her ability to walk again if she ever wakes up. Jimmy sits at her bedside, the hospital security seated outside the door, and he talks out loud to Caroline, asking his wife to be at their daughter's side. Occasionally, his daughter will smile, a slight wry grin with one side of her mouth drooping and the other side in a perfect grin. A tear escapes as he thinks his daughter must be with her mother. He dreams of the years that Caroline tended to their children, taking them by the hand at the beach and entering the cold and frigid waters, only to be knocked over by the impending wave.

He is in such a deep sleep that he snores himself awake only to find Charlie standing there over his sister. Charlie just smiles, fixes her pillow from behind her head, and pulls the sheet to her chin. He leans in closer, and nudges her ear.

"When you decide to wake up," he whispers, "we'll have everything ready for Christmas. Then," he continues, "we'll talk about that bed-and-breakfast you should be starting on, huh?"

He stands beside the bed as Adele enters the room with a hot cup of coffee, and squeezes her husband's hand. The three of them peer at the figure before them, laying softly in her bed, as her lips begin to part, and sighs, "h...e...l...p." Her eyes are closed tight, and they lean into her.

"I'm here, sis," he says.
And she lays still as ice, her lips parting ever-so-softly, "Where," she forces from her lips... "Where" she grunts.

"The girls are on their way, Mel," he says, which forces out a tiny smile from his sister. "Dad's here, too," Charlie says, "and Adele."

This time, parting her eyelids, barely, but visibly. "Mom," she rasps.

"Have you seen your mother?" Jimmy asks, leaning forward eagerly onto the

293

bed. "Caroline," he says, scanning the room for a presence.

"Mom." She rasps again.

"We're listening," Adele says as Macy walks into the room.

"She's talking," Adele cries out excitedly.

"What?"

"Mom…" Melody stutters.

"I think she's trying to say something about Caroline," Adele says.

"Mom?" Macy exclaims as Marlene enters the room.

"She's talking, Mace," Charlie says.

"What?" Macy nearly drops her coffee. "Oh, my God. What is she saying?"

"She's trying to say something about your grandmother," Jimmy strokes his daughter's hand as he continues to look around the room.

"It's so good to hear you speak," Adele says, holding her other hand.

"Mel?" Charlie says from the foot of the bed, arms around his nieces as the doctors and nurses enter the room, checking her charts and vital signs.

"Her vital signs are improving," the doctor says, glancing at the monitors

"She's trying to talk," Charlie says.

"Just might be a matter of time now," the doctor explains. "It'll be a process after this, but she's doing well so far."

"She's a trooper," Adele says, smiling softly.

"That she is," Charlie says as Mel's eyes flutter, and begin to open. Slowly, she turns her head to the side, first at Jimmy, then at the other.

"Mom," she says again.

"What? What did you see?" Jimmy asks, as she inhales deeply.

"My legs," she moans.

"You won't be able to feel your legs," the doctor says. "The car accident has caused some damage to your spine. But you're very lucky to be alive."

"We're happy to have you back, Mel," Charlie says.

Chapter Eleven

A week or so later, as November begins to blossom, Priscilla tends to Melody on the sun porch of the farmhouse as Melody's own home was sold as opposed to going into foreclosure. Wheelchair bound, she is unable to work; the spaciousness of the farmhouse allows for ample maneuverability and she enjoys looking through the fields at the bare almost frost covered trees that line the property.

Priscilla brings Melody a hot cup of tea and they sit together with quilts placed across their legs. Melody doesn't miss a great deal about her home; being with Priscilla and her Dad provides more than the extra help she needs to do the things in life that require legs – like bathing. She is getting used to the process of spinning her rump over the side of the tub while Priscilla turns her naked, skinny legs inward.

Melody talks about her divorce from Macy and Marlene's father when Marlene was nearing junior high school and she raised Macy and Marlene alone – the three of them becoming best friends. Now, Marlene has transferred to the University where she studies education, and Macy has graduated with a degree in veterinarian science and wants to have a rescue organization of her own. Macy especially likes to adopt homeless animals and has acquired some kittens from the local ASPCA alongside two dogs she rescued from breed-specific organizations: one Beagle mix and a Border Collie. Melody describes how working at the veterinarian clinic as a technician inspired Macy to pursue working with animals. Macy now rents a single bedroom apartment with her boyfriend Tom who studied computer science and works in a small computer repair shop. Melody also talks about how she isn't displeased about not re-marrying, but thinks about how she might be open to meeting someone *when the time is right.*

"Most things are just a matter of time," Priscilla says, her cold hands wrapped around her coffee mug.

"Speaking of time…" Melody says, twirling her hair in her fingers. "I was waiting for the right time to tell you about Mom."

"I'm listening." Priscilla shifts slightly in her seat to face the young woman.

"I saw Mom…"

"Where?"

"At the hospital. She was standing before me, I guess at the foot of the bed…"

"How did she look to you?"

"Youthful. Like she was my age again," Melody says smiling, sipping gingerly from her mug.

"Do you want to tell me about it?"

"Yes, but I was waiting because I didn't want to upset Dad."

"Well, I'm all ears."

"Mom was right there in front of me, but I couldn't see the room." Melody starts, a faraway look in her eyes. "I couldn't see all of you there...I could only see Mom. She was looking at me, she was smiling...I tried to ask *where am I*, but the words wouldn't come out of my mouth."

"Did she say anything to you?"

Melody shook her head. "No. I heard Charlie's voice. She just smiled, as Charlie talked to me. Mom was so beautiful, magnificent, and she smelled so good, like a garden, and she was subtle and sweet like I remembered her...then she spoke, but only to extend her one hand toward me, and she said *go.*"

"*Go?*"

"Yes." Melody sighs. "Then I opened my eyes and she was gone. You all were there. And I found out about my legs."

"She wasn't ready for you to come to her, Mel," Priscilla says, eyeing her with compassion, and a serene grin.

"But there's more."

"Oh, please do share. That is, if you're ready."

"I saw myself in the car." Melody picked at an invisible thread. "I saw my car, and me in it. I was inside the car, wedged between the seat and steering wheel – I saw that I was unconscious, and my body was contorted and twisted. I looked awkward and there was blood on my face."

"You mean you had an out-of-body experience? What else happened while you were looking at your body? How did you feel?"

"I didn't feel any pain, and I remember feeling bad for *her*. "Melody laughs slightly and shakes her head.

"Like you weren't in the car?"

"No. I was a separate entity from that body. I remember feeling weightless, like being the wind."

"What else?"

"Then a masculine voice spoke to me."

"Like God?" Priscilla smiles, shifting her cup to another part of her cold hands.

"Yes, someone like him. He had a hearty laugh. "He was warm and comforting. I didn't feel a sense of fear … but a sense of well-being."

"Could you see him?"

"No, I could only sense him being there."

"What did he say?"

"He told me I was going to be alright."

"Don't you think your father would like to know about your experience?"

"I'm not sure that I want to…because I told him he was being delusional. I didn't believe him," Melody wipes a tear from her cheek.

"It's alright dear." Priscilla reaches over to wipe away a tear that has fallen from Melody's other cheek.

"I miss Mom, too…but I couldn't believe him."

"I know sweetheart…"

"She was just gone," she hiccupps. "And he walked inside that hospital…"

"He was in a lot of pain."

"But we all were. She died unexpectedly. We didn't have time with her. Then he came in with that gun, while she was still in the morgue."

"I'm sorry, Melody."

"But I'm so selfish …"

"Why do you say that?"

"Because I thought he should be here for our family."

"That's not selfish," Priscilla leans over to give Melody a kiss on her forehead.

"Yes, yes it is. We should have been there for Dad."

"But weren't you?"

"No. Not really. We sent some money, but we couldn't pay the ridiculous bail amount."

"You did what you could. I think your father forgives you."

"It's so hard without Mom. I miss her."

"I know you do."

"This has been much harder than getting divorced," Melody laughs slightly.

"I don't know about divorce," Priscilla says, "but death certainly is devastating for most. Especially when sudden or unexpected."

"How much do you miss Henry?" Melody asks, sipping her now cold coffee.

"Every day."

"You also lost a father?"

"Yes. I was still in my twenties."

"That's very hard."

"Yes it was."

"I have a question, what do you know about an out-of-body experience?"

"Mystics report that a person can leave his or her body at any time, through practices like meditation. You should look into the phenomena of astral travel or astral projection which is leaving the body to travel the cosmos," she grins.

"What?" Melody nearly spits out her coffee.

"Scientists have studied out-of-body experiences by scanning brain waves while a person is provided with the illusion of seeing his or her body."

"Have they found anything significant?"

"They say that we take for granted the feeling of possessing our own bodies."

"I know what they mean," Melody sighs, scanning the surface of her legs.

"You do now, Melody," Priscilla smiles, patting her quilt covered knee. "But not permanently perhaps."

"No. Perhaps not forever," she says, forcing a smile.

"But you do have the feeling of owning a body."

"Partially," she shrugs.

"Imagine those who become one without the ownership of a body; a transformation takes place. One like you and others have experienced."

"Only permanently."

"Yes." Priscilla nods.

"Do scientists know what is taking place?"

"Not yet. They say they don't quite know what is going on in the brain."

"What do the mystics say?"

"They don't know either." She laughs, "They just enjoy doing it."

"Sounds like a drug addiction."

"I guess it induces a sort of utopia–like anything out of the ordinary."

"Maybe it will one day become common place to believe in miracles."

"I think it will...just a matter of time," Priscilla grins.

Chapter Twelve

Priscilla wakes to the sound of Melody in the kitchen and Macy coming through the front door, flashing her fingers forward, bent at the wrist. Melody glides toward her, staring in awe at the carat diamond beset in white gold. The diamond shimmers in the light above and she twirls on her toes, "I'm getting married," she sings.

"Oh Mace, I'm so happy for you, sweetie," Melody cries, taking her by the hand.

"Thank you, Mom," she hugs her, walking toward the kitchen.

Priscilla stands before the sink, one hand on her hip and the other clutching a tea towel.

"What is this?" She motions with the towel.

"He proposed," Macy says, hugging her tightly.

"Isn't that grand!" Priscilla exclaims, switching the *on* button to the coffee maker.

Over coffee, in the living room, they talk about plans for the wedding, about marriage and the excitement and challenges it presents. Macy listens as Priscilla tells her about being in a home with the only one she ever loved and Melody nods when her daughter asks to marry Tom at the farmhouse during a Saturday in May, hoping the weather would not be hot nor too cold.

"What piqued your interest in starting a bed and breakfast?" Priscilla asks after they exhaust wedding planning talk, her elbow resting on the grand piano.

"Mom," Melody says, "my mother wanted to have a bed and breakfast here."

"It does have a lot of space," Macy says, looking around fondly.

"We could make arrangements after the wedding," Melody says.

"I think that's a nice idea," Priscilla says.

"I do, too. Mom was so busy with my brother and I, then we gave her six grand-babies, so she never had the time."

"Perhaps this is going to be a good time then," Priscilla smiles.

"If Dad can handle it," Melody interjects.

"I do believe he can."

"What about his mental health?"

"Just something else that kind of subsides with time."

"Time can heal, I guess."

"That's all we have Melody, is time."

"You're right about that."

Macy twists the ring around her finger, admiring the glint in the light.

Jimmy walks into the house, flipping through the mail. Discovering one addressed in his name with the return addressed: Duke Hospital. He withdraws a letter that is hand written in a metallic gel pen. Ignoring the commotion coming from the parlor, he sits at the table to read the note.

Dear Jimmy,

My name is Lorellei Willard and I am a nurse at Duke Hospital. I do remember who you are as I had been at the hospital working as a nurse during the nine months you stayed in room 309 awaiting a heart. I remember that you were always kind and courteous to the nursing staff at the hospital.
I also remember that you had a heart donor that suddenly hadn't worked out, forcing you to wait even longer before another heart came in just for you. You are one of the many successful heart transplant patients at Duke Hospital and patients like you give us the strength and the encouragement to work every day in the face of adversity. You may remember me, but you

may not know that my mother worked with your wife around 1968 as nursing students. My mother's name was Lucille Willard but her maiden name was Gooden. She also worked at the hospital for the next thirty years and retired by the time you were admitted in the hospital. I followed in my mother's shoes also becoming a nurse myself. My mother had mentioned your wife's name before her death as being the wife of the man who entered Duke Hospital that day, because his wife had not survived a surgery herself. I tended to your wife at the hospital while she awaited her surgery.

I want to say that I am sorry for your loss and I wish you and your family the best in wellness, happiness and health. I sincerely apologize for the death of your wife Caroline and I wish that I knew the two of you personally. I too lost my mother at Duke Hospital, from stomach cancer one year after her diagnosis. She is missed, as I presume you also miss your dear wife.

I also lost my husband many years ago in a boating accident and mourn his loss to this day ten years later. Perhaps your heart is still healing and perhaps you can open your heart to the prospect of making some friends who do know your pain. I wish you the best in your recovery.

Best,

Lorellei Willard

Jimmy folds the letter and places it onto the table and stands. Limping to the double pane glass doors he opens it and steps into the frigid November air. He inhales a deep breath and then staggers, falling face down into the paved concrete and lets out a moan – the door ajar behind him.

You have about ten years with a new heart, he recalls the doctor explaining to him a little over a decade before, *you won't know if you're having a heart attack since the nerves have been severed,* Jimmy hears the voice of his surgeon as if it's the present day. He rolls gently onto his back, his face peering at the sullen sky before him – its blueness all around with patches of gray and white surrounding his sights.

Priscilla, shivering slightly from the cold, makes her way into the outdoors, "Jimmy, Jimmy," she hollers as his eyes squint at the sound of her voice as if the sounds pierce right through him. He lays with his chest heaving and his face contorting in pain.

"Jimmy, I'm calling 9-1-1," Priscilla says before yelling upstairs for Melody and Macy. She runs into the kitchen to grab her cell and punches three digits before returning outside. She grabs Jimmy by the hand and holds onto him.

"Pappy, Pap?" Macy hollers from behind the door leaving Melody in the bedroom, unable to drag herself onto the electrical escalator that was installed in the home. Someone has to fold the wheelchair and carry it down the stairs, but Melody is stuck upstairs, hollering to the floor below.

"Dad! Dad!" she yells down the stairs, unable to hear anyone.

Priscilla holds Jimmy's hand tightly to her chest as she speaks into the device that is wedged between cheek and shoulder. Macy leans over him, "Pap we're here," she says. His eyes grow wide and he utters the word *Caroline* and lets out a light gasp as he exhales, into his last breath before he extends his other hand into the emptiness of the air and wind. A slight breeze of warm air nudges between them and Jimmy's face becomes lighter. *Caroline,* he says again.

Melody leans heavily forward in the wheelchair until her upper body becomes top heavy, and she falls with a sharp thud to the floor. She tosses one leg and then the other over the edge of the stairs. With one hand and then the other, she pulls onto the banister to a pain-staking crawl and lets out a loud wince until the pain becomes sharp – so sharp that her legs begin to ache.

"I feel my legs," she says, staring down at her thighs and feet-her right toe twitches slightly and then the nerves in her toes become sensations in her feet, then up through her legs.

She pulls, tugging at the railing of the stairs, one leg at a time, pulling and shoving with her hips until the pain surges in her entire lower body, so much pain that she calls out in a loud screech.

"Dad I'm coming!" she says and pulls with a sideways hip, forcing the muscles in her upper thighs to react to her commanded movement. Her left leg moving an inch, then the other even further, then she adds weight to each leg when the movement becomes something like walking – something like a movement intended to run, the way that her mother had run in her youth. She drags each foot with each step at the bottom of the stairs; then drags and pulls herself across the cold kitchen tile until she lands in a thud against the door.

"Mom!" Macy yells from behind the glass; Melody pulls her body from behind the door and lands mercilessly upon her father's chest with her face pressed to his gasping breath when the paramedics arrive, gurney in tow behind them.

Chapter Thirteen

"I'm sorry but your father didn't make it," the doctor says as Melody weeps into Priscilla's shoulder, with the same ferocity she felt for her mother.

"He called to Caroline," Priscilla explained to Melody as she cried in waiting room at Duke Hospital.

"I called to him," Melody explains, "I wanted Daddy to see me walking again," she says and smiles to her daughter.

"He knows," Macy says casually, her hand to her mother's shoulder.

"He sure does," Priscilla says, rocking the young women in her arms. She is their rock as funeral arrangements are made at the Gateway Funeral Home, and when they spend their first Christmas without Jimmy and Caroline.

"I'm happy to be here," Melody says, smiling radiantly to her daughter.

"I am too, Mom," she says back.

Melody walks her daughter down the aisle; Macy looks radiant in a long white, satin gown with a laced veil over her beautiful hazel green eyes. Tom's eyes sparkle in the sun. Marlene and her boyfriend, Rich, stand opposite to one another as the groomsman and maid of honor. Macy gets married to Tom Heart on the tenth day of May in sunshine in the backyard of her mother's childhood home – newly painted white and accented with rough wood finishes. "It's country chic," Macy told her mother on the day they opened the bed-and-breakfast the month before the wedding. Priscilla planted large deep, purple irises in the front, on two patches of earth that bare large erected stones in the memory of their mother and father.

Charlie smiles radiantly and kisses Macy on the forehead. "You are stunningly beautiful, like this garden," he says to her.

"We couldn't have asked for anything more," Tom says as they make their way down the aisle to greet the one-hundred guests.

"What a most perfect day," Priscilla says as the wind kicks up, filling the air with the scent of irises.

"There's Mom and Dad," Melody says as Charlie and Adele exchange a hug.

"I'm sure they wouldn't miss it for the world," Adele says, and they wave – sending Macy and Tom off on their honeymoon to the Virgin Islands where Tom plans to rent a villa at Charlotte Amalie in St. Thomas.

Over the next several months, letters became an everyday occurrence. It began with one or two then turned to four and on to a dozen per day of letters: letters addressed *Dear Jimmy.* Then, *Dear Jimmy and Family,* and *Jimmy and Caroline.* The letters come from patients at Duke Hospital – those who have heard about the incident of the man who lost his wife (and his mind): a man who was lost without his beloved Caroline.

The letters are of remorse, grief and loss but many others are also about the continuation of life. There have been letters saying that Caroline frequents the hospital from time-to-time, while the spirit of Jimmy calls her name in the hallway – a sound of love and compassion followed by a bout of happy laughter. Others talk about having a heart transplant at Duke Hospital and others talk about having survived breast cancer. The letters almost always end the same: we hope for a love like that.

"What would you like next?" Priscilla asks.

"I want love like Jimmy and Caroline," Melody says, "just like the letters say."

"That's right." Priscilla says, "Then it's just a matter of time."

"A matter of time," Melody says, with a sideways glance.

And they share a wink.

Just a matter of time...

Epilogue

The bed-and-breakfast at the farmhouse on Heide Cooper Road fills with the families of patients for Duke Hospital. *My dad's awaiting a new heart* one of them says, *my mother's a candidate for a lung transplant* another says. They converse about small miracles – like the one with the heart transplant that didn't work out, only to receive another heart in the same week – and only after waiting for nine months.

The bed-and-breakfast fills with *hopefuls* who are there to talk about life and almost always – never mention a word about death. The letters still arrive by the day and come from all states – and all countries.

"The world it seems is talking about us," Melody says, thinking of her own miracle – a survivor and one who would walk again. How, it seemed, her mother was there to guide her down the stairs against the anguish of excruciating pain to be with her father as he was dying. Their guests talk about the love between them and the spaces that are filled when love is there.

"Love is a dear friend," Priscilla says as Macy and Marlene hold their babies to their chests and Melody tends to her grandchildren. Charlie and Adele sit in the living room with their four children and growing grandchildren.

"Love is having each other," Melody says, fixing the curtains of the parlor room. *Amen,* they say in unison as the light falls behind the horizon and Melody pulls open the front door to let the remaining guest in.

"Hello," the woman says, "My name is Carolyn. And I was a nurse in 1967."

"Welcome," Melody says, "so was my mother. Her name was Caroline."

"Yes." The woman says. "Caroline owns this bed-and-breakfast."

"Yes." Melody says, with a sparkle in her eye. "Yes, she does."

And the door closes behind her.

The Marathon Runner

Preface

It's not a matter of determination
but a matter of I must walk, then run, many
miles to my destination.

Candace Meredith

Prologue

Vivian and Maverick were married on a white sandy beach in Puerto Rico in front of 200 of their closest family and friends. Maverick promised to love her until death do them part. He kept that promise while they lived in a furnished condo in New Market and purchased a carat diamond with matching necklace and earrings on their anniversary. She worked for her father in real estate; he purchased their Mercedes and leased the Jaguar.

They spent the month after their anniversary in the Virgin Islands. The following summer they went to Cabo; that was all before her unexpected business trip took her to Florida. Her father wasn't prone to plan trips in advance. Often, she packed for a night or two, but this trip was different and didn't go as planned.

Chapter One

The Man on the Street

Maverick sits with his back against a dogwood tree on Valley Street. He leans over his right knee to extract a pair of flashy purple *Athlete's* shoes with neon green trim from the sidewalk. Maverick turns the shoe over to examine the sole where *Marathon*, and the date of a year prior, is etched in permanent marker.

He ties the laces together and tosses the shoes over his shoulder. He also carries a knapsack that he tosses over the other shoulder, and walks in the direction of the state park. He notices a man with a *Homeless Veteran* sign scribed onto a piece of cardboard, who leans over an abandoned bike; he turns the wheel with the pedal in his hand and examines the linked chain; a few spokes are broken, but the bike otherwise appears well-kempt.

Maverick has been homeless for three years since his wife Vivian called to tell him she would not be returning from Florida.

He has his own yacht, she said before slamming the phone down after she had ignored his texts and calls. He had a job in advertising sales that earned him a six-figure income but he left that job, and its money, and sold his house and the rest of his belongings before heading to the mountains.

He began his hike on the C&O Canal in the Western Appalachia of Maryland where he got off the train; the trail lay only a mile ahead. His plan was to hike toward the North on the Appalachian Trail and reach Maine in six months. The months, however, turned to years as he exchanged his former life for the greater outdoors. He visits parks that offer free showers in the out-buildings, and makes a life as a homeless vagabond who can pitch a tent made from a simple poncho and cord tied to tree branches.

His hair has grown long and lays in wavy layers upon the middle of his back. His beard has also grown in a shaggy thicket past his chin. Sometimes at night, beneath a street light, he will twist it into numerous tiny braids.

As he walks briskly in the spring breeze, he passes a sign advertising an Easter egg hunt scheduled in two weeks. He hunches his back and pulls at the straps to his knapsack containing his poncho, thermal container, and survival kit complete with matches and his reading material. He collects what he can from the local convenience store where he enjoys the company and conversation with its owner, George.

He rarely eats hot food after drinking hot water from a canteen daily during his hike on the AT, except when George offers up a cup of coffee. He eats fruits, vegetables, sandwiches and cold tea. His body is lean, at five-feet ten inches with strong calves and a packed torso. He grins at the passerby who is jogging in his direction, sweating from top to bottom, sporting a headband and ear buds. To the left, the homeless veteran pedals off the sidewalk, his cardboard box blowing from the wind, and continues to the entrance of the park.

The BMX track is busy with youth who cycle the dusty hills sporting cycling gear and helmets. The veteran passes, heading further toward the golf course. Maverick parks himself at the bench of the state park and takes the weight off his shoulders. He removes a shapely pear and crunches into its firm outer layer, juice seeping from his mouth.

He removes the knot in the strings of his shoes and unties them. Taking them off, the left sole coming loose, he tosses them to the side. He stuffs one foot into his new shoe snug against the thickness of his green wool socks. He wiggles his toes and stands to walk, checking for comfort. Glancing at the word *Marathon* and the date *5-19-16,* he wonders about his journey ahead, thinking about his time on the trail.

Counting on three slender fingers the years that have passed since Vivian left, he etches onto the sole of his muck boot *The Appalachian Trail 4-6-14 to 10-11-14.* He tosses the boots onto the deserted pavilion. He trots carefully in his new pair of purple sneakers, peering over his left shoulder for the jogger.

The next day is raining and Maverick steps into the convenience store at Millwood Avenue in a small city within Virginia. Removing a bill from his pocket, he slaps his palm onto the table. George emerges from the freezer with ice cream sandwiches in tow.

"What can I get ya?" George says, setting the box onto the counter.

"I'll take the usual," Maverick responds with a slanted grin.

"I didn't have to ask," he smirks, "the usual with a side of slaw."

"That's right," Maverick says, eyeing the sandwiches.

"So that's one Italian cold cut with extra salami," George says, working the register.

George's skin pales in contrast to Maverick's honeycomb bronze skin; even his eyes are iridescent to Maverick's deep-set brown eyes – the palest of blue with large black pupils. He stands above the counter at an average height but built like a bull. His biceps bulge beneath a tight black tee tucked neatly into his blue jeans and accentuated with a leather belt with a biker's insignia on his buckle. Behind Maverick's head, a bell clangs against the glass as a customer enters the door.

"How you doing, Bill?" George says. Maverick turns to see a veteran of about fifty walk in.

"Hey, George," Bill says, slapping his palm onto the counter. "Just give me the usual."

"Two dogs?"

"And add the chili," Bill grins.

"Hey," Maverick pipes in, "I just saw you with that bike the other day." Maverick smiles as George hands over a freshly made Italian sub. "The bike appeared in good shape."

With his hands in his pocket, Bill steps back, "I had seen that bike for a few days," he says, "thought someone might go back for it."

"Must have thought it was busted."

"The spoke poked through the tire so I ran it to George's garage, got a patch and fixed it up."

"Oh, so you also know the garage?" Maverick says, his mouth full of salami.

"Sure he does," George interjects, "but he hasn't been around for six months or more."

"Winters are too cold," Bill says, taking the first bite of his chili-smothered hot dog. "Got a cup of water to wash it down?"

"Sure thing," George says, pouring water from the fountain into a Styrofoam cup.

Maverick excuses himself and takes his lunch to the park where he eats with the grazing geese. The day wanes and he sets up shelter under the stars, gazing at Orion's belt, softly drifting off to sleep under the canopy of a pavilion.

Chapter Two

The Garage

George's garage houses his motor bikes and a collection of random vintage items including metal, rusted casino signs, and Vegas memorabilia. He's offered up some of his belongings to Maverick, like the junked-fixer-upper Saab in his backyard, but Maverick explains how he's takin' up living on foot and prefers his nomadic style. Maverick has on occasion, especially during the past season's blizzard, takin' up his cot in the garage. On cool spring nights, they would have a beer over the bonfire and talk about fishing.

Maverick had never met Bill and was shocked by the fact that they hadn't crossed paths at the garage. George has a small home set in the middle of forty acres, but the one bedroom doesn't offer a place to sleep. George also offered up his garage to Bill, who he knew would decline for reasons unknown to him, aside from Bill's keen determination to remain nomadic and proud in his independence. Bill had the drive to stay on foot, and often followed the good weather. Bill ended up in Georgia after catching a ride on a coal train out of West Virginia and hitch hiked his way south. Bill wasn't one to stay cooped up in some garage, but he appreciated the offer and left George some CD's on the fender of an old Cadillac in thanks.

That evening, Maverick, George and Bill end up in George's garage tossing a collection of CD's onto the disc player – cranking up bluegrass, smoking marijuana from a corn pipe, and throwing burgers onto the grill well past midnight. They easily talked into the night with the light of dawn bringing on the need for sleep.

"I've been meaning to ask you," George says through the mist emanating from his corn pipe, "where did you get those purple shoes?" He exhales a light cloud of residue.

"I've never seen some purple shoes," Bill lights the end of a pipe with tarnished fingers.

"I got them from the same place you got that bike," Maverick says waving his hand to pass on the pipe.

"Where I got my bike," Bills says, "well, I got it off Valley Street."

"And that's where I got these shoes," Maverick tosses his empty beer bottle into the box marked for recycling.

"You got those shoes from the street?" George asks, wrinkling his brows.

"Sure thing," says Maverick.

Bill laughs, then coughs, trying to catch his breath, "You happened to find shoes to fit your feet?"

"Well, almost," Maverick explains.

"Almost?" George asks.

"They're half a size too big but with these here wool socks," he taps his ankle, "they fit just fine."

"Those wool socks are going to give you athletes' feet," Bill says, spitting a cud onto the earth.

"Not these feet," Maverick laughs, "they've stood the test of time."

Bill guffaws, "Shit, you ain't even forty yet, is ya?"

"Thirty-nine," Maverick insists.

"Well, hell then, what test of time you talking about?"

"Hiking on the AT."

"What the hell is an AT?"

"The Appalachian Trail."

Bill lets out a wry grin, "That ain't like the miles we walked in Nam my friend, but you ain't the only person to not know about that."

` "I'm going to be sixty," George offers, "and I don't know nothing about it."

"Well, I'm getting too damn close to seventy," Bill says, "but I was only seventeen to get into Nam."

"I was already thirty-five to get to the AT," Maverick says, "but I was nowhere near a war at the age of seventeen."

"And it's best you weren't," Bill admits, with a nod.

"And we can leave it at that," George says.

"No problem," Bill shrugs, turning over ash in the fire.

In the morning, Maverick sets off to his favorite park to stand amid a training ground obstacle course likely intended for military and police. In front of him are the parallel bars, the laughter of children at the nearby playground reaches him. He places his knapsack on a nearby bench and begins to flex his muscles across the bars; his calf muscles burn and he leans forward to increase the tension and repeats the motions to stretch both legs. In the distance, he can hear a woman yelling *Malakai! Malakai!*

"Hey, loser, go get a job!" A young man, leaning out the driver side of a black Viper screams, interrupting his exercise. From the passenger seat another male, decked out in a trendy sports jacket, laughs vehemently, "Sorry bastard."

The driver stops the car and opens the door. They walk toward Maverick, but stop at his knapsack on the park bench. The driver picks up the knapsack and flips the green canvas bag with the thermal shell upside down, dropping everything in the dirt.

"Hey, assholes," Maverick yells as the two derelicts pick up his book on outdoor survival first and begin tossing it back and forth. The passenger kicks open a bag of trail mix, then begins collecting the items, tossing them into the bag. They run toward the vehicle slamming the door behind them, Maverick running at full speed toward them.

"Hey!" He yells, as they start the engine, "Who the hell are you?"

"I'm Flip," the driver, behind dark sunglasses and a high fade, screeches, "and this is Dick."

They peel out of the park, kicking up dust, and Maverick slows to a brisk pace, palming his pocket, relieved to feel his keys. Although he had sold nearly everything, he rented a small storage shed for a mere thirty bucks a month. The shed housed his collection of photography, especially his shots of the AT, before he sold the camera along with some of the prints to a nature enthusiast. He happened to capture images of carnivorous plants at the Cranesville Swamp, one of Maryland's wetlands preservation.

Maverick had been contemplating setting up a photography display at the local Arts Council.

Maverick tosses both hands to his head, throws back his hair, and turns back to the course to finish the remaining pull ups on the bar.

He jogs the five miles to the storage shed site, stopping at intervals to give his knee a rest. He throws open the shed door, with sweat staining his only shirt, and finds his boxes still stacked the way he had them – hoping to find bags of survival gear and fresh clothes. In the last three years, he has thinned out considerably. In the far left sits his bag of briefs, thermals and a toboggan – the clothing he purchased for his hike on the AT.

It is a cold, windy April night, so his stash of clothes are only good for tonight. But the following week temperatures are due to spike to 81 degrees. Maverick's stash of $25,000 is dwindling; he has five grand left. He confiscates the envelope from the sealed box and secures the money in his interior pocket and slips into warmer clothes. Outside the wind is howling. Huddled behind ten boxes, he places the thirteen gallon bag onto the ground, and dozes off until early dawn.

Chapter Three

The Past and the Future

The day after is fifty-eight, mostly sunny, with almost no wind. He puts on his dried tee, cargo pants, his inside out thermal socks and his now dry purple joggers. He secures a lantern, wool blanket, and a *North American Birds Guidebook* he forgot about inside the bag for easy access later. Blinking in the bright light of the early morning, he steps out of the shed to pay a months' storage to the office clerk. He recalls he was last quoted a cost of four grand to rent a gallery and print and frame his large collection of photography; his work mostly consists of nature and landscape photos. If his artwork does not sell then he's out four thousand dollars, plus the costs of van and storage rental for transporting and containing his beloved photography.

The words *get a job* ramble through his mind – exactly what he left behind so he could search for his heart and soul, and what he found before him was the landscape (not a cubicle). In his previous life, he spent twelve-hour-days writing creative for an advertising business to market and sell whole food products for a major vendor. He produced copy for radio, television, and billboard advertisements to promote the brand. After twelve years, he grew tired and frustrated and deeply needed a profound interruption. So he found nature, the trail, and the outdoors where he became a tour guide in his own right – his photography being the means to showcase that adventure.

He started hiking after purchasing a camera from an online ad by a local photographer. Setting out solo with a pack and a digital SLR, he started keeping everything light and easy. For his first destination, he began hiking where the towpath flanks the C&O Canal. Bog turtles, wood ducks, and cranes were among his first images – the canal provided several miles of a rich scenic view which included Maryland's old city, Cumberland.

From that point, Maverick set his sights on hiking the Appalachian Trail all the way into Maine. The six-month trip began in April of 2014 and ended in October. In Maine, he planned to live in a hostel and work in during the coldest months. Before getting to the AT, he took a route across the Potomac River from West Virginia and arrived in Harper's Ferry – the midpoint of the 2,178-

mile trail. His plan was to carry his pack and the essentials, and camp where he could get off the trail, avoiding paying for the luxuries he left behind.

He felt that a six month hiking period beginning at mid-point would give him sufficient time to make use of his photography skills while sight-seeing. He studied photography in high school, and then as a hobby during his off time. In college, he majored in marketing and business, earning his Masters by the age of twenty-four.

He didn't mind that Vivian left, and he certainly preferred his solo quest for mindful enrichment over entertaining her friends who wanted sparkling wine and caviar. Maverick always preferred a simple lager or pale ale by comparison. Today, Maverick is two years past the AT with a thousand miles on his boots – now he contemplates how to put the miles on his jogging sneakers.

Inside the café, Maverick orders a cold beverage and a ham and swiss on rye bread. He scans the café for reading material and locates the paper. The Easter egg hunt that attracts about a hundred patrons at the local park is featured on the front page. Below the main headline is a marathon scheduled for the following month, held to raise money for the *Heart Association*.

The entrance fee to the *Race for the Heart* is a donation charged at the participant's own discretion. Entrance forms are obtained at the library. He digs in his pocket and extracts a one-hundred-dollar bill and places it onto the table. Leaving the café, he makes his way to the post office after a visit to the library where he prints the registration form for a mere ten cents per page. He tucks away ten one hundred dollar bills into an envelope, along with the registration form, and deposits it into the drop box on his way out the door.

Chapter Four

Training Begins

He begins with one mile, taking four laps around the track at the local community college. He's testing out his bum knee since he plummeted several feet into a ravine during his hike on the AT. The knee, prone to giving out, is wrapped in a brace. Maverick hasn't seen a medical professional in four years and he's not interested in knee surgery.

To save his knee, he glides like a gazelle, using his toes as springs to lunge him forward. After four laps, Maverick's knee is on fire and he sprawls out onto the ground, rolling over in the grass to stare at the picturesque blue sky. Above his head an owl sours by – a sign he takes as good luck.

Maverick makes his way to George's market with a slight limp and looks forward to an ice pack and his usual. The bell clanks as he walks through the door. George shimmies up to the counter taking off his gloves.

"What'll it be?" He glances at the door.

"Just the usual," Maverick insists.

"I'm out of salami," George says, "My meat truck is running late."

"Well, what else you got?"

"Just what you see here," George points to the storage container.

"Well, then I'll have the chicken and provolone."

"You got it," George removes thin slices of cold chicken from the fridge.

"You expecting someone?" Maverick asks.

"Just thought they were calling for rain," he says, slicing the chicken.

"No, not anymore," Maverick says. "They changed the forecast twice already to cloudy skies with a high of seventy."

Maverick excuses himself after his lunch, still wearing his muted orange tee that features a mountain alongside the words *Come in, We're Open* and khaki colored cargo pants. He sets up camp in a clearing between the park and his storage unit that is not marked as private – an area owned by the University, but the only building on this side of campus is condemned and in need of renovation. He plants himself beneath a tree on the side of the park closest to the duck pond and begins to eat. Across the way children are tossing their prize into colorful baskets. He turns his face towards the sun when a woman and a boy, about the age of five, walk a small white dog. The boy chases a rainbow-colored kite across the grass. Suddenly, a car comes to a screeching halt and the driver turns a sharp one-eighty, kicking up gravel.

"Hey, asshole," the driver says as Maverick recognizes Flip. "Hey, you still looking for handouts?" The passenger hangs a baseball bat from the window.

"What are you going to do with that bat?" Maverick stands on his feet.

"Don't worry what I'm gonna' do with it," yells Dick as he gets out of the car and levels his bat at Maverick, swinging it at his head.

"What's your problem?" Maverick ducks.

"You know what our problem is," Flip says, standing outside the car.

"No, I don't actually."

"We don't care for assholes like you," Dick spats, slinging his bat haphazardly, while Flip makes smoke rings, smirking.

"You planning on doing something with that bat?" Maverick bellows.

"Just did," Dick hollers, taking another step toward Maverick.

"Then you better get it over with," he says, flicking his fist to the air when Dick slings his bat, whirling it toward Maverick's face. Maverick blocks him as Flip approaches from behind. Maverick grabs the bat at the tip, shoving Dick. Flip kicks the back of his leg sending Maverick down onto his knees, his head to the ground. Flip kicks his spleen. Dick gets to his feet, retrieving his bat and ball. Flip takes Maverick's remaining lunch, spreading the remnants where he lays and Maverick rolls onto his back.

"They kicked ya' while you were down," Bill says in George's market, tightening a bandage around Maverick's swollen knee cap and examining his possibly fractured wrist. "Shouldn't be anything a tight wrap can't fix."

Bill learned basic first aid in the Army. A Navy Corpsman lent him his medical bag once to treat a shrapnel wound in his leg Bill acquired from an ambush. Bill wanted to dress his own battle wound while his friend tended to the critically wounded.

"Those assholes don't know me," Maverick says.

"Unfortunately, men don't need to know men to decide if they don't like them," Bill says, "and they don't know you from a hole in their head but that doesn't stop them."

"You've experienced something like this?" Maverick asks.

"I've been in your shoes," Bill replies.

"Could have been worse," George says, filling a bag with ice, "you might want to put this to that wrist."

"Thanks, George," Maverick puts the ice bag on his arm.

"Any time," George says, shutting the door to the deli, turning the lights down.

Chapter Five

The Gallery

The next day Maverick limps, glaring at the obstacle course before him. With a swollen wrist, upper body is a chore and with a blown left knee running is hell. His torso and his thighs burn as he moves on to one-handed push-ups and rolls onto his back for another set of reps. To his left, a high school track team runs through the park. At night, Maverick takes coverage from the spring rain huddled beneath a poncho beneath the shelter of George's garage. It's Friday night and Maverick enjoys the company of his friends.

"Hey, Bill," Maverick says the following Friday night, sipping from the six pack he purchased at the market, "Did you happen to see a red-haired woman, her son, and her dog at the park lately?"

"Can't say that I've noticed," Bill says, "Why?"

"Well, never mind," Maverick says, "It's nothing."

"It must be something," Bill hollers over the music.

"I just used to know a red-haired girl," Maverick hollers back.

"Well, what are the chances of that?" George says.

"Numerous," Maverick says, sipping from his lager, "And in the street were a pair of running shoes...what are the chances they've been worn in a marathon?"

Three weeks go by and Maverick kicks up gravel beneath his feet, during this dry and hot May morning. The trail at the Berryville Park is lined with stone and dirt; the air is dry and hot. The wild flowers flanking his path fill the air with honeysuckle. He begins with stretching his calf muscles, bending to the side and leaning the other way, pulling at his ankle. There is a brace on his weak leg he purchased at the downtown Mountain Trails store along with a pair of jogging shorts. His wrist has healed.

Naked from the waist up he flexes his legs briskly, shaking out the kinks, and starts at a slow and steady pace. The trail veers ahead for ten miles. This is Maverick's first run since his injuries caused by the Viper duo. As he steadily increases the miles, he increases the pace and learns to steady his breathing rhythm. Happily, he achieves two miles in seventeen minutes on a bum knee.

After his run, he sets off for his storage shed: a total three miles run west of the trail. He jogs rhythmically and stops at the trail store once more to buy a watch to count his steps so he can keep a more accurate time. He already missed the marathon, but is consoled by the fact that he could contribute to the cause.

In three more weeks there is a 10k to raise awareness for autism and Maverick has already signed up. He's running at three miles in twenty-three minutes, but he must increase his stamina and double the mileage. He arrives at the storage unit to retrieve his negatives to bring to the Arts Council where Patricia Pattison will examine his work and place him on the waiting list. He collects his single box of negatives leaving the remaining box of his memorabilia: photos from college, baseball cards, and the jewelry he salvaged.

He closes the storage container and places the items from his box into a bag and carries them toward the exit, tossing the empty box into the recycling bin. Maverick makes his way to the Arts Council. Patricia meets him at the front desk with a toothy smile and an elegant demeanor; she has silky short blond curls, above the shoulder, and angled at the chin. She shimmers in light lilac colors.

"Hello, Mr. Hall," she says.
"Hello, ma'am," he replies.

"Oh, no need to call me ma'am, Mr. Hall," she grins like a Cheshire cat.

"And you can call me Maverick," he grins back.

"Maverick, I'm Patricia, but most just call me Pat."

"It's very nice to meet you," he chimes in.

"Well, I have to say there's not a great deal we have to do," she pauses and taps her finger to the schedule, "I have you penciled in right here-had a cancellation."

"Is that right?" He asks, startled with the news.

"For next week," she says.

"Next week?"

"Will you be ready by then?"

"I wasn't expecting…"

"I'm afraid the waiting list is booked two years for the gallery."

"Then I got lucky," he winks, "what day?"

"Monday. But you can get set up Saturday – I'll make sure you get a good crowd."

"Not even the end of the week?" He swallows the lump in his throat.

"It's only Tuesday – I have faith in you. You frequent George Mason's place."

"I do, and how do you know George?"

"He's an old friend," she says, "I have been going to his market for many years."

"It's the best little convenience store, market, deli, I've ever been to. Not only that, but he serves the best coffee made from slow roasted beans."

Maverick shifts back and forth, waiting for George to answer at the knock on his door. George emerges from the locked door, sporting a fishing pole and tackle.

"Where are you off to?" Maverick asks.

"Heading over to Bill's place by that boat dock across the way from the BMX complex and the golf course."

"How did he manage that?"

"Put his name on the waiting list out there at the Martinsburg, West Virginia VA clinic. Been waitin' for about six months but they set him up in one of those tiny houses, gave him an ID card, along with medical benefits."

"A what?"

"You ever seen them on TV?"

"I kinda don't have one right now, George."

"It's a one-hundred-something square foot tiny house set up by the park – parks and recs donated acreage for the veterans who were granted tiny houses."

"Sounds like a real nice set up."

"Hell yes it is," George exclaims, "gave him veteran's compensation, enough to live on."

"Hey, I'm happy for the old man…"

"Oh and Patricia Pattison came to my store."

"That's exactly what I'm here for. I wanted to know if you had something to do with my gallery spot?" Maverick asks, shifting his feet.

"I only asked her if you were going to show some photography there."

"Why didn't you just ask me, George?"

"Because you wasn't in my store, but she was, you see." George laughs. "So, you came here to tell me you got a spot?"

"I got a spot," Maverick mocks back, shaking his head.

"I'm by no means a magician Maverick – I didn't use hocus pocus to get your name on the books."

"You just asked."

"That's right. You don't think I held her at gun point and demanded you a spot, did ya?"

"You never know," Maverick jokes.

George's cheeks flush as he laughs heartily. He taps Maverick on the shoulder. "Why don't you take a load off your back and get ya a fishing pole, they're over there in the garage," he gestures.

Several hours pass as the trio reel in fish. The big mouth bass Maverick yanked onto his dock chills in the cooler. Trout fill the buckets beside them.

"How about we head inside and fry up some fish?" Bill says as they head back to the tiny house. The home gleams like a gem with rustic wooden charm and industrial simplicity. The exterior is a light honey wood and the metal A-frame roof is red. Inside, the interior is also a combination of traditional wood and modern trim with modern amenities such as a sizable stand-in shower, compost toilet, small sink and a dorm room size oven and range, standard refrigerator and two lofts on each side. The tiny home is spacious enough for a queen size mattress, but Bill settles for a small chair and table to sit and eat.

"They're taking care of our veterans," George says as he prepares the trout. As they cooked they spoke about the weather, camping, hiking the AT, setting up the gallery, preparing for a 10k, the women they wanted and the women they'd never have.

Bill removes a paper from the shelf where he keeps a collection of paperbacks and places it onto the table before Maverick. The front headline appears above a smashed shiny black Viper that reads: *Two Winchester locals face charges for nearly causing the death of a family of four.* The article details that Richard "Flip" Bossie and Dick Richards injured a family during a racing incident while traveling on the wrong side of the street which resulted in a head-on collision. The family were in intensive care after being evacuated by medivac to the Charlottesville UVA Hospital.

"What's with those childish jerks?" Mavericks sniggers.

"Keep reading, they're not kids," Bill says. "They're adults and they're going to be charged like adults."

Maverick spoons the first taste of fried fish between his lips and savors the tiny morsel on his tongue. After eating, they talk until they crash at midnight.

The next morning, Maverick crosses the BMX track, past the basketball court beyond the playground and the outdoor pool and onto the obstacle course. He places one foot on the rung to the *stairway to heaven* and leans forward applying pressure to his left leg. On the rung, the sensation to his feet feels like the eight hundred fifty-foot elevation of Monson, Maine where he ended his hike.

The 282 miles through the Northern-most point on the Appalachian Trail was rugged and noted as being one of the wildest on the AT in the remote state. He hiked past the wilderness cabins and Lake Hebron into the market and the café; the quaint atmosphere reminded him of George's place – likely the reason he felt at home there. The café provided him with his first cold drink since his ascent through Vermont.

He takes another look at his left leg and flexes his muscles, feeling the sharp pains through his knee-cap; it was his hike through an unabridged Kennebec River in Maine that became hazardous after heavy rains that took out his leg for a second round. Now, he's almost certain the leg requires surgery but he still feels he can gain strength by slowly working and conditioning his muscles and training feverishly to gain the stamina he had on the AT.

Finding the pair of running shoes marked with a marathon is now a personal quest to re-gain strength, increase energy, drive and focus. He has been in the same place for too long and feels there was nowhere to go until now. But possibly, he thinks, there is something he's missing.

Chapter Six

An Old Friend

With each passing day, his body grows leaner, stronger, and more defined. His leg has grown stronger beneath the knee brace and he moves effortlessly through the obstacle course. He has taken up running on the trail at the park by the lake and stops abruptly in his tracks, pulling off his ear buds at the sight of a woman and a boy leaning over a small bog lined with rocks.

"We're just checking out some snakes," she laughs.

"Snakes?" Maverick asks.

"Yeah," says the boy, "on the rocks."

The woman turns gracefully, peering at Maverick.

"Tessa?" He exhales tossing his earbuds over his shoulder.

"Yes?" She says inquisitively.

Tessa has long locks of reddish hair and striking dark blue eyes. Her physique is tall, thin and well defined. She wears a tank top and silky floral shorts.

"You probably don't recognize me," he shifts his weight to the right leg. "I'm Maverick," he smiles and offers his hand.

"Oh, my gosh," she says lightly.

"I know I look different."

"Older, but that's to be expected," she says, matter-of-factly. "How are you Maverick? It's been how many years?"

"Nearly twenty-five years," he says, "I was only fourteen when you left…"

"That means a lot to catch up on," she says.

"Who is this?" He nods at the boy.

"My son," she says, "Malakai."

"Malakai?" He exhales. "You were at the park…I heard you calling his name."

"Yes, we frequent the park often," she says, "and he likes to play on the big slide, don't you buddy?"

"Yep," the boy shrugs.

"And how old are you?" Maverick asks.

"I'm five."

"Do you like to ride bikes?"

"Yep."

"How long have you been in the area?" he asks, turning his attention back to her.

"I've been here in Winchester since we left."

"All these years? I must have been dancing around you."

"How long have you been here?"

"Just a couple of years," he explains, "I met George on a hike and just kinda stayed."

"George?"

"He owns the deli, but he's good company. Likes to collect things like old billboard signs, souvenirs, and old cars. He's got a few acres full of the stuff he's collected for over thirty years. He jokes how they're older than I am," he chortles. "It's like walking back in time."

"I'm sure it is…" she pauses, "It's wonderful to see you, Maverick. How you have been?"

"It's sort of complicated," Maverick shifts his weight to one side and runs his hand through his hair. "I mean, I'm not sure how you'll take to it."

"Try me," she smiles softly.

"Well, I'm training for a 10K, raising awareness for Autism."

"Really?" She says, her eyes lighting up. "I'm a social worker for some of the kids who benefit from those events."

"That's really wonderful."

"Thank you," she says, "I'll have a booth set up to promote raising awareness and getting donations that will contribute to their education and activities."

"Then I do hope that I can make this one. I intended to make the last one but got side-tracked, or attacked," he chuckles.

"Oh, my," she gasps, hand to her mouth. "What happened?"

"I don't know how, but I offended someone."

"You don't know how?"

"No, I mean they mostly just didn't like the look of me."

"That's pretty bold of them."

"That it was."

"Who are you?" Malakai pipes in, his fist full of rocks.

"I'm Maverick."

"We were friends when we were little," Tessa explains.

"Like my age?"

"Just a little older," she says.

"Oh," Malakai says, and attempts to skip rocks across the water.

"So where do you live?" She asks.

"That's the hard part," he shrugs.

"Oh, okay," she says, "well, I live by the University."

"Really?" He grins, "I pass by there all the time, and I'm just now finding you."

"You've found me," she jokes with a beautiful smile.

"Tessa, I have thought about you many times over the years."

"I have as well." Her smile threatens to escape her face.

"I mean you just took off one day and then I never saw you again."

"I know, Maverick," she whispers, "we need to catch up."

Tessa, Maverick and Malakai walk the shoreline trail of the Shenandoah River to the parking lot. They exchange a handshake that swiftly turns into an embrace, and agree to meet one another at the café to catch up.

Maverick continues training but this time at the gym. With a membership, he has access to the pool, a sauna, tanning booth, weights, machines and the hydro massage bed – but most importantly a shower. Maverick spares another thirty bucks a month because Tessa. If he wasn't already determined before then he's beyond more-so now.

On the treadmill, Maverick runs a steady pace, his heart-rate beating rhythmically, his ear buds pumping The Clash in his ear; he has accelerated to pumping-out three miles in seventeen minutes and on the fourth mile his knee aches. The muscle twitches behind the brace and he slows down the pace to a power walk, making sure not to blow out his knee before the race.

On the AT his ankle got wedged between the rocks, the current twisting his body onto a large protruding boulder. His kneecap twisted and became dislocated – his leg left dangled midstream when a passerby in a small boat pulled his ankle at an angle well-enough to get him loose. Maverick laid in a heap atop his knapsack, adrift and nearly unconscious.

When Maverick came to, he gave his knee a sharp twist, cringing at the sickening sound of bone on bone – his knee was straight again. Howling loud enough to shake the fur off a mountain cat, he shuddered. Maverick then wrapped his leg in tape over his tee shirt and limped bare-chested to his destination – a place the boatman told him about called Pete's.

The owner of Pete's Place offered him an omelet and a hot cup of coffee, but Maverick asked for a cold deli sandwich: tuna on rye. He then packed up a cold cut with provolone and honey mustard feeling energized. Alive but in need of a nap.

Maverick steps off the treadmill with his knee like putty in a tight brace. He limps into the men's room and stands naked beneath the shower cascading down his back – a luxury he doesn't take for granted.

Locked muscles slowly unlock as he spends fifteen minutes in the hydro massage bed where he lays and dozes into reverie. Again.

The next day he heads off to the storage unit to retrieve a box of jewelry he purchased for Vivian; when she came back from her exile in Florida to retrieve it, he assured her it was nowhere to be found. When she tried to reclaim her jewels in front of the judge, he told her to furnish the receipts. Maverick was able to keep his property and with her re-marriage, he was able to put a stop to the alimony. He pawns the jewelry to a gold collector for six thousand dollars – money he intends to use toward his collection of photography.

Chapter Seven

Like Old Times

Maverick marvels over seeing Tessa for the first time in over a decade. He puts on his dark blue jeans and short-sleeved collared shirt. Thanks to seeing her again, he is now the proud owner of a razor, a comb and aftershave, and sports performance men's deodorant. Instead of his pack, he carries a men's case and ties his laces to a pair of classics and tosses his joggers in the old pack.

He walks through the glass door of the sparsely populated downtown café to find Tessa seated at a table for two; the remaining tables are sparsely filled. Each wall of the café is painted a different color: muted yellow, green, brown and beige, each displaying original art marked for sale. Tessa places the literary journal onto the table that she picked up from the free books rack, and stares at the clean-shaven Maverick.

"Hello, ma'am," he smiles, tipping an invisible hat to her. "Do you mind if I sit down here beside you?"

"Maverick, you shaved," she beams.

"That I did. It was time," he says, pulling at the chair.

"Well I hope you don't mind if I ask…"

"You don't have to," he says, "I'm homeless."

The café employee delivers a hot latte and tomato and basil grilled Panini to the table. Maverick orders a sweet tea and the turkey club sandwich with a side of chips.

"Homeless?" She asks sinking her teeth into whole wheat bread, tomato and mozzarella.

"Yes," he says, "it started when my wife left but she's not the reason."

"What started?" She asks, sipping from her white chocolate latte.

"My hike on the Appalachian Trail."

"Oh, well that's not being homeless, is it?"

"I guess I've been homeless since I sold my house along with all my possessions."

"What else did you sell?"

"Mostly everything. Like the car I bought for my wife and the house. When I went out to hike the AT for six months – I just didn't go back to my former life."

"Why not? What didn't you like about it?"

"I worked, even when I was home. It consumed my life."

"What was your former job?"

"I was in sales and I did a lot of marketing for a whole foods distributor. I wrote copy for advertising, but if they didn't like my proposal I had to adjust my work around their liking which basically means I had to scrap what I finished and it was back to the drawing board. It was consuming. To say the least."

"You were drained."

"To a point, but when my wife left, I decided to leave it all and I'm glad that I did."

"Tell me what you've been doing, being homeless I mean."

"I spend a lot of time at George's place."

"George from the deli?"

"Yes and Bill an Army vet, who was homeless until recently – he got some benefits through the VA and they gave him a place to stay."

"Is he happy?"

"He seems to be. We do a lot of fishing, and spend some time at his place."

"Do you foresee having a place to live?"

"No, I didn't for a long time, until possibly recently I guess."

"What's changed?"

"I didn't have a job. Didn't know what I wanted to do…"

"You do now?"

"I have something coming up – I got a spot to display my work in a gallery."

"You paint?"

"No, photography – I took a good bit of photos while I hiked the AT, then for about a year after that."

"Why did you stop?"

"I didn't know what I was going to do with all of it – so I stuck the proofs in some boxes and stored them in my storage unit outside of town. I earned enough to live on. I mean, I live pretty modestly," he grins, "but it's about time to be making some other considerations."

"Tell me about the gallery…"

"I have a spot at the local Arts Council to display my work, and they work in conjunction with the local museum where I can display the other half."

"How much do you have?"

"I have thousands of shots."

"Can they display that much?"

"Between them I can, but I have to get them developed, framed and transported."

"And you don't have the money?"

"I actually do. I could rent a van but they require some kind of credit and I don't have that."

"I can help you," she swallows while Maverick slurps on his tea that's turned to water and ice.

"You'll help, Tessa? I mean, I don't want to inconvenience you."

"It's no inconvenience at all. I'll help you rent a van, but I need to ask how much money do you have?"

"I'm going on almost 10k since I sold the jewelry I bought Vivian."

"That's certainly enough for the van, but how about the rest?"

"It'll be about four grand for printing and framing. I already have a place lined up."

"No problem," she says, "just let me know when and I'll be there. Sounds like you have everything else taken care of."

"I do, it's awesome to see you again."

"Likewise." She smiles.

Tessa and Maverick make plans to begin printing and framing at the downtown studio for mid-week, just three days before his showing. With his prints ordered, he has decided to get back to his training. He ties the laces on his jogging shoes and steps onto the treadmill while dialing in the numbers to increase his speed – today he is hoping to complete six miles. After thirty-five minutes, he has managed over four and his leg has stiffened up. In order to take weight off his pounding knee, he completes a two mile course by bike and he wonders if he'll muster the miles it takes to complete a full race.

Tessa meets Maverick, along with her son and her dog, at the state park that evening.

"Just like old times," he says, as they walk around the pond.

"Just like old times," she beams.

Malakai brings a fishing pole and small orange tackle box. Sitting in a shady spot, Malakai casts his reel without help. The pond is stocked with catfish and small mouthed bass.

Maverick learns that Tessa is a single mom, the birth father left early in her pregnancy because he was not willing to leave his band. He met another woman, started touring and they moved to somewhere in Arizona.

Early in her pregnancy, she decided to take a trip to Hawaii that was sponsored through her employer – an incentive to raise money for orphaned children and she fell in love with its beautiful beaches. She named her son after the place where she retreated because they were there together, just the two of them.

Malakai pulls at his reel, the line waving in the water, and a catfish the size of his fist flops on the shore. Tessa uses her

smartphone to capture a shot of his first fish.
He holds it proudly, then lets it go.

Chapter Eight

Another Encounter

That evening Maverick is invited back to Tessa's townhome in a gated community complete with a recreational center. He has a van rented for the week with his prints ready for pick up on Saturday. The lot includes two hundred fifty of over one thousand shots total to be featured at the gallery. Freshly showered, Maverick enters Tessa's home. Malakai trots up to the door, grasps onto his leg as Maverick enters the threshold.

"Hi, buddy," Maverick says.

"He's not shy," Tessa laughs.

Tessa beams radiantly in a cute navy blue romper and her hair pulled back loosely; small strands dangle about her face accentuating her jawline. On her fingers, she wears four plastic and metal rings – tokens from her son. Malakai grabs Maverick by the hand, leading him to the finished basement where he removes a couple paddles from the yellow basket and ushers Maverick to the Ping-Pong table. Tessa enters the doorway, her fingers twirling her necklace with the Infiniti pendant, a smile of delight on her thin, round face.

"Can I get you something to drink?" She asks, her foot dangling from the last stair.

"Sure," Maverick says.

"Yep," Malakai replies, tapping the small plastic ball with a wooden paddle.

"What do you have?" Maverick asks, awaiting a turn, holding his paddle up.

"All natural energy tea," she winks.

"I'll need that," he laughs, "if I'm to keep up with this guy."

"A juice box for you, sweetheart?"

"Sure, Mom," Malakai responds astutely.

After a game of ping pong, Malakai leads Maverick to his room where he asks him to play a game of dinosaurs, build with blocks, read a book and shoot at the target with dart guns. Maverick stays into the early night, entertaining Malakai, who chats about school, sports and the dog park – explaining to Maverick that he named his dog after he was hit by a car. His mother stopped their vehicle, pulled over after noticing the dog moved but appeared to be injured.

"He's a *Chee-wa-wa* and something else," he explains, sipping on his straw. After dinner, he sits on the sofa, aside Maverick, placing his head upon his shoulder, and dozes off.

Friday rolled into Saturday and in three hours they would deliver an entire gallery display to the Arts Council and the museum. Maverick's spot was slated in the books for Monday, but after making some arrangements, Patricia bumped Monday to Saturday to allow for more publicity.

"The museum and the entire display will be televised," she said, "and from your proofs I decided you'd make great coverage for the local artists section."

Maverick was apprehensive, but Patricia was determined to show his work as "fine photography by a local photographer," especially since Maverick took a year to photograph the region. His regional pieces include: a close shot of a butterfly atop Milkweed, a deer amid the grasslands with her fawn, some ancient buildings in ruin, a fisherman's boat in the horizon, a falcon atop street lighting, abandoned warehouses, other condemned places, and nature amid the ruin.

The doors opened at noon and his display was featured for three solid days. A small production crew set up toward the back of the gallery to film. The local artist section was featured in the paper and the news station, alongside a feature for graphic art and creative writing. The local literary journal is on display in the book case, and pottery is featured in the window display for another participating artist.

They greet their guests with a smile, a hand shake, a nod, and a toast over red wine while answering questions about photography, hiking the Appalachian Trail, and the arts in general. For three hours tourists are in and out of the museum. In the evening when all becomes quiet, Maverick and Tessa are ready to turn in for the night. Tessa offers her couch for him to crash on a few nights.

Maverick awakes early as daylight glimmers over the hills. He begins with a run to the park to re-start a regime of obstacle time twice a week and the gym three days a week, leaving the weekend to spend time with Tessa and Malakai.

On Monday morning, Tessa goes to work after driving Malakai to the charter school. She said goodbye to Maverick camped on the couch. He makes his way to the gallery and eventually to return the van to the rental center. Maverick drives only two miles bypassing the park when he sees Dick Richards on foot, in the rain.

"You need a ride?" Maverick asks, from the driver window, ushering him from the rain.

"Yeah, man," Dick jumps in the passenger side.

"Where to?" Maverick asks.

"Heading to the Mill," he replies.

"Don't you have any wheels?"

"Not right now I don't," he says, turning to the window.

"Why is that?"

"Couldn't pay the ticket, got it impounded–so I'm trying to work to get it out," he sighs.

"Well, I'm Maverick," he says, with a grin.

"Hey man, I'm Dick."

"That's right. You are. But you don't recognize me, do you?"

"Do I know you?" Dicks asks, fidgeting in his seat.

"Well, let me see…I've recently shaved and a few inches taken off the top."

"That doesn't help me out much."

"Let me put it this way–you have a few things of mine."

"I'm sorry man, but I'm not following you."

"I'm the guy you sacked and took what belonged to me."

"Oh, man," Dick runs his fingers through his hair.

"Well, where is my shit?"

"Man, I'm not sure, but look, all I can say is I'm sorry."

"I have a hard time believing you."

"No, look, really, I am. I mean we just got carried away."

"Is that the kind of shit guys like you do?"

"No, well," Dick pauses, looking for the right words, "Flip and I have been friends for a long time, and…"

"You go out looking for trouble?" Maverick finishes.

"No, not really…I guess there's no real reason…"

"Okay, but what I'm telling you is, my stuff you stole from me, it was personal, and you took the shit that meant the most, I mean as far as shit goes, and I want my shit back."

"Your shit is gone man," Dick stutters.

Maverick turns a sharp left, hitting his fist to the steering wheel. "That shit was over a thousand miles on the AT, not that you'd understand that, but it's my blood, sweat and tears. I want all of it back."

"Listen man, it could still be in Flip's car, but the car is impounded and Flip's incarcerated," Dick lisps, pausing for exaggeration, "and my man is going to be doin' some time."

"Yeah," Maverick insists, "I read that in the paper. Well, with this job you have you can get that *Vipe* out of the impound and why aren't you in there with him? What the hell were you two guys thinking racing on the wrong side of the street?"

"They're just prosecuting the driver, a no fault for the passenger of the car."

"How the hell is that guy driving a ninety-thousand-dollar ride like that?"

"His dad's a criminal defense attorney, he's got money."

"Isn't that just perfect," Maverick says, pulling into a gravel driveway.

"Right, but he can't represent him in court or nothin' like that."

"Maybe not. But my guess is he'll keep getting off easy."

"Maybe," Dick says, reaching for the car door. "Hey," he says, softly, prying the door open, "thanks for the lift."

"No problem," Maverick says, putting the van in reverse.

Candace Meredith

Chapter Nine

Reservation for Two

Maverick steps out of the shower at the gym. He made it to mile five before his leg felt like it had been sawed off like a tree stump. He props his leg onto the bench massaging the salve into his knee cap, letting the menthol penetrate deep into the tissue before putting on his clothes. He plans to meet Tessa at the Italian restaurant at seven.

The restaurant is in the plaza adjacent from the sports complex and Maverick makes his way on foot. He enters the front door and is taken to the outdoor balcony that has been reserved for two. The balcony is lit with red and green lights on floral garlands and leafy green plants. Running water cascades from a fountain and artificial lights illuminate a gas burning fireplace.

"This place is brilliant," Tessa says, setting her purse on the empty seat, wearing an above-the-knee red dress and black heels.

"Stunning," he says as he takes his seat across the table.

"Yes it is."

"I mean you, of course," he insists.

"Oh," she blushes, "thank you, Maverick."

"I'm dying to hear the good news," she opens her menu and folds her napkin on her lap.

The waitress appears, taking down two ice waters and a glass of Merlot.

"You might not believe it," he pauses, "but my work was sold…"

"Really?" She beams. "Who? Or by how many?"

"Patricia said all of it."

"Wow, Maverick," she gasps. "Are you pulling my leg?"

"Not at all," he says, squeezing a lemon onto ice water, "Patricia says the new medical center bought out my work. They're putting it in their new buildings."

"I'm impressed."

"I thought you would be," he says, pausing to order a chicken parmesan platter with a chef side salad and house vinaigrette. Tessa orders the cheese stuffed manicotti with a side salad and the house dressing. Maverick takes Tessa by the hand. "Tessa."

"Yes, Maverick?" She whispers.

"They are paying me a quarter of a million dollars to purchase my art."

"Maverick, this is really wonderful."

"And I never would have ever imagined it those nights alone on the AT, but now I really can't believe it."

"Believe it." She smiles widely.

The next day, Maverick boards a train after hitchhiking into Maryland, to the Western Appalachia that inspired his six month trip into the mountains. The forty-mile route in Maryland blazes the C&O Canal Tow Path where Maverick began along the Potomac River and headed into West Virginia. He begins a more arduous run on the loop of the man-made lake that comprises of a five-point-three mile trail of moderate incline. Maverick completes it in under thirty-five minutes and afterwards stretches his leg muscles. His knee is throbbing and he is limping.

I better slow down, he thinks as he passes over the watershed, wishing he'd kept the van another week. He sits to rest his aching leg and contemplates heading to the in-town car dealer to purchase a set of wheels for the first time in three years.

He makes his way to the area bath house to make use of the park facility. The hot water cascades onto his back, relaxing his aching muscles. The money from the gallery purchase should post to his bank account today.

After hitching a six mile ride with a truck driver, Maverick spots a small car dealer in the city limits. Maverick had hitched the ride after he had assisted the trucker with one of this tires.

The Henderson Dealer featured a Subaru Sport that Maverick felt would be efficient – complete with roof rack and a back rack for a bike. He imagines a smooth transaction now he can pass for someone other a hobo. He is greeted by Ted, who guides him to have a seat at the desk. After forty-five minutes worth of credit checks and insurance calls, Maverick explains that he'll be paying in cash which leaves the salesman perplexed. Maverick steps out of the dealership, swinging the keys to his new twenty-five thousand car, and starts the engine. Delighted, he puts the transmission into drive and makes his way through the mountains and to Tessa's.

"Where have you been?" She asks, removing the chain to the door.

"Mind if I come in?"

"If I can get the damn door open," she laughs. She glances in the driveway as Malakai steps outside wearing his favorite super hero tee shirt and red basketball shorts. "Whose wheels?"

"They're all mine."

"Hi Mav-Mav," Malakai tosses up his hands for Maverick to lift him onto his shoulders.

"What do you have going on tonight?" Maverick asks.

"It's Mal's first tee-ball practice tonight," she says, "you should come."

"Absolutely." he says, "Wouldn't miss it."

"Malakai has been batting a ball since he was two," she says, ushering them through the door, closing it behind them.

Two hours later, they are eating hot dogs from the concession stand. With each toasty bite, he is reminded of how he spent so much time drinking dirty water from a warm canteen. A crack of the bat and Maverick looks up to see Malakai laughing with his foot on the plate. He's safe on first, taking two to home plate.

"Practice is a success," he says, wiping ketchup from his upper lip.

"If only they play this well on Saturday," she says, "But I have faith." "Saturday?"

"His game is at six. I can make it to the marathon. I have to be there, my company is promoting awareness by setting up a booth, passing out flyers, pins, posters."

"I hope to see you there," he says, "but I understand if you're too busy."

"I shouldn't be," she smiles, tugging at the collar to his shirt. "I had to fix that," she shrugs.

"Thanks?" He grins.

"You should thank me," she winks.

"Oh, yeah? Why is that?"

"You're becoming your old self again."

"But that's not who I want to be."

"I'm not talking marketing frozen chicken," she says earnestly, "I'm talking about the young guy I knew."

"You make me sound as if I'm regressing," he laughs.

"Not regressing as in level of maturity but in happiness and personality."

"That's right," he says, "in that way I do feel like my old self again – like the freedom I felt at the park, on my bike, at the BMX stadium, hanging with you and Maxi."

"And I was happy, too," she whispers as Malakai approaches, taking his water bottle out of the packed cooler.

"How you doing, Buddy?" She asks.

"Good," he says mid sip.

"Ready to go home?"

"Yeah," he says, removing his cleats, knocking the dust off his shoes.

"You can change in the car," she pats his mussed helmet hair.

Chapter Ten

The Marathon

After three days of rest, relaxation and light stretching exercises, Maverick feels ready. Orange cones are placed as markers throughout the downtown district, blocking off motor vehicles. There is a "Race for Awareness" banner that marks the beginning and the end, and at the end is Tessa and her booth: The Psychiatric Association Board, which is decorated in blue ribbons with the words "Autism Speaks" ascribed in white. They are also handing out flyers that describe the range in spectrum disorders: different challenges and strengths experienced by individuals with the disorder.

Maverick wears number 501 out of the thousand who have showed to participate in the race. He sips from the grape flavored water that was passed out to the participants and he stretches his muscles, before he begins what looks like a steady ascent on Main Street. The runners litter the streets wearing light spandex, some of them shirtless, others in light neoprene, dressed for the eighty-eight-degree weather with partly cloudy skies.

When the gun goes off, adrenaline pumps through Maverick. He passes the first marker, sporting his purple runners with the green laces and his lucky matching green wool socks that feel like soft gloves on his feet. His thinks about Bill and George who he intends to visit by the end of the week, but for now his mind is on Tessa and this race.

Breathing rhythmically, he moves along at a steady pace, intending to speed up towards the end. Patrons cheer, clap, and pass out plastic cups filled with cool water. Maverick takes the small cup and swallows quickly, hoping not to lose his rhythm. He gracefully darts past the second marker then onto the third when his knee begins to throb. His tight muscles wobble at the sight of the last marker Grunting, he howls loudly and thinks of something to push past the pain.

He thinks about Tessa and her gorgeous smile, how she used to carry a loaf of bread for the ducks at the park, her spiraled curls and her exquisitely beautiful turquoise blue eyes. Suddenly, his leg buckles under the weight of his body. He crashes down into the asphalt, rolling onto his back, his hands bracing his throbbing knee. He feels the hands of two men flanked at each side. The two men toss an arm around his neck and another arm about his waist – they steady Maverick between them for the 1.2 kilometers ahead – taking Maverick the full distance, one hard step at a time.

He succeeds, then, in step with strangers who bare his weight and hold him up at the victory line-finishing not last, but in record time.

"I thought my face plant meant the race was over," Maverick winces, wiping his brow.

"Never man," one man says, "I'm Tony...the other guy I've never met before. Hey man," he says, tapping him on the shoulder, "can we get your name?"

"Oh yeah," he says, "of course–name's Rick."

"Awesome," Tony says, "that was a good run."

"Sure was," Rick says, "and how about your name?"

"I'm Maverick," he says, jetting out his hand for a shake.

"Thanks for helping me get this guy across the line."

"Hey, no problem," he says, waving a hand in the air.

"Heck yes," Maverick says, "thanks to both of you."

A woman in a peachy-pink skirted suit with jet black hair and blue eyes approaches, and touches Maverick at the shoulder.

"I have to take off," Tony says, shaking Maverick's hand and turns to his friends and family.

"Maverick," the woman says, as he swings around with her lipstick smile in his view. "Maverick I've got good news," she says, clasping her hand onto his shoulder.

"Mom," he says, taken aback, "what are you doing here?"

"Don't mind why I'm here, but I have to tell you…oh, well, I'm here to let you know she's coming back to you." she exclaims, delighted.

"Mom, what?' He stutters, "who is coming back?"

Before he can finish, Vivian appears wearing athletic gear and sporting a pink hat atop platinum blond hair. She places both hands to each side of his face and forces a kiss. Engulfed in the moment, he places his hands to her shoulders but Tessa stops dead in her tracks – she doesn't take another step closer.

"We saw you on television," his mother says exuberantly.

Behind his mother, Maverick spots his father's gray hair and receding hairline as he makes his way past the crowd toward Maverick and places an arm around Vivian.

"We found her in Aruba," he grins like a Cheshire Cat.

"You went looking for her?"

"No silly," Vivian says, "we went looking for you."

"After we went to Aruba," his mother pipes in, "and Vivian was there, out on the back dock, out the window. We were dining when we saw you on television."

"We just thought that it must be meant to be," his father chimes in.

"Don't you think so?" His mother asks, puckering her lips.

Disappearing into the crowd, Tessa makes her way back to the booth. Putting on a brave face, she greets the crowd and begins collecting her items.

"I heard how awful things were when I left," she purrs, forcing him to look at her, "I didn't know that leaving would cause all these things to happen."

"What things, Vivian?"

"You going crazy and homeless and all that. You poor man."

"So you heard all that about me, but you didn't want to come back then?"

"If only I knew that coming back would change all that…"

"That's not what I'm saying and you're not the reason. Why are you trying to come back now?"

"I didn't know all that. Your parents told me all about it while we were in Aruba."

"Then why did you leave in the first place?" He sighs. "You know what, never mind...and you're not the reason I'm homeless."

"No need to lie to us," his mother says.

"That's right, son," his father says, eyeing his mother, "we're all together again."

Maverick turns to walk away, towards Tessa and her table. However, he forgot his leg is jelly, and he collapses to the ground. His knee cap is no longer straight but set sideways the same way he found it after falling to the ravine, confirming his worst fear, it's likely he'll need surgery.

"Son, let us help you with that leg," his father says, kneeling, looking directly into his eyes.

"That's fine, Pop," Maverick says, "but..."

"No but, dear," his mother chimes in, her hands upon her hips.

"Here, Maverick," Vivian says, lifting him beneath the arm, "let us get you to the hospital."

Ten minutes later, Maverick takes a seat in the hospital waiting room. Glancing on the wall, he notices one of his photos: the Paw Paw Tunnel in spring among the falling water and wild flowers. Aside the photo is a small plaque that reads:

Local Resident Photography
Maverick D. Hall

Maverick smiles, feeling momentarily famous then he thinks about Tessa again. Angry that he doesn't have a phone and that he never thought to get her number.

Two hours later, Maverick exits the emergency room wearing a full brace and leaning on a crutch. He knows Tessa was attending her son's tee ball game this evening as he reluctantly accompanies his parents' home. His mother's home is decorated in glass: crystal chandeliers adorn the rooms and large mirrors occupy the space. They have a seat in the formal living room and Maverick is handed a cup of hot tea. He barely takes a sip.

"Thought it was going to be cold," he says, and adjusts his legs across the ottoman. Vivian sits on the beige leather couch and tosses a pillow playfully onto his lap.

"Look," he shifts in his seat, feeling uncomfortable and manipulated. "I have a woman," he says forcefully.

"You have a woman?" His father scoffs, "and how long have you had this woman?"

"Just a couple of weeks," he explains matter-of-factly as Vivian stifles a laugh.

"I see," his father says.

"Well, who is she?" His mother asks, plopping some ice into his cup.

"It's Tessa."

His mother gasps, "you don't mean that girl from the trailer do you?"

"It wasn't a trailer, Ma," he says.

"I don't know what else you call it."

"A housing unit, Ma. Typically called a row home or a townhouse."

"For low income families," she says.

"Doesn't it sound," his father says, "a bit low class to you, Maverick? You know, a bit trashy?"

"Tessa isn't trash," he growls, "she's highly intelligent. She works in social work, aiding children who have disabilities – she was at the marathon today…"

"I see," his father waves his hand dismissively, "isn't real estate humanitarian enough for you?"

"It's not exactly the same, Pop."

"It's not the same how?"

"In principle."

His mother chuckles. "You know, your sister is making quite a living – the way that you used to."

"I chose to leave my profession."

"Everyone at some point in time has made the wrong choice Maverick – but it is time to take the bull by the horns."

"I just have to choose the right bull this time."

"Then let's put it this way," his father begins again as Vivian flicks back her hair. "It's likely you need surgery on that leg. How are you going to afford it? With what job?"

"I do have money, Pop."

"What money?"

"I sold some of my photography."

"I know. I saw you on television."

"Pop, then why did you ask?"

"Because that certainly cannot be enough."

"We are happy for you, Maverick," his mother says, "about your photography, I mean."

"Nonsense," his father says, a wave of his hand, "you can get a job with your mother."

"Dad, I'm not getting a job with Mom."

"You'd rather be homeless? A bum?" His father scoffs again.

"I'd just rather be me, myself ..."

"And who, or what, are you?"

"I'm a carpenter by trade."

"Since when?"

"On the AT. I had to be good with my hands."

"You weren't getting paid."

"Not yet."

"Then when?"

"When I leave here. I've been making plans to start a business."

"What kind of business?"

"It'll be a repair shop."

"Computers?" His mother raises a well-manicured eyebrow.

"Yes, but I don't know how to repair computers."

"Then what do you repair?"

"I'm skilled in craftsmanship, Pop, so I'll have a job again soon."

Heaving himself off the couch, Maverick leaves the house. He pulls his gimp leg into the car, shoving the key in the ignition. After a twenty-minute drive, he arrives at Tessa's door. The lights are off and no one comes to the door – he is uncertain if the garage is empty. He hurries back to his car, looking for pen and paper – jots down a note stating he was there, then takes off.

Her fingers pry open the curtain as his tail lights fade around the corner.

Chapter Eleven

Bill

Maverick slept in his car until the early hours. Getting out of the car, he pulls his crutches out of the backseat and hobbles up to George's door. Before he can knock, George exits the house, his keys swaying from his finger.

"Where have you been?" He says, rushed, "get in the car."

"Where are we going?"

"You'll see in a minute. Just get in the car."

They hop in the car and make their way onto the interstate heading north. They pass a sign for the Department of Veteran Affairs; they get off at the next exit.

"Where have you been?" George asks again.

"I had the gallery, the marathon, Tessa – then my family showed up."

"You'll have to tell me about it," George tosses an empty cigarette pack onto the floor. "Bills' got cancer," George chokes out as he pulls on a cigarette.

"What? Shit."

"You couldn't guess it but he was smoking medical marijuana. I mean I smoke marijuana because I like marijuana, but Bill was different."

"Do you know what type?"

"A rare brain tumor. And he doesn't have long. That's why I'm taking you...he's in hospice."

"How long? I mean how long has he been in?"

"Three days. Surprised he's been in that long."

After a thirty-minute drive, they end up at the VA Medical Center. George tosses the car into park and they make their way to Bill's room. Inside, Bill lays stiffly on his back, his chest rattling deeply as if he is in a thick soup. Maverick takes a seat at the side of the bed and leans into him, whispering.

"Hey, old man," Maverick begins, "I came here to tell you a few things..." George is too wound up by his friend's impending demise to do much else than mutter at the ceiling.

Maverick begins with Tessa, then Malakai and on to the Gallery, the sale, training for the Marathon and running the marathon – on to the family visit, then almost forgetting about Dick Richards. A ghost of a smile plays around Bill's mouth. Then he starts grunting and wheezing for several minutes. In the middle of his breathing episode, a man walks into the room.

"How long has he been diagnosed?" Maverick asks, standing.

"I don't know." The man replies, "I just handle the contracts."

"What contracts?"

"His living will, also referred to as an advanced directive. Are you Maverick?"

"Yes," Maverick responds, curious.

"Mr. William Collier has left you his estate."

"Estate?" George scoffs.

"Yes," the man responds, "he's left Maverick Hall his entire estate–everything he owns."

"Bill," Maverick says, placing his hand on Bill's as a nurse walks in to change his bedding.

"Sir," the man says, "would you mind if I get a few signatures? We can step out into my office down the hallway."

"No problem," Maverick assures him. After twenty-some minutes, Maverick returns to the room to find the medical doctor with George.

"Thank you," George says, wiping his face with a bandana he shoves in his back pocket. The medical doctor leaves the room, nodding to Maverick as he walks past. Bill's eyes are closed and he is no longer breathing.

"I'm making the burial arrangements," George says, "he didn't want a funeral – just cremation and burial at the cemetery. Can you believe he's already got a plot? Doc said he was diagnosed two weeks ago – he denied treatment, and they prescribed the marijuana."

"Did they say anything else?"

"He had brain cancer, then it spread to other areas of the body – he had large masses that would be hard to operate on so he thought it best to get the medically prescribed stuff."

"Can't say that I blame him."

"No, I don't either. Just wish I knew."

"Must be a reason he couldn't say."

"Didn't want us to ruin his mood," George feebly jokes.

"That's right," Maverick says, "didn't want us to ruin his good time."

"That's it," George says fighting back the tears.

A few days after his last wishes are carried out George stands besides Maverick, peering at the headstone that reads:

Vietnam Veteran
William Collier
11-12-1946 – 05-14-2017

"You went and died on us you old goat," George says, still finding the humor in his soul that Bill was so fond of.

"Doctors told me I'd never run again," Maverick shrugs, removing an ink pen from his pack.

"That's what they told Bill after he took that bullet."

"And they were damn wrong," Maverick insists. He clicks the top to his pen and removes the left shoe from a gimp leg and stencils *Marathon 05-07-17* into the sole.

"Told me I'd never run again….Do you think this guy, the one who wrote this date," he says pointing, "do you think he finished the race?"

"Don't think that we'll ever know man."

"Once I have that knee surgery," he continues, "I'm going to get through that physical therapy they have planned for me."

"Gotta get through the surgery first, Maverick man," George pats Maverick on the shoulder as they turn to leave, gazing at the expanse of the clear sky.

Later that evening, Maverick and George sit perched on the front stoop of Maverick's inherited home. Between them, Bill split his insurance policy fifty-fifty so that the money he earned as a war veteran could be used properly. The evening breeze brushes past the burning fire as George grills hot dogs. They want to do right by Bill so they talk about what to do with his money, investing, donating, and family.

"You know, that guy that Vivian met," Maverick says, sipping a beer, "He's been locked up for everything from theft, to forgery, check fraud – embezzlement…"

"Oh, yeah?" George raises an eyebrow, "how'd you hear that?"

"Overheard my father speaking about him," Maverick explains, prying back the lid to a can of beans. "I don't find it a coincidence she's trying to make her way back now."

"Well, now it's just a matter of what you're goin' to do about it."

"I'm going to see about a woman," Maverick says smoothly.

"You'll have to bring her around sometime."

"I plan on it George, hoping she's around."

"Were you supposed to see her?"

"Yes, but Vivian showed up instead. Possibly the doing of my parents. They saw her in Aruba."

"What's the chance in that?"

"She goes every year," Maverick snickers, "her daddy pays for that trip and has done so every year since she was in high school."

"Then you're saying the odds are strong?" George laughs heartily.

"Pretty much. They stay at the same villa every year, too."

"Then I'd say they knew right where to find them. But why this long?"

"To tell her all about what they saw on the TV."

"Then if that's the case…," he pauses, "well, what's their reason for that?"

"Because they see no wrong in Vivian," Maverick stands to stretch and leans on one good leg. "She comes from money," he says, throwing water onto the fire, "but what were you going to say first?"

"Well, that if that's the case, seeing you on TV and all that then there's a chance Tessa saw you, too."

"What are you saying?"

"Whatever happened between you and Vivian," he shrugs. "She might have seen it."

Maverick nearly runs to the car, kicking up stones from his crutches as he extends an arm out the window, waving a farewell to George and drives into the night.

Chapter Twelve

Tessa

Maverick pulls into the driveway at 109 Terrace Boulevard to find the lights are out, the garage door is open and empty, and in the front yard is SOLD sign. Maverick slams a fist onto the horn and his head onto the steering wheel, first Bill, now Tessa. He wonders how this too has gone wrong.

He pulls into his own empty driveway – no one is there either. In the morning, he bathes in the outdoor shower – a feeling of familiarity, but far from relief. His knee is a crooked sight with his brace off. He schedules the surgery he has been advised to have and then decides to resume training the better half of his body until he can come up with a plan. He rotates his crooked leg a little less angular onto the floor undermining the pain and begins one arm push-ups putting his mind at ease.

He moves on to one-footed squats and a pantomime jump rope then to pull ups using the shower rod. In the tiny house, he hangs from the loft with his torso over the edge and his feet between the rungs to the stairs in a dead man hang. A moment later the receptionist calls with his surgery scheduled for three weeks from Thursday, and with that he takes off back to Tessa's place.

Knocking on the neighbor's front door, a woman wearing leggings and a baggy shirt with an infant cradled on her hip answers.

"Hello," Maverick says quickly, "I'm looking for Tessa – I just got a phone – I never got her number. I'm Maverick."

"Maverick?" She smiles faintly, "yes, she's mentioned you a few times."

"I'm hoping you might be able to tell me where she's gone."

"She's mentioned Miami a few times but I'm really not sure."

"Miami?" He says quizzically. "Any idea, why Miami?"

"I think her mother and maybe for work."

"Okay, thank you," he says as he heads back to his car.

"Best of luck," she hollers back and shuts the door.

Maverick rushes to the nearest library on Handley Street and looks for every Lucille Sweet and Markle, both Tessa's maiden name and stepfather's name, he can find but the only Lucille Sweet in Miami is ninety according to the search engine. The remaining search arrives at a dismal conclusion being that the only other Lucille Markle lives on Tulip Street in Clearwater is twenty-nine. He clicks the main screen to another page, one last hope being case records, finding nothing and no one to match either description. Tessa may or may not be residing with her mother who may or may not reside in Florida.

He clicks out of the screen and stammers from his chair, clutching at his crutches – his leg feeling half broken. The next marathon hangs on his mind.

I have to get my thoughts off Tessa for now, he thinks as he considers the pending surgery. He soaks his body in the trough that replicates a soaker tub in the tiny house. Maverick crunches his body into a half fetal position, feeling the intense heat from a hot temperature and rubs his thigh to loosen the leg muscles. He lets out a deep breath as the pain from his nerves reaches his toes – he grimaces and shuts his eyes briefly to lament on how he nearly made it to the finish – but his body gave out and refuses to endure any more. But now he must go – his body must not fail him in finding Tessa across a span of hundreds of miles.

A home needs to have its Queen, he thinks. *I almost had her,* he, thumps his fist into the soapy water. *I've got to get her back.*

The cool air rushes past his face as he opens the door to the outside shower. He tosses the crutch onto the cot he uses as a bed and places both hands on the skinny rail and drives it home – one crunch at a time. After he dries off, there is a honk in the driveway. He spots George, waving a fishing rod out the window.

"It's a nice day," he says, "and I've got to eat." He chokes, "can't retire Bill's old fishing pole, thought you'd like to give it a try."

"Might test my luck with an old fishing pole," he grins, shimmying to the truck and closing the rusted door.

After catching several sizable fish, they head back to George's house to fry up a hot meal. George pulls the bone from flesh and pan fries white fish in hot butter. The smell of churned butter permeates the room and George and Maverick have a seat on the front porch.

"You're not going to light one up?" Maverick asks, sucking butter from his fingers.

"Not anymore," he says, tossing a log onto the fire.

"Why not?" Maverick asks, peering into the fire.

"Because I don't have cancer," George says matter-of-factly, "and it don't seem right no more." He cracks open a can.

"Then we'll just have a cold one," Maverick says, grabbing a can from the cooler. "He was one good veteran."

"That's right," George says, "he served this country, so I feel like I owe him one."

"But he'd tell you to smoke another one," Maverick jokes.

"I quit in his name."

"To Bill," Maverick says, raising his can for a toast.

"That old goat," George huffs.

In the ensuing weeks, Maverick doesn't give in to the pain – with every flinch he pushes for another rep, pushing past the limitation inflicted by his aching body. On the day of his surgery, George waits in the hospital, paper in hand.

"Flip Richards was released," he hollers as Maverick is pushed between two heavy doors in a gurney, followed by nurses.

Four hours later he lays on his back in the recovery room, George by his side, sipping from a mug filled with black coffee. Maverick's leg is elevated, tucked away in a full cast. He can feel the staples pulling at the mesh.

"Treating it like a broken leg," George says, tapping his fingers to the side of the hot cup.

"Might as well be one," Maverick twists his torso for a better look.

"Nothing to look at," George says, "I can assure you it's all there."

"Kind of nice not to feel anything," Maverick gasps.

"Got you the good shit," George grins.

"Is that what it is?" Maverick jokes, "I guess that's why I don't feel anything then."

Maverick spends a week in the hospital recovering before he is discharged. In his pack are the papers to begin physical therapy, which will take months the doctors say, to use again. His new replacement knee needs strengthening and conditioning but for now he maneuvers within the tiny house on one leg. George is a regular visitor and Maverick begins physical therapy starting with the pool, taking the weight off the leg, he does simple leg raises one painful stretch at a time.

Chapter Thirteen

Mark

Tessa walks Malakai on the fishing pier overlooking the Atlantic Ocean. It's a beautiful hot day full of sunshine, and she opens a book while Malakai uses his super hero fishing pole. She moved to Florida to move up to a managerial position with the Department of Social Services.

Malakai's birthday is approaching and Tessa arranges plans with her mother, who is now married to a gentleman by the name of David Blake. Her stepfather is charming, five years younger than her mother who is fifty-nine. Her mother is slim, one hundred thirty pounds with strawberry hair and hazel eyes. Her smile is sweet and her demeanor is feminine but stern. She has moved to Florida to take on a flight attendant position in a warmer locale. Tessa was tickled to get a position in the same state as her mother, who is also her best friend.

Tessa feels that Walt Disney World is an appropriate place to take her going-to-be six year old son for his birthday. Her mother makes her appearance on the pier looking twenty years younger in her coral colored swimsuit studded with jeweled accents.

"Hi, Mom," Tessa looks up from her suspense novel.

"Hi, Daughter," her mother says taking a seat, fanning her face. "Who's the guy?" she asks, rubbing tanning oil onto her skin.

"What guy?" Tessa asks, amused.

"That one over there" she points subtly, "the one who's been looking over here."

Tessa glances at the beach below them. There is a guy in Hawaiian shirt seated in front of a ripe red colored frozen daiquiri. He glances upward toward the pier and tosses a hand into the air in a gentle wave. Tessa and her mother wave back.

"I'm hungry," Malakai says patting his round tummy.

"I could use a bite to eat myself," her mother says followed by a mischievous wink.

"Mom," Tessa warns, trying to get ahead of her mother's thought process. Before she could say anymore, her mother takes Malakai by the hand, guiding him toward the restaurant below. Lucille takes a seat in clear view of the man with the dark features and a Hawaiian shirt while Malakai plops down beside her, Tessa behind them.

The man pays for his drink, leaves his seat, and saunters over. "Hello," he says, his daiquiri dripping water in the hot sun.

"I don't mean to be too forward," he says, patting his hand to his chest, "but I just want to introduce myself."

"I'm Lucille, or you can call me Lucy," her mother says, extending her hand to his.

He takes her hand, smiling widely, "I'm Mark," he says, "it's very nice to meet you."

"Likewise." Lucy smiles, "and this is my daughter, Tessa," she places one hand on her daughter's shoulder.

"It's also very nice to meet you as well," he grins.

"Thank you," she blushes.

Malakai glances at his mother and then back at the man with the Hawaiian shirt. "Where is Maverick?" He asks.

"Mommy already told you," Tessa grimaces, placing crayons and a placemat in front of her son. A woman in a black bikini, a martini in her hand, stops at the table.

"I couldn't help overhearing," she says with a wry smile, "you must be Tessa."

"Yes," she admits, laying the menu in her lap. "Vivian?" She asks, slightly amused.

"Yes," Vivian tosses her long blond tresses from her shoulder. "How did you know?" She squints at them as she removes her sunglasses.

"Everyone knows the girl who's painted on the yacht," she muses.

"I'm sorry," Mark says "but am I interrupting anything?"

"No," Lucille replies with a wave of her hand.

"I heard you ask about Maverick," she smirks, "he and I are both doing just fine," she huffs haughtily. Her friend to her right in the turquoise swimsuit nods, looking to one another out of the corner of their eyes.

"Well, I'm happy for you both, Vivian," Tessa says, motioning for the waitress who approaches the table.

"We have to order our meal," Tessa explains dismissively.

"Enjoy," Vivian smirks and flounces away.

"A yacht?" Her mother inquires.

"The Vivian." Tessa explains, "her spouse named his yacht after her, then got himself hacked by the FBI or something like that."

"Ouch," Mark whistles, "doesn't sound so good, that Maverick guy."

"Oh no, Maverick is her first husband, the one she replaced for a yacht."

"Double ouch. Hate to be that guy."

"Didn't he lose his mind?" Lucille asks, taking her margarita from the waitress.

"Mom," Tessa interjects.

"What? I don't know what you call it."

"He just needed a change."

"Evidently not," she huffs, "if he's opt for the same old thing."

"The same thing he said he wanted to leave," Tessa says, "something doesn't make sense."

"Does anyone?" Lucille laughs, turning to Mark. "You've been so patient, please sit with us" she says, guiding him to have a seat with her hand.

"What brings you ladies to Florida," he asks, "or do you live here?"

"Relocated," they say in unison. "We both found new employment," Lucille explains.

"In the area?"

"Just outside Miami."

"I just re-located here myself. I'm an engineer, I just got a job working for Disney," he explains, "I love it - just bought a new house, a few nice cars."

"Sounds glamourous," Lucy says, squeezing on a lime.

"I don't know about that but it's pretty nice."

"Well I'm a flight attendant and Tessa works for the Department of Social Services with orphaned children."

"You're a humanitarian. Working for other people like that shows a lot about your character."

"Do tell," Lucy says, nudging Tessa with an elbow.

"She's a real sweetheart," he grins.

"My Tessa is so sweet it's her last name," Lucy laughs.

"You mean that literally?

"Yes. Yes I do. Well, no longer mine, I'm married, but Tessa – she's single."

"Mom," Tessa groans, burying her head in her hands.

"Oh, okay. Have you ever been married?"

"No," Tessa says faintly, removing her hands from her face, "his father didn't stick around."

"I'm sorry to hear that."

"Yeah, he didn't want to leave the band."

"That's his loss then."

"Yes, it sure is," her mother says, patting Malakai on the back.

"What's your name, little man?"

"Malakai."

"Malakai, like Hawaii?"

"He's named after a beautiful place in Hawaii. It's where we vacationed before he was born."

"Ah, okay. Got ya."

"I can't say that I've ever been."

"Tessa won that trip," Lucy interjects, "she decided to go at it alone."

"Really? How did that happen?"

"An online casino game."

A cell phone rings and Lucy dives into her bottomless purse and retrieves a touch screen phone. "Oh, it's David," she says, "I'll take this call in private," and moves to the bar in the far corner.

"Your mother is an outgoing woman," he says, "I like her personality."

"That she is. And she was joking about the casino game by the way."

"How's that?"

"I went on a work trip."

"She's a funny woman."

"She has tenacity, ever since she moved away with me, years ago. She had to make it on her own, then she met David. I'd say he's real outgoing, too."

"You look a lot like her."

"It's where I get the red hair. My eyes came from a dead beat father."

"I take it you two don't talk?"

"Not since she left him and she took us to where we could have a better life. She always kept her promise."

"What promise is that?"

"To make up for choosing a loser to be a father," she jokes.

"What's Me-Me doing?" Malakai pipes up.

"Talking on the phone, sweetie."

"To who?"

"To Pap-Pap."

"I want to see Pap," Malakai says, jumping in his seat, "and Maverick."

Tessa shakes hands with Mark after scheduling a date to meet up one evening. He provides his number so she can call when she is ready, saying he hopes to see her again.

That night, Tessa searches for the name Mark Sportsman into the judiciary database. To her relief, none of the profiles match his age, name or location. Her mother mentions him often. He has a good job. He's good looking. He's got a nice personality and good taste in alcohol.

It takes Tessa three weeks to make any contact and she decides to text him *hello.* Which he promptly responds, *Tessa?*

Chapter Fourteen

Back on His Feet

Maverick is four weeks into his recovery via physical therapy – and all the training and agility strengthening he can muster. He perseveres past the agonizing pain starting with just one mile – his knee is full of staples, but he leaves the brace off. Today, George has met Maverick at the track, this time he's not following him in his truck, but running beside him.

"I bet you ain't got a mile in you," he spats, sporting spandex and a tee he scored at the thrift store.

"I bet I can beat you with two broken legs, old man," Maverick insists, pulling his left leg as he tries to hurry up. He then begins with a sprint, taking a stride half way around the track with George at his side.

"Tell you what," George begins, "if you can't out run me then you're pretty damn slow." He groans, catching his breath.

Maverick slightly increases his speed, building his endurance around the junior high track. The track team approaches from behind, and Maverick begins to feel lighter on his feet.

"Can you beat the young bucks?" George hollers from behind.

"Hey, man," one student says passing on his right side wearing red shorts and a white sports top – his school uniform. Maverick focuses on the backs of his legs, watching as his calf muscles flex appearing light on his feet like a gazelle.

Maverick begins to sprint again, his knee no longer feeling like two nails rubbing on bone. He throws out his arms to endure a full sprint, not losing speed he passes a runner who is grunting. He keeps pace with the runner edging on his tail and inhales deeply, releasing from his mouth, inhaling through his nose, steadying his breathing rhythm. He has surpassed where he started, knowing the first mile was complete. This time he continues to keep going, picking up the miles, extending his leg's capacity beyond the limitations set by the physician who said he'd never run again.

"I didn't think you were ever coming back," George says, sitting atop his Cadillac. Maverick doesn't know the miles he ran, but he knows he's ready to make another mark in his shoes.

Back at the garage they crack open a cold one.

"Be prepared for the obstacle course tomorrow, old man," Maverick says, rattling his already empty can.

"Damn it, Maverick," George says, "You're liable to take the life out of me."

"You're not passing over Rainbow Bridge on me just yet anyway."

George spats, laughing, and drinking from a cold can, "Bet you had nothing like this on that trail you was on."

"Nah," Maverick agrees, "nothing like any of this. I didn't even pack a tent. It was too much work – so I just threw up a poncho and slept under it."

"Didn't worry about the bears any?"
"That's funny, but I actually bought a deterrent spray. Must've worked because the only bear I saw was higher on the mountain– didn't come around either."

"What's something like that smell like?" George snickers.

"You gotta look that up yourself, I was just trying to not get eaten," Maverick shrugs.

"I've been seeing that guy around town," George says, between sips of a cold beer.

"What guy?"

"The one who had that Viper, who they call Flip."

"Oh, yeah? You tell him to give my gear back?"

"Thought you already did."

"I did. To his friend from the passenger seat, named Dick. He said the gear was still in the Viper."

"And what happened to the car?"

"Impounded."

"Wonder if he got it back then."

"Was he in it?"

"I don't know. He was coming out of the bar down on Amherst Street. Didn't look for the car."

"How you know what he looks like?"

"I recognize him from the paper. Anyway, Maverick, I'm wondering what you're planning to do?"

"When?"

"I mean now… you got any plans?"

"Yeah, I do," says Maverick.

"Tell me about it."

"For starters, I'm not giving up on nothing I set my mind on and second, I saw that bike shop for sale on Boscawen Street."

"What do you want with a bike shop?"

"I want to buy it. Own it. Sell and repair bikes."

"Shoot," George says, "well hell, you can fix bikes right out of my garage."

"Your place isn't right in town," Maverick explains, crushing another can.

"Let me ask you another question…"

"Shoot."

"Why this running?"

Maverick inhales, "Because I feel something inside myself. I like the way it burns – like every step up that mountain. It reminds me I'm alive, and then when I found out Tessa would be there…"

"That was fate," George muses.

Tessa returns Mark's simple question with an equally simple answer: *yes.*

Hello. He responds. *How are you? Nice to hear from you.*

After about thirty minutes of texting back and forth, Mark asks if she would like to meet up for a dinner. Delighted, she agrees to meet him at restaurant that serves authentic Mexican food at 8 that night.

She leaves her best knee-length red dress and black heels in the closet and opts for a pair of blue jeans instead. She pulls on a silky burgundy tank over her head, and calls a sitter, who arrives on time. Tessa leaves her home knowing she will arrive late.

Chapter Fifteen

Anew

Maverick paces among the quads, squats and hamstring fitness machines at the sports complex, wanting to test out his new knee, but the machines are full. After a few shoulder and hip rotations and leg stretches, he settles for the stair climber and begins to test his new knee. His staples have been removed and the new artificial, plastic knee is seemingly as good as his real knee.

The new knee is strong, bending rhythmically in place and not giving in as his old knee had in the river and again during the marathon. With his new body part, he feels like he could move mountains. Slowly he increases the speed, his leg no longer feeling like a slinky. His left leg feels stronger, but he knows he must work harder to perform like he had on the mountains.

Maverick returns to his tiny house after purchasing a smartphone. A piece of him feels as though he is returning to the life he formerly had, but this time feels different too and he wants access to the internet. He has scheduled a road trip to Florida, although he's uncertain if Tessa is located somewhere in Miami.

George drives up and honks quickly in the driveway. "Where are you off to?" He asks, as he gets out of the car and leans against it, watching Maverick.

"Taking a road trip," he says, preparing the hitch on the trailer, "right after I trade in the car for a truck."

"Taking the house with ya?"

"That's right," Maverick says, closing the door to his tiny house, "I'm heading out now, found a good truck – a 2013 Colorado."

"You planning on stopping by before taking off?"

"Well, I planned on being back, I guess, at some point."

"But you have something you have to do first."

"That's right."

"What happened with the bike shop?"

"I own it. Same management – he'll run things while I'm away."

"You going to run out of money?"

"Not for a while, but that's why I got the bike shop – a modest living."

"You are real modest," George grins, his hands in both pockets. "Have you tried looking on the internet?"

"That's why I got a cell phone. I can use the net."

"You're getting fancy."

"I've been off the grid for long enough I guess. She's on there – but nothing's been updated for a few months. And I haven't received a response so I'm heading off to Florida. I'm done sitting around here waiting. Something happened to make her leave like this without saying a word – and I've got to find out what."

"Isn't heading off to Miami kinda like searching for a needle in a haystack or winning the lottery?"

"Not at all," Maverick insists, "it's kinda like finding the girl I lost."

"I'd say good luck but I don't think you'll need it."

"Why is that?"

"Because you'll find her," he says.

"You know that?"

"I do," he says.

George and Maverick shake and part ways. Maverick heads to the dealership in town. After paying in cash for a duel tire truck, he's able to transport the tiny house in tow and heads south on the interstate.

Thirteen hours later, on interstate 95 south Maverick parks his tiny house at Pomano Beach, Florida outside of the downtown district at an inlet that overlooks the Atlantic Ocean. He's not certain how he's going to do his search except for some local newspapers. He places an ad that will run online and in the Sunday paper:

Desperately seeking Tessa.
Hoping we can talk.
Call Maverick 402-995-6665.

Three days later, he receives calls from women claiming to be Tessa and another claiming to have seen Tessa. The call is a possible lead from a bartender who says that a woman and a man were having a conversation and he distinctly recalls hearing the name. Maverick got a description of the woman and man, but it has been years since he has seen Tessa's mother or father and cannot place the description. He thanks the bartender who works at *The Pub* in Coconut Creek.

He then makes another call to a paper and places an ad with the same caption. During the week, Maverick receives an anonymous call from a man claiming he received a generous tip from a woman who had been with a man, who was cut off from ordering another mimosa. He found it strange that the woman paid for the tab, but felt the man may have been too inebriated to handle the bill. When Maverick asked for her description he was relieved to find out she matched Tessa's description. He now feels certain that there cannot be another Tessa who has curly bright auburn hair. The bartender also distinctly recalled her having deep blue eyes.

Tessa has been planning for her son's birthday all week, and Mark has graciously opted to show them around the park. Malakai occasionally asks about his friend Maverick, who he likes because he rides on his shoulders. Tessa weeps not knowing how to tell her son that Maverick chose another woman. She bends on one knee to tell her son that he is not forgotten and that sometimes friends have to move away from one another.

"But Mark isn't fun," Malakai told her one evening while Tessa was baking cookies that made her entire condo smell like vanilla.

"But he could open up," she gives Malakai the spoon to lick the icing, "and become more warm." Malakai sighs and informed his mother that he missed his friend. Tessa waits for Mark to arrive, hoping that his birthday at Disney will ease his mind.

Five minutes after finishing getting Malakai and herself ready for the big day, Mark shows up. Tessa lets him in. As he passes by her to pat Malakai on the head, "Hey kiddo," he says, entering the hall, "Hey, uh, do you have a restroom I can use? Had one too many last night."

"Down the hall on the right," she points.

"One too many what?" Malakai questions.

"Nothing," she responds, grabbing an umbrella.

After several hours, they get out of the car and head to the amusement park. Malakai cannot contain himself with the excitement. He marvels over the Star Wars characters, particularly his mother snapping a photo of Chewbacca and the droids. Tessa giggles as Malakai points to a live Mickey Mouse.

"Mickey is for babies," he says.

"Aren't you a baby?" Mark asks.

"No. I'm five," Malakai insists.

"Who just turned six," Tessa says. "He's not a baby," she whispers.

"Oh, I meant that as the same thing as a kid," he says.

Tessa's mother sends her a quick text to check in on progress. *I hope you're making out great with that handsome bachelor,* she says, followed by a blushing emoji. Tessa responds quickly – *I don't know, His time spent weight lifting equals his binging,* Tessa places her phone into her purse and ignores her texts for the rest of the day. On the ride home, she types her message: *I need to talk to Maverick.*

That evening, Tessa joins her mother over a martini while Malakai has a sitter. Initially, Tessa wanted to be near her mother because of her great job, but has second thoughts about giving up on Maverick so easily – or is she just playing the fool? Tessa's mother's husband is five years younger than her mother but they get along well. Lucille has never been impartial to a good drink, so his ownership of the hottest tiki bar on this side of the Atlantic wasn't to her distaste.

"Tessa, darling," she says, sitting daintily at the bar, one hand folded in her lap over a tight black skirt, "what have you been doing with this Maverick?" She sips.

"Mom," Tessa groans.

"He wasn't so bad in youth," she continues, "but turned out treacherous by what you say."

"I said he turned out homeless," Tessa gulps, speaking before thinking.

"That's putting it mildly," she sneers.

"He was getting his life turned around. We got close, so close something doesn't seem right. Or is off."

"You should always follow your instincts," her mother rolls her eyes.

"Mom, I mean, I'm not sure what or who I can believe."

"Believe what you saw, dear."

"Maybe if I gave it another minute."

"His hand would have been up her skirt?"

"Mom, you don't know that."

They both jump when there is a scream behind them.

"Ladies," Mark hollers, placing both arms around each shoulder, a sweaty hand grasping a large chilled mug.

"Having a beer on the house," he yells in Tessa's ear, "from the bartender over there."

"Owner you mean," Tessa says as David waves from behind the bar.

"Oh, you ladies know that guy?"

"My husband," Lucille says.

Mark's commotions caught the attention of a group of women from across the bar. Vivian ducks behind a friend, but Tessa ignores her. Mark clamors between them, appearing to have had a few more than one on the house.

"Husband, huh?" He grins widely, "How can you be Tessa's mother when you don't look a day older than twenty-nine?"

Her mother coyly places her hand to her chest. Tessa, distracted, glances around to see Vivian engulfed at the bar by a man who wears tight jeans and a muscle shirt.

"Tessa." She hears faintly over the music coming from the speaker overhead. "Tessa," her mother says again.

"What, Mom?" She asks, not wanting to take her eyes off Vivian, who has placed both hands around his neck, running her fingers through his short brown hair.

"Mark has offered to buy you another drink."

Tessa hasn't noticed her glass sitting empty and opts for another to not blow her cover, feeling she hasn't been noticed by Vivian. To her dismay, Vivian leaves the bar, exiting with her man in tow, unfortunately unable to snoop any further.

"Excuse me for a minute," she grabs her purse, "I have to use the ladies' room." She makes a hasty exit behind them.

"Tessa, sweetheart," her mother hollers, "the ladies' room is the other way."

But Tessa continues to the window where she can see Vivian followed by the same man and a group of friends. Standing outside a flaming red Ferrari, he opens the door and she climbs in the passenger side. As he peels out of the lot, Vivian glares from her window, they lock eyes and Tessa turns away.

Chapter Sixteen

Heading Home

Tessa makes haste back to Virginia, back to her old job, and back to Maverick. She stays in a hotel for the time being with Malakai and their small dog. She left it to her mother to explain to Mark where she has gone by leaving a note on the table. She did not return to the martini he ordered for her and the note simply said: *I love you Mom, but my home is back in Virginia.*

Her first stop is the park. She and Malakai along with their dog make their way to the place where they found one another. Malakai skips rocks in the water and occupies his young mind by collecting sticks.

The small lake is occupied with fishermen who use electric operated boats to maneuver in the water. The Blue Ridge Mountains encompasses thousands of acres with trails for hiking. As Malakai returns to the path from the water a motorcyclist makes use of the ATV trails and stops to park his motorcycle. The driver removes his helmet and gloves, kicking out his stand, and leaves his bike to approach them.

"Hey," he hollers, brushing his hand through his flattened hair, "have you seen a guy around here, might have a backpack, recently cut his hair, looks totally different."

"You're not talking about Maverick, are you?"

"Yeah." He says, taken aback, "I didn't really expect you to know him but he used to frequent the park here."

"Are you a friend?" She asks.

"No. Not really." He admits.

"Are you the guy he told me about?"

"That's a possibility." He says, "Name's Dick."

"Yeah," she says, "you're that guy."

"I am, but look, just tell him Dick is looking for him when you see him."

"I'm looking for him myself," she says.

"You'd think we'd find him pretty easily online, ordinarily everybody's on social media these days."

"Maverick just isn't the ordinary kind of guy," she says, tucking long locks of hair behind her ear.

"Yeah, I've noticed that," Dick says. "What are the odds of the two of us being at the same place looking for the same guy?"

"Better odds than finding Maverick evidently."

"I haven't seen him in weeks," Dick says, "used to see him on that obstacle course across from the playground."

"What were you doing at the park?"

"Scoping the place out for some good ATV trails, me and my buddy Flip cruise by often."

"And where is this Flip?"

"Gone. Most of the time. Got a job working for his father – finishing a degree," he pauses, "a lawyer."

"Pretty ironic for him to be a lawyer and act like that."

"That's why I don't see him no more. And he's already helping Flip expunge his record."

"Must be nice to have Daddy."

"Must be," Dick snickers.

"Well, alright," she says, "but why are you looking for Maverick?"

"I got something that belongs to him."

"I see. Well, I'll tell him you're looking for him when I see him."

"Alright," he says, at the start of his bike, "I appreciate that."

Dick fades into the distance out of sight when Malakai asks, "Who was that?"

"Just a friend, sweetie," she says, "just a friend."

Maverick has been searching every bar in town since he received the anonymous phone call. But the city is large, and the caller would only say they were on the cove nearest the water – narrowing the search to the Miami River. He heads east toward Bayshore Drive locating Bayside Bar adjacent to a Fit 2 Run store. *Its fate again,* Maverick thinks as he heads into the store, buying nothing more than new shoelaces for his Marathon shoes.

The hunt for Tessa turned out to be futile at Bayside Bar. The bartenders there have never heard the name and none of them made a call – at least none of them would confess to it.

"Have you looked online?" One of them asked while wringing glasses in a sink, bar towel slung over his shoulder.

"I've looked," Maverick responds, "hasn't been updated for a while."

"Maybe she doesn't want to be found," another protests.

"Thanks anyway," Maverick says, exiting the bar. He feels no closer than before the phone call made him aware that Tessa reached Florida.

Tessa's search leads her to the internet, although Maverick has never subscribed to social media. She types on her wall: *Maverick we need to talk.* She wonders if his recent kinship with technology will take him to the internet so they can finally talk.

Maverick sweats profusely as his run takes him to five miles alongside coastline. His only way of defeating the aggravation is to run, to prepare for the Miami Marathon held in support of the troops. The run reminds him of Bill, and he thinks of returning home for some time to visit George.

As the weeks pass, Tessa has grown desperate from frustration. She becomes obsessively flashy and showy, hoping to stand out. She purchased an ostentatious pink Beetle with a license plate that says *2 Sweet*. Through social media, she discovers a marathon approaching on the 29th of June for a Marine Corps 10k to take place in Washington DC in conjunction with a 10k to take place in Miami and in Fairfax, Virginia. Honoring service members is just the kind of support Maverick would partake she thinks. Tessa pays the donation of $35 to run in the 10K and pencils the date in her notebook and places a reminder in her calendar.

Tessa purchases hot pink running gear, fluorescent wrist and headbands and a tee to announce her participation. She runs in town early in the mornings while Malakai sleeps in the presence of a trusty sitter named Mandy: a 25 year old medical student who has certifications in First Aid and CPR. Tessa runs the park, bypasses the obstacle course and within downtown. She searches the ATV trails surrounding the mountains and the running trails at the local parks... She laments that Maverick is nowhere to be found; she should have waited, waited to speak with him personally. At the time, action spoke louder than words; besides, perhaps he simply does not know of Vivian's infidelities toward their re-kindled relationship – but she knows nothing without first speaking with Maverick. She also knows not whether she should buy a home because her heart tells her that she does not know where home should be.

Chapter Seventeen

The Cove

Maverick he has nailed it. *The Cove* sits on the corner of Northeast 3rd Street. He puts on a clean, pressed shirt and newly creased cargo pants and heads out the door.

The bar is rather quaint and tucked away beside a faintly lit back alley that leads to the back patio where the band plays eighties British popular music and classic rock. He makes his way to a small bar that serves bottled beer and asks for a pale ale house brew from a server who wears punk rocker clothes styled from the eighties. Maverick enters the back of the bar where he meets two male bartenders and a handful of female servers. He has a seat on the red-seated bar stool and glances at the posters of deceased rock artists and hears faintly a tribute being played for the late David Bowie. He turns his back to the crowd recollecting what he was told by the anonymous caller.

"Hey, man," he blurts out, "I thought we might've had a conversation the other day

443

on the phone. I'm the guy who's looking for a girl."

The bartender wearing the rock-n-roll tee and black jeans looks slightly amused, "Nah man," he says, "sorry, it wasn't me."

"No problem," he says, and thinks for one more question. "I am looking for a woman by the name of Tessa," he says, nonchalantly.

"I don't know her," the bartender says calmly, "but you might want to talk to the guy who owns the place – he may know her."

"Can I get a name?"

"Sure, his name is David. He's in here all the time," he says, collecting a bar tab and ringing the bell—a sign for a generous tip.

"Do you know when you'll be expecting him?"

"No, sorry, he owns the place so he doesn't really have hours."

"In fact," interjects the other bartender with the platinum blond hair and green eyes, "he's gone on vacation, so you don't have to waste your time looking for about a week."

"Alright," Maverick says, grabbing his brew, "thanks."

"Hey, no problem. And you want another one? And what's the name you're looking for?"

"Tessa," Maverick says, "yeah, give me another," sliding his empty bottle across the table.

"I'm pretty sure she was with the guy who kept buying all the drinks."

"A guy?"

"Yeah, man, I mean he's in here all the time, and I'm pretty sure the boss has mentioned them."

"I think you're right," the other bartender says, taking the cap off his bottle, collecting bills from the bar.

"That guy is in here all the time, but I can't remember who he was with."

"I only know that she has red hair," the blond haired bartender says. "The boss seemed to know them though, I mean he was serving their drinks."

"And you said his name is David?"

"That's our boss. He owns the place and he'll be back later next week."

"Well, Tessa has red hair."

"Sorry man, we don't know any names."

Maverick knocks his knuckles on the wooden bar top. "Hey, thanks again," he says, turning to leave.

"No problem," they say in unison.

Tessa has a long, lean stride. She sports her super pink fluorescent running shoes and makes her way to the obstacle course. She places one foot on the bottom rung of the *stairway to heaven* flexing her calf muscles and feeling his presence all around her. Running is no problem to Tessa; she spends mornings refining her body on the elliptical and making great strides on the stair master.

Maverick pushes his body to its limit using the treadmill. He sets the pace at maximum speed and gains three miles in under nineteen minutes. *Not too shabby for someone who wasn't supposed to run again*, he thinks slowing down his pace for a drink of cool fountain water. He sets the pace again knocking off another three miles in twenty minutes – his body wants to falter from exhaustion, but not dehydration. He drinks up to 40 ounces of water per day knowing that hydration makes up at least ten percent of success if not more – 90 percent is preparation.

The days feel long and Tessa occupies her mind by playing games with Malakai. They play hide-and-go seek, building blocks, and tinker toys and Malakai enjoys reading stories to his mother. He's in kindergarten and attends a private charter school. Tomorrow, Tessa returns to working with children and families who suffer from mental or emotional disturbances, and they are relieved to have her back as their case worker. One child commends her efforts at training for a marathon, especially since she is a major supporter for the Special Olympics; last year Michael got to hold the torch standing alongside Tessa.

"Anyone can run," she tells him.

"But not everyone can succeed," he responds.

"But what is the measurement of success?"

"You have a strong point. A level of success is the amount of effort you put into it, Tessa," he explains.

"You are so smart, Michael," she hugs him before she goes back to work to re-file for her tax forms and other on-the-job formalities.

Now she feels as though she can never leave them, at least not permanently, because her clients are like family to her. And because of Michael, in addition to her yearning to see Maverick, she trains vigorously. One foot in front of the other, in long strides to reach her goal all the way to the finish line.

Maverick trains diligently on the cardiovascular equipment and outside beneath the Florida sun—in preparation for the

Miami Marathon. His leg feels strong and his knee bends fluidly. The week following rigorous training, Maverick feels powerful and athletic, and Tessa feels as though she is gliding like dancing on air. She is two miles into the race of her life – to get to a finish line where she feels that Maverick will be waiting. She paces her stride at a comfortable level for the slight elevation ahead of her. She breathes mildly, beads of sweat dripping from her hairline, pieces of bangs dangle in front of her eyes that she swipes with long fingers. Her arms dangle limply at her sides to help her maintain a steady rhythm. She continues to glide on air rounding the next corner and a marker signaling the finish line is up ahead. The participants wear "support our US Veterans" tee shirts, some of them walking, others are running, like Tessa, scanning the distance before them. This marathon enables the Veteran's Administration to collect donations that are used to aid and bring awareness for the needs of vets.

Tessa feels wild inside; helping others gives her the motivation, determination and the drive to succeed. Thinking about Michael, about her son, and thinking about Maverick. She yearns to be past the finish line, embracing in thankful resolution.

Maverick nears the remaining mile of the Miami Marathon. He thinks about Bill, about George, about Tessa and about Malakai. He has the stealth of a raging carnivore that has found its prey. He nears the end, runners dodging past him like bullets, but he does not give up. His focus and his drive is geared toward achieving a summit. He finds the marker signaling the last of his run is just minutes up ahead.

Tessa can see the finish line. She is exhausted, her legs are cramping, but success is a measurement of the amount of effort one puts into a certain task. She screams, not wanting to give in, or to give up, she keeps running, one foot in front of the other she runs, light on her feet despite the exhaustion and the crowd of on-lookers can be heard cheering up ahead, she keeps reaching. Her lungs are burning. She inhales deeply through her nose and out through her mouth. *Almost there* she reassures herself, nearing the finish line just feet away.

Maverick is nearing the end. He feels strong and comfortable until suddenly his feet buckle beneath him. He is fatigued and he wants to keep going, but his legs are a twisted tangle beneath him as he lays face down panting, and thinking *what is the problem?* He tells himself to get up but he cannot. He sees before him the finish line that is merely a few seconds before him.

Tessa passes the finish line before exhaustion takes over her entire body.

"I have done it," she says, as Michael moves in to congratulate her the way she does at Special Olympics when he won for tossing the shot put. Tessa finishes third at a pace of 06:05 minutes per mile and a time of 22:32621 minutes total on the clock. Michael smiles with wide brown eyes looking at her in awe. She is a hero to him, as he is to her.

Chapter Eighteen

Reunion

Maverick lays in a Miami hospital emergency room awaiting to be admitted to a permanent room. His knee is broken. The doctor has already informed him that it will be another month of recovery – first to replace the knee and second for the physical therapy. He is anxious. *The Cove* bar is on his mind as well as speaking to David, but now he cannot reach it laid out in a hospital like this.

"You're a real trooper." His father says, seated at the side of his bed.

"What do you mean by that?" His mother asks.

"You know what I mean Debbie, he's always off on some wild crusade, or more recently, a wild goose chase."

"What are you talking about, Pop?"

"You know what I'm talking about."

"How do you know about that?"

"What else would you be doing in Florida if it's not for Vivian?"

Ignoring his father Maverick happily accepts pain pills from one of the nurses and falls asleep. He wakes up as the first light of dawn breaks through the curtain, noticing that he's been transported out of the ER. Fully awake he notices the figure of a shiny red-haired woman standing at the foot of his bed with her arms folded.

"Your broken knee replacement is all over social media," she begins, "and it took you a while to get here. I was all over Virginia looking for you."

"Looking for me?" He stutters.

"Yes, looking for you," she says, half anxious. "I thought we needed to talk after I saw you…" she pauses unhappily, "you and Vivian kissing in front of everyone…"

"You saw Vivian and I? So George was right."

"How could I not? Everyone could see you!" she yells.

"But you have to let me explain."

"Explain what?"

"I didn't kiss Vivian – she kissed me, but you must understand that I didn't kiss her back despite how it looked – I didn't push her away and should have. Instead I just waited for her to let go."

"She told me the two of you were doing fine. As in together."

"She said that? I swear that is just like Vivian."

"Then I saw her at the bar with another man."

"That's also not surprising, Tessa. Vivian is just interested in money... and she's so egocentric she thought I would want to take her back. Like I just went crazy for losing her. But I've explained before – that's just not the case."

"It looked like you were taking her back."

"But you know how looks can be deceiving and she's entirely deceiving you. That's Vivian."

"A condescending, manipulative, egocentric bitch?"

"Yes."

"Then you haven't come to Florida to be with Vivian?"

"No," he says, extending his arm out to her, "I came here to look for you."

"How did you know where to find me?"

"Don't be upset, please, but your neighbor..."

"Clara," she says, nodding.

"She said you mentioned Miami."

"I did." Tessa agrees.

"You left before I could tell you anything."

"Like what?" She says curiously.

"I've gotten a house. I've gotten a truck, a phone. I've looked for you on your media accounts."

"You got a house?" She interjects quizzically. "I'm still living in a hotel because I've been uncertain what to do."

"It's a house in miniature, like a camping cabin on wheels. Most people refer to it as a tiny house–it's only about one-hundred-eighty square feet.

"I've heard of those," she says, shifting her weight to the other leg.

"What's wrong?" He says, observing her discomfort.

"My legs are still stiff from running."

"From running where?"

"A marathon. Because I thought you would be there."

"Not when I've been here looking for you." He muses, "Which marathon?"

"I n Fairfax."

"For a cause?"

"To raise awareness for veterans."

"How did you do?"

"I came in third."

"You always impress me."

"Stop." She blushes.

"No, really. You can do just about anything."

"Well, Malakai was with the sitter but I had Michael to cheer me on."

"And who is Michael?"

"A client. Ten years old."

"That's special," he says warmly.

"Yes, he is very special," she sits on the chair, stretching out her legs.

"Maybe we can run the next one together," he says, adjusting himself in the bed.

"Maybe," she says keeping her focus on his gaze and not his leg.

The door to his room opens. The doctor comes in, explaining that he is to be discharged and must admit himself to the therapy ward for his treatments following the surgery.

In the following weeks, Maverick begrudgingly remains at the care facility where he receives continued physical therapy. Tessa returns from Virginia to take Maverick on his first outing – to her stepfather's bar where she can introduce him to her mother.

Tessa's mother sips gingerly from her martini beneath the hot August sun. Maverick walks with crutches and a full leg brace for another six weeks. They enter *The Cove* that is at full capacity during high tourist season.

Lucille wears a frumpy hat to shield the sun from her face and thick white framed sunglasses and an orange sundress with flower accents. Tessa wears a light yellow sundress with small pineapples on it and brown leather flip flops with yarn wedged at the toe. Maverick has a seat beside Tessa at the bar as the bartender approaches.

"Hi, I'm David," he says, with a thin lipped smile.

"David?" Maverick says back.

"I'm married to Tessa's mother, and I am the owner of this bar."

"Yep, that's my stepfather," Tessa says. "And this is my mother Lucy," she explains, turning to her mother who is on her right side, and taking a mojito from David.

"Hi, David. Lucy," Maverick says, "it's nice to meet the both of you."

"Likewise," David says, "what can I get you to drink?"

"I'll have the special house lager," he says.

"Have you found a job yet?" Her mother chimes in.

"Mom," Tessa says, turning in her seat, "he's still in therapy."

"Actually," Maverick says, "I haven't told Tessa yet but I've bought a bike shop in Virginia and I'm trying to franchise so I'm opening another store here in Miami."

"A bike shop?" Her mother says cheerfully.

"What kind of revenue does that bring in?" Maverick's father says as they approach behind them. Frank and Debbie Hall introduce themselves astutely to Lucy and David, ordering themselves a frozen daiquiri and a Blue Island Margarita.

"A house special," David says, grinding the ice.

"I bet," says Frank, tossing one arm around Maverick, patting him on the shoulder.

"I raised Maverick here to be another great Hall," he begins.

"Frank," Debbie rolls her eyes.

"Now Debbie, I'm just saying that our son here was raised right."

"And how do you think I raised my daughter?" Lucy breaks in.

"I know how you lived off taxpayers dollars."

"Dad," Maverick barges in as Lucy gasps. "That's enough of this."

"Enough of what?"

"Acting as if you're better than everyone else."

"At least I have your sister."

"Frank!" Debbie protests.

"That's right, Dad," Maverick says, "at least you have Natalie to show off and be proud of…"

"You're a homeless bum, Maverick," his father growls.

There is commotion at the bar. A man wearing a red and white Hawaiian shirt and navy blue shorts approaches.

"Hey," he hisses "are you Maverick?" His fist is curled tightly in a ball and there is a mimosa in the other hand.

"Yeah that's, right," Maverick says as he receives a face full of fist square against the side of his jaw, his head knocked backwards.

"What the hell?" Maverick says, standing on one leg off the chair as Mark throws another punch to his face and Tessa breaks in between them.

"Don't you hit, Tessa," Lucy cries.

"Who the hell are you acting like this?" Debbie commands back.

"I'm just a guy who's pissed," Mark says, "and I'm Mark by the way."

"And what does that mean to me?" Maverick glowers.

"You never could fight back," a female voice cackles from behind blond hair.

"Vivian," Maverick growls, "could you try to be a little more manipulative?"

"It wasn't all my idea," she snickers with a shrug.

"What are you saying?'

"I just wanted you to be happy," his mother confesses, "I thought you lost everything when she left you…you lost your job, your mind, your house, the car…"

"Mom," he says. "Tessa and I…"

"We what?" She asks.

"We were getting to know each other," Mark insists, "until this jackass here…"

"He's not a jackass," Tessa says.

"I don't know what in the hell to call it." His father exclaims, tossing his hands into the air, "but losing your mind over a woman… I mean the way you did…"

"I know most of you don't understand," Maverick pleads casually, "but you have to understand that I've always known money," he pauses, looking Tessa in her eyes, "but more than that – I knew companionship. Before you left, Tessa. Then and now."

Tessa's mother drops her jaw in resignation and Tessa's eyes become watery. Maverick's mother sulks as Vivian rolls her eyes and Mark walks away.

Candace Meredith

Chapter Nineteen

Keeping the Pace

Tessa's son holds onto her tightly by the hip. She wears the number 501 upon her chest. Maverick holds her other hand while Michael assists with his mobility chair. Maverick has not begun to walk yet and he moves along faster without the crutches.

"Okay, get ready," she says to her son as he bounces when he walks, plopping onto Maverick's lap. At the sound of the gun the race has begun, a 6k to raise awareness for children and adults who have disabilities. Michael pushes the wheelchair with Maverick and Malakai in tow as Tessa takes off, running like a starved cheetah about to catch her prey. She takes her stride in leaps and bounds which leads to cramped legs and mild exhaustion.

"Hey, Maverick," a familiar voice yells from behind, bearing the number 293 on his chest. George is running, sweat cascading from his head, his face flush, "Couldn't let you tackle this one alone." He sprints ahead.

"You go on, old man," Maverick chuckles, tossing Malakai onto his shoulders. Maverick's weather app calls for fifty percent chance of storms but the 6k is hundreds strong and not one of them has succumbed to fatigue or exhaustion. Malakai waves to the crowds of onlookers.

"I didn't know you could run," Maverick says as Tessa finishes in second place.

"I used to run track in high school," she says, Malakai hugging around her neck.

Behind them, George staggers to finish but makes it across the finish line along with dozens of others who are greeted by friends and family who offer cold drinks and a dry towel. Maverick's mother and father make their way through the crowd along with Tessa's mother and David.

"We are proud of you two," Tessa's mother says.

"But I'm not Mark," Maverick says with a grin.

"And I'm not Vivian," Tessa says.

"We just wanted your happiness," Debbie says, fighting back the tears.

"When we get you on your feet," Frank says, "you'll have another marathon to complete, I'm sure."

Maverick laughs, "Well, I'm not so sure, but I'll have this guy to run for me," he says, tossing his hand for a firm shake.

"I think this is my last," George pants, exhausted and sweating profusely as it begins to rain and more runners continue to cross the finish line. George takes a step back, "I'm an old man," he winks. "If I can do it – you should be able to do it on one leg," he chides.

"In due time," Maverick says, patting his arm. "In due time."

August gives way to September as Tessa and Maverick celebrate the Labor Day weekend from the front stoop of a tiny house. Malakai plays with a fishing pole and tackle before asking to go play on the slide.

They walk across the street, with Maverick's knee supported by a leg brace and a cane George whittled from wood. Maverick visits the garage on occasion, and George assists as needed at the bike shop. Knowing how to repair things is his specialty and a bike is no exception. When they get there Dick steps out of a white utility truck to greet them.

"Oh," Tessa says, "I forgot to tell you that there's a guy who's been looking for you."

"Name's Dick, in case you forgot," he says as he approaches them carrying a brown trash bag in tow. "I've got all your gear in here," he hands over the bag to Maverick.

"Not even sure I need this stuff anymore," he says, tossing the bag over his shoulder, "but I appreciate you returning them to me."

"Not a problem," Dick says, turning to leave.

"Have a nice day," Tessa calls after him.

"Thank you. You, too," he says, opening the driver door to the utility van.

"There was a time when this stuff was important to me," Maverick says, turning toward Tessa, "but I'm not so sure anymore."

"Then it's just time to move on to other stuff," she says, then they embrace. His thin lips touch her voluptuous mouth and they stand there together, amid where it had all begun – from the desire to run in a marathon.

Epilogue

Tessa and Maverick were married by the lake beneath the dogwood tree. Their guests seated twenty, many of them runners. They re-located to the lush, green mountains of Vermont in a tiny house nestled by a mountain with a dog Malakai named Lucky, where Maverick set up his third bike shop. On the wall hangs the bike that Bill confiscated from the sidewalk above a sign that reads: *Bill's Place*. Every year, they coordinate a marathon in support of persons who are diagnosed with disabilities. On their anniversary, Tessa purchased a tee for Maverick: *The Mountains I Must Go!*

"But this time you have a partner," Tessa said.

"My perfect companion," he agreed, pulling the tee over his sweater, "worth all its weight in gold – all 123 pounds."

Tessa throws her arms around Maverick and her son every morning before she heads off to work. Maverick's leg has healed and, on occasion, George pays a visit with his rescue pup Bentley. They find in one another happiness, contentment and completion. Tessa's nor Maverick's family attempts to push on them a relationship or a job position, and for that reason they have finally found in one another a reason to keep smiling.

"So, what's next?" Tessa asks, taking his hand into hers.

"Well," he says, looking her in the eyes, "there's this triathlon I've been thinking about."

"I'll be there to pull for you," she says, and they embrace there on the front stoop of a tiny house. Intimately. Together.

About the Author

Candace Meredith earned her Bachelor of Science degree in English Creative Writing from Frostburg State University in the spring of 2008. Her works of poetry, photography and fiction have appeared in literary journals Bittersweet, Backbone Mountain Review, Anthology 17, Greensilk Journal, Saltfront and The Broadkill Review. She currently works as a Freelance Editor for an online publishing company and has earned her Master of Science degree in Integrated Marketing and Communications (IMC) from West Virginia University.

Visit Candace's Author Page At:

www.ctupublishinggroup.com/candace-meredith.html

10480751R00260

Made in the USA
Lexington, KY
23 September 2018